Henry Clay Trumbull

The Knightly Soldier

A Biography of Major Henry Ward Camp

Henry Clay Trumbull

The Knightly Soldier
A Biography of Major Henry Ward Camp

ISBN/EAN: 9783337098360

Printed in Europe, USA, Canada, Australia, Japan

Cover: Foto ©Raphael Reischuk / pixelio.de

More available books at **www.hansebooks.com**

A RECORD OF COLLEGE, FIELD, AND PRISON.

THE

KNIGHTLY SOLDIER:

A BIOGRAPHY

OF

MAJOR HENRY WARD CAMP,

TENTH CONN. VOLS.

BY

CHAPLAIN H. CLAY TRUMBULL.

—oo⚬⚬oo—

BOSTON:
NICHOLS AND NOYES.
NEW YORK: OLIVER S. FELT.
1865.

STEREOTYPED BY C. J. PETERS & SON, BOSTON.

PRESS OF GEO. C. RAND & AVERY.

To the Parents

TO WHOSE

JUDICIOUS TRAINING AND EARNEST PRAYERS

HENRY CAMP

OWED SO MUCH, AND WHOM HE LOVED SO DEARLY,

This Tribute of Affection

IS DEDICATED IN TENDEREST SYMPATHY.

PREFACE

This book is not an attempt to prove that Henry Camp was brave, accomplished, and upright in all the course of his beautiful life here, or that he was fully prepared for the future to which God so early called him. It simply shows him as he was, grouping the memorial sketches of those who knew him best in the various relations of student, soldier, and Christian; with copious extracts from his own letters, written in all the freedom of family correspondence.

It was undertaken in behalf of his home friends, college-mates, and army comrades, who are sure to prize whatever concerns his record, or honors his memory. Yet, it is believed, it will have special value to many who, without knowing him, were his campaign associates in the Carolinas and Virginia, and who here find narrated the more striking incidents of their own army experience. Nor can any reader fail to admire his glowing details of personal adventure, and his graphic description of events national in scope and of historic significance.

One thing demands explanation. The relations between the compiler and the subject of this volume were of peculiar and rarest intimacy. The two were, during the years chiefly considered in this record, united in well-nigh perfect oneness. To have left out all the references to Henry Camp's friend, of whom almost every page in his later writings made mention, would have been impossible without destroying the fullness and coherence of the narrative, and distorting the picture of army life to the eyes of those familiar with the seldom-equalled attachment of the friends to each other. Very much of this nature was stricken from the record, — all indeed that could be with seeming propriety. It is hoped that what remains will be ascribed to the affectionate partiality of him who has fallen, and not to any want of good taste on the part of one who was loved by and who mourns him.

H. C. T.

RICHMOND, VA., April 21, 1865.

CONTENTS

CHAPTER I.

CHILDHOOD AND SCHOOLDAYS.

CHAPTER II.

COLLEGE LIFE.

CHAPTER III.

TEACHER — LAW-STUDENT — SOLDIER.

CHAPTER IV.

ROANOKE AND NEWBERNE.

CHAPTER V.

CAMP-LIFE AND CAMPAIGNING.

CHAPTER VI.

THE FIRST CHARLESTON EXPEDITION.

CHAPTER VII.

JAMES ISLAND AND FORT WAGNER.

CHAPTER VIII.

CHARLESTON AND COLUMBIA — PRISON LIFE AND ESCAPE.

CHAPTER IX.

LIBBY PRISON — HOME — CAMP PAROLE.

CHAPTER X.

CAMPAIGNING WITH THE ARMY OF THE JAMES.

CHAPTER XI.

DEEP BOTTOM — STRAWBERRY PLAINS — DEEP RUN.

CHAPTER XII.

IN THE PETERSBURG TRENCHES.

CHAPTER XIII.

LIFE AND DEATH BEFORE RICHMOND.

CHAPTER XIV.

MEMORIAL TRIBUTES.

THE

KNIGHTLY SOLDIER.

CHAPTER I.

CHILDHOOD AND SCHOOLDAYS.

HE short lives of some who have fallen on the field of the new American conflict contained more of romantic adventure and of heroic daring than the material of which the novelists and the poets of our language have wrought their most attractive narratives during the present century.

Another Cooper could find a Leather Stocking and a Harvey Birch in almost every camp of our army. Another Tennyson could sing of exploits of American battalions which would pale the brilliancy of the charge of the Light Brigade. Dumas could bring out of the truth from Andersonville and the Libby such tales of horror as would commonplace the ghastliest stories of the French Bastile.

The familiar, every-day home letters of young officers of culture and of nobleness, who have had widest experience in campaigning, and greatest vicissitudes of fortune in this now-closing war, furnish a variety of description and incident, possessing permanent interest even to those who have no special knowledge of the writers. To present such material from the record of one of whom his brigade-commander said, " Our cause cannot boast a nobler martyr," and his colonel, that " the service has never suffered a heavier loss in an officer of his grade," is the purpose of this volume.

HENRY WARD CAMP, son of Rev. Henry B. Camp and Cornelia L. Baldwin, was born February 4th, 1839, in Hartford, Conn., where his father — formerly pastor of the church in Bradford — then resided as a professor in the American Asylum for the Deaf and Dumb.

To the judicious training and Christian faithfulness of his parents, young Camp was indebted for the preservation of his rare symmetry of mental and moral character, and for its full and delightful development. Unusually gentle and retiring, even for a child, he shunned the boisterous companionship of city boys, and clung to his home, contented with its quiet occupations and satisfied in its enjoyments. Almost unaided, he learned to read at four years of age, and, from that time onward, found his chief enjoyment in books. His love of reading was so great, that, after he had devoured all the children's books in the house, he resorted to those far beyond his years. He gained an excellent knowledge of history before taking it up as a study, and was ever fond of books of travel. Too close devotion to reading, with too little out-door exercise, began to affect his head seriously ; and he was so troubled by somnambulism that, during his eighth year, he was sent to Durham to spend some time with his grandfather on a farm, where books were entirely forbidden him. This rest to his brain, with the exercise and other advantages of country life, quite re-established his health ; and, after a few months, he returned re-invigorated to his home.

One of the earliest observed peculiarities of young Camp's character was the exquisite sensitiveness of his conscience. He shrunk from every appearance of evil, and was oppressed by a fear of doing wrong. When he was five years old, a sister was born to him. As he first looked at the baby treasure, with childish joy and wonderment, a shade of thought came over his face, and he went alone from his mother's room. On his return, his mother asked him where he had been. " I've been, mamma," he said, "to pray to God that I may never hurt the soul of dear little sister." Although too young to have a consciousness of responsibility for others, the incident is in keeping with his whole course in boyhood.

A year later, he exercised himself in writing a little book of sermons, taking a text, and making on it brief comments as striking and original as the employment was unique for a boy of his years. In looking over the manuscript, his good mother observed frequent blanks where the name of God should appear. Inquiring the reason of these omissions, Henry informed her that he had feared he was not feeling just right while he was writing, and, lest he should take the name of God in vain by using it then, he had left the blanks in its stead. The strictest letter of the Jewish law could scarcely exact more reverent use of the ineffable name of Jehovah than was demanded by the tender conscience of this pure-minded boy.

His fear of transgressing induced habits of self-examination which gave him no little discomfort. Recognizing the standard of absolute right, his rigid scrutiny of motive and purpose, with his discriminating review of each outward act, revealed to him his imperfections of thought or deed ; and, as a consequence, he sometimes suffered keenly from unmerited self-reproach. At five years old, he joined the Sabbath-school infant-class of the Centre Church (Rev. Dr. Hawes). His teacher there was Mrs. Roswell Brown, who has held the same position for a quarter of a century. Writing little notes to her, young Camp said in more than one, with his uniform sensitiveness, " I am sometimes afraid I shall love you better than I do my mother. I don't think I do, but I am afraid that I shall. " " Mrs. Brown, " he said, one Sabbath morning, as he took his place by her side, " I am afraid I did wrong last Sabbath. While you were talking to us all, I wrote my sister Cornelia's name with my finger on the seat. I didn't think it was wrong then; but I've thought it was, since, and I've wanted to tell you of it." No misdeed of his during his four-years' stay in that infant-class was greater than the one thus candidly confessed. His teacher there says of him, with warmth, "I had nearly four hundred and fifty children under my care in that room, but never but one Henry Camp."

Yet, in spite of his quickly-reminding and often-accusing conscience, Henry Camp was of cheerful temperament, and richly enjoyed life. His refined sensitiveness made him only more lovely to others, and he was the light of a happy home. No laugh was more merry than his, and no one did more than he to provoke a laugh at every proper time.

With the exception of a few weeks at the district school, he studied at home until he was ten years old. In 1849 he entered the Hartford Public High School, which he attended for six years. It was there that he first mingled actively with his fellows. Although he did not seek to lead, he found himself ahead. His comrades looked up to him. In the recitation-room, the play-ground, and the gymnasium, he was a pattern. Loving out-door sports and athletic exercises, he practised and strengthened his muscular powers until his form and figure were a type of his compacted and well-rounded intellectual development.

S. M. Capron, one of his high-school teachers, says of him, "There was a charm about him even then, which attracted all who knew him. I never had a pupil who

2

possessed a purer character, or more completely won the respect and even admiration of his teachers. He despised every thing mean, every thing vulgar; and his generosity and manliness in his intercourse with other boys made him a general favorite among them. He was remarkably truthful also, and this, never from a fear of consequences, but with a spontaneity which showed that truth was at the foundation of his character. As a scholar he was very faithful, accurate, and prompt in his recitations; especially copious and rich in his choice of words; of superior talent as a writer. No one stood above him in his classes; and he took some prizes, while in the school, for English composition and other exercises. But it was chiefly his uncommon nobleness of character which made him conspicuous then, as in later years."

In the summer of 1855, Camp passed examination for admission to Yale, and connected himself with the Brothers' Society. But as he was yet only sixteen, and had been so long in seldom intermitted study, his judicious parents strongly advised his waiting another year before entering on his collegiate course. The disappointment to him was severe, yet he yielded gracefully, as always, to the judgment of his parents, and for a twelvemonth occupied himself in out-door exercise, in attention to pencil-sketching, and in the study of French and German. He joined the freshman class of Yale, in September, 1856. Then commenced his life away from the home he had so dearly loved, and in the possession of which he had been so favored. Then, first, he was obliged to forego the privilege of speaking in all freedom of the experiences of each day to those whose sympathy and affection were not to be doubted.

Perhaps it was the missing of home confidences, with the accruing sense of personal loneliness in a crowd of comparative strangers, that, soon after he entered college, caused thoughts to centre, as never before, on his need of fellowship with a loving and sympathizing Saviour, who alone could fully understand him. He had long been a prayerful, reverent worshipper of God, approaching him in conscious need, in reliance on the one Mediator; and his life had for years given delightful evidence of the power of grace in his inner being: but not until now did he make open profession of faith in Jesus as *his* Saviour. Just when his heart was transformed into Christ's image by the power of the Spirit is known only to the Omniscient one. During his spring vacation, in May, 1857, he connected himself with the North Congregational Church at Hartford, of which the Rev. Dr. Bushnell was pastor. That pastor's counsel he had often sought, and to him he had confided his doubts and fears. Of Henry Camp as an inquirer concerning divine truth, and as he showed himself before 'and later, his good pastor writes thus in glowing eulogy : —

HARTFORD, Nov. 7, 1864.

REV. H. C. TRUMBULL.

MY DEAR SIR, — I most deeply regret that I cannot do more to help you in your difficult but laudable endeavor to prepare a memorial for our young friend, Major Camp. It is my great misfortune that I do not remember facts and conversations so as to be able to report them. I only remember impressions, or resulting estimates and opinions; and these will give you little help in the sketching or living presentation of a character.

It was my privilege to know this young patriot and soldier from his childhood up. The freshly vigorous, wonderfully lustrous, unsoiled look he bore in his childhood, made it consciously a kind of pleasure to pass him, or catch the sight of his face in the street. I do not recall ever having had such an impression, or one so captivating for its moral beauty, from any other child. And it was just as great a satisfaction to see him grow as it was to see him. I used to watch the progress of his lengthening form as I passed him, saying inwardly still, "Well, thank God, it is the beautiful childhood that is growing, and not he that is outgrowing his childhood."

The noble man-soul was evident enough in the child, and when it was bodied forth in his tall, massive, especially manly person, it was scarcely more so. Indeed, the real man of the child was never bodied forth, and never could be, without a history of many years, such as we fondly hoped for him, but shall never behold. He died, in fact, with his high, bright future shut up in him, — it will only come out among the angels of God ; and, I doubt not, will make a really grand figure there. Seldom have they hailed the advent among them, I think, of a youth whose kinship, and peership and hero-life begun, they will more gladly acknowledge. Indeed, I have never been able to keep it out of my mind, since I first heard of his death, that there was some too great aptness in him for a place among these couriers and squadrons of glory. It seems to be a kind of extravagance to say this, but I know not how otherwise to describe real impressions. He was such a man as, going into a crowd of strangers, would not only attract general attention by his person, by his noble figure and the fine classic cut of his features, by the cool, clear beaming of his intelligence, by the visible repose of his justice, by a certain, almost superlative sweetness of modesty ; but there was, above all, an impression of intense PURITY in his looks, that is almost never seen among men, and which everybody must and would distinctly feel.

But I am only describing here what others felt as truly as I, and could describe, if they would, much better than I ; though, perhaps, the acquaintance I had with Henry's interiorly personal character and struggles in the matter of religion may have prepared me to note more distinctly than some others would the signs outwardly appearing. He came to me a great many times, from his early childhood onward, to lay open his troubles, and obtain spiritual direction. My conviction, from the very first, was that I had nothing to do with him but to put him in courage, and enable him to say, "I believe." I never saw him when I did not think he was a Christian, and I do not believe that he ever saw himself early enough to properly think otherwise. Still he did think otherwise much longer than I wished. The difficulty was to get him away from the tyranny of his conscience. It was so delicate and steadfast and strong, that his faith could not get foothold to stand. I feared many times that he was going to be preyed upon all his life long by a morbid conscience. Still there was a manly force visible, even in his childhood; and I contrived, in what ways I could, to get that kindled by a free inspiration. To get him under impulse, afterwards, for the war was not half as difficult, I presume, after the point of my endeavor was already carried; for, having now become a soldier of Christ, by a clear and conscious devotion, he had only to extend that soldiership for the kingdom of heaven's sake.

As far as he was concerned, the kingdom of heaven was not worsted when he fell; but the loss to his country and his comrades in arms was certainly great, greater than most of us will know. Besides, it is a great and sore disappointment to us all, that we are cut off abruptly from that noble and high future we had begun to hope for him. Let us believe that he can have as high a future where he is, and resign him gladly to it!

Sympathising deeply with you in the fall of your heroic brother and friend, I only wish I could help you more effectively in the very tender office you have undertaken.

Wishing you all the success which the beautiful subject of your memoir deserves,

I am truly yours,

HORACE BUSHNELL.

CHAPTER II.

COLLEGE LIFE.

T the commencement of his sophomore year, Camp became especially interested in boating; finding pleasure in both its exercise and its excitement. He joined the Varuna Boat-club, and was soon as prominent there for his strength, skill, and energy in the use of the oar, as he was distinguished in every other pursuit to which, at any time, he devoted himself. So well established was his reputation in this line, that he was one of the picked crew to represent Yale in the University race, at the Worcester regatta, in July, 1859.

That regatta was an era in his life, and its influence was important in shaping his whole future course. In it he first realized the keen enjoyment of exciting endeavor, and attained the satisfaction of accomplishing something, through the straining of every nerve, in a contest with his fellows, while stayed by the consciousness that he held the honor of those whom he loved, in his keeping. He gave himself up to the struggle, both in preparation and performance, with his whole heart and soul, and seemed to secure thereby a relish and a fitness for the work to which he was subsequently called for his country. A plain but massive ring, made from the gold of the regatta prize, he wore to the last, — refusing to part with it, even at an extravagant price, when most pinched for the comforts of life in a Southern prison; and he yielded it only when the enemy wrenched the sword from his grasp, and drew the ring from his finger as he lay in the helplessness of death on the field of his last battle.

The Yale and the Harvard crews in the Worcester races of '59 were,

Yale.	Harvard.
H. S. Johnson (stroke),	C. Crowninshield (stroke),
Charles T. Stanton, jr.,	W. H. Forbes,
Henry W. Camp,	E. G. Abbott,
Joseph H. Twichell,	H. S. Russell,
Charles H. Owen,	J. H. Wales,
Frederick H. Colton,	J. H. Ellison (bow),
Hezekiah Watson (cockswain),	

It is a noteworthy fact, that every man of the Yale crew, and a majority of those from Harvard, were subsequently in the Union army.

Of Johnson, Camp wrote, when he met him in North Carolina on the staff of Gen. Terry, "He is an Aide, ranking as lieutenant, — very nice little position, — left the signal corps some time since to take it. Signalling, he didn't like at all, — no fighting, — slim business, — at it through the whole Peninsular campaign, and was heartily sick of it.

At Fair Oaks, he volunteered on some general's staff, and went in — lively time — horse shot under him. *That* was more like it." Stanton, as captain in the 21st C. V., was wounded at Drury's Bluff. He was subsequently commissioned Lieut.-Col., but was mustered out in consequence of the severity of his wound. Owen, Camp's early playmate, school-fellow, and always attached friend, was in the 1st Conn. Heavy Artillery, and later on the staff of Gen. Robert O. Tyler, receiving at Cold Harbor a wound, the effects of which he must carry to his grave. The fair and stalwart arms of Stanton and Owen were often admired by enthusiastic boatmen in the days of college racing. The right arm of Stanton and the left of Owen dropped powerless by their sides in the same good service for their country. For three years, Twichell filled with rare usefulness and acceptance, the chaplaincy of the 2d Regiment, Excelsior (Sickles') Brigade. Colton, as an army surgeon, had Owen under his skilful charge at the Douglass Hospital, in Washington, D.C. Watson has fought long and nobly as colonel of the 143d Regiment, N. Y. S. V. Crowningshield and Forbes are, at the writing of this, colonel and lieutenant-colonel of the 2d Mass. Cavalry, the former command of the lamented Gen. Lowell. Abbott fell at Cedar Mountain, while Russell, going out a captain in the 2d Mass. Infantry, returned a colonel of a colored cavalry regiment. Surely a noble record of noble men !

The following graphic and thrilling sketch of the Worcester regatta is from Twichell's graceful pen : —

THE WORCESTER REGATTA.

"In looking back to Henry Camp, as I knew him in college, it is impossible not to recall his singular physical beauty. The memory of it harmonizes very pleasantly with the memory of his beautiful daily life. Each became the other so well, while they were joined, that, though now his body has gone to dust, I find, while musing on my friend, an unusual delight in continuing to associate them. He furnishes a perfect example of the truth, ' *Virtus pulchrior e pulchro corpore veniens.* ' His handsome face, his manly bearing, and his glorious strength, made that gentleness and goodness which won our love, the more illustrious. I well remember, while in college, riding out one day with a classmate of his, and passing him, as, erect and light of foot, he strode lustily up a long hill, and the enthusiasm with which my comrade pronounced this eulogy, ' There's Henry Camp, a perfect man, who never did any thing to hurt his body or soul ! ' That was before I knew him well; for, as I have intimated, we were not in the same class : but what I heard and saw, made me so desirous of a better acquaintance, that when, in the summer of '59, our crew was made up for the college regatta, to take place at Worcester, and it fell out that he was assigned to duty in the boat, as No. 3, while I was No. 4, I was more than pleased.

"The six weeks of training that followed, culminating in the grand contest, witnessed by far the greater part of all our personal intercourse, for after that time our paths diverged. That was the last term of my senior year, and the end was not far off. We parted on commencement day; and though I afterward heard from him, especially of the fame of his soldiership, and hoped to see him, we met again no more than once or twice. But, at the distance of five eventful years, the news of his death struck me with a sense of my bereavement, so deep and painful, that, looking back to those six weeks, I could not realize that they were nearly all I had intimately shared with him. Nor am I alone in this: I know of others, whose private memories of Henry Camp, as limited as mine, stir in their hearts, at every thought of his grave, the true lament, ' Alas, my brother!'

" During the training season of which I speak, the crew had, of course, very much in common. We ate at the same table, and took our exercise at the same hours; so passing considerable part of every day together, beside the time we sat at our oars. Our hopes and fears were one, our ardor burned in one flame; we used even to dream almost the same dreams. The coming regatta was our ever-present stimulus. To win, — there was nothing higher in the world. It quickens the pulse even now to remember how splendid success then appeared.

" Camp gave himself up to the work in hand with that same enthusiasm of devotion that carried him to the fore-front of battle on the day of his glorious death. He was always prompt, always making sport of discomforts, always taking upon himself more than his own share of the hard things. Severe training in midsummer is something more

than a pastime. It abounds in both tortures of the body,
and exasperations of mind, as all boating men bear witness.
Under them, not all of us, at all times, kept our patience; but
Camp never lost his. Not a whit behind the best in spirit
and in zeal, he maintained under all circumstances a seren-
ity that seemed absolutely above the reach of disturbing causes.
The long, early morning walk into the country, the merciless
rigors of diet, the thirst but half slaked, the toil of the gymnasium, the weary miles down the Bay, under the cockswain's
despotism, the return to childhood's bed-time, and other attendant afflictions, often outweighed the philosophy of all but
No. 3. He remained tranquil, and diligently obeyed all the
rules; serving as a sort of balance-wheel among us, neutra-
lizing our variableness, and making many a rough place
smooth. He had a presence, — almost the happiest I ever
saw, and a temper that betrayed no shady side. He carried
all his grace with him everywhere, and had a way of shed-
ding it on every minute of an hour, — no less on little matters
than on great, — that gave his company an abiding charm,
and his influence a constant working power; and so he went
on working with all his might for the college, doing us good
daily, gaining that skill and muscle, which afterward enabled
him to pull so brave an oar through the stormy waves of
Hatteras.

"He had soldierly ways about him then. Discipline was
his delight, and coolness never deserted him. We were upset one day, in deep water, under a bridge; and, at first, each
struck out for land, till Camp, remaining in mid-stream,
called us back to look after the boat, which was too frail a

structure to be left to chance floating. That Hatteras exploit, when we heard of it, did not seem at all strange. It was just like him to volunteer, and still more like him to be the last man to give up what was undertaken.

"At last the day came,—the day big with fate, dreaded, yet longed for. Noon of July 26th found us sitting in our good boat, 'Yale,' on the beautiful Lake Quinsigamond, near Worcester, ready at the starting goal, for the signal to 'Give way.' The waters of the lake glittered and dimpled under the summer sky, as if mocking our deep cares with levity. Each grasped his oar, and, though it was a vain attempt, tried to be calm. A mile and a half away up between the woody banks fluttered the white flag, that marked the turning goal. Beside us was the 'Harvard' and her splendid crew, gentlemanly fellows, whom we had liked at sight. There was also in the line a boat from Brown University, with a son of Adoniram Judson at one of the oars. Many thousands of spectators clustered on either shore, among whom were hundreds of college men, all eager and emulous, but with no stirring of bad blood. The grace of generosity presides most happily over those congresses of youth, and keeps out bitterness from their rivalries,—or did, at least, in our day. But the bustle of the crowd did not reach us as we sat watching the slow preliminaries of the judges and umpire. We only heard the music of the bands, which then seemed a call to battle,—almost as much so as the terrible bugles that nearly all of us were destined yet to hear. At last the suspense was ended. The first signal gun sent its sharp echo to the neighboring hills,—'Ready to give way!'

Every oar quivered in its place. A second gun, whose echoes we did not hear, —' Give way all!'—and we were off.

" In twenty minutes, the first day's race was over. All the college-boating world knows we were beaten in it, and that at evening, Harvard bore into Worcester, with songs and shouting, the colors that pertained to victory. We shook hands all round,—the two crews,—and tried to appear to take it easy on both sides, though it was not, of course, exactly in the same mood that we returned to our quarters, and our friends to theirs. But Yale was used to it, and so was Harvard. It was the old thing over again: the Fortune that prospers oars was too coy to be propitiated by us. Yet we had hoped for a change: undoubtedly we had expected it. Then was Henry Camp a refreshment to us. He had done his best, he was disappointed; but he radiated a quiet resignation that was contagious. It was a comfort to talk with No. 3 that night.

" The next day there was to be another regatta given by the city of Worcester, open to all comers. The Harvard men had signified their willingness to try it again with us; but we were not immediately of one mind, and did not jump at the offer. Worthy as our rivals were, it was not pleasant being beaten by them; nor was the desperate work of a three-mile race, at mid-day, in July, to be coveted for itself: yet it gave us and *Alma Mater* one more chance, and that was not lightly to be thrown away. Camp's counsel was unhesitating and spirited. He was for re-entering the lists from the first instant it was proposed; and so it came to pass, that we took heart of grace : and noon of the morrow found us again on the lake, grasping our oars and waiting the signal.

" This time there was no boat against us but the 'Harvard.' An accident early in the first race had disabled the representative of Brown, and she was withdrawn, not to appear again. The same fair multitude, shining in bright summer attire, was gathered to witness the scene. Signs of the previous day's event were not wanting. On land and water, the Harvard head was high, as was not unmeet ; but our fellows among the crowd observed a modest demeanor, and we in the boat were not disposed to vaunt ourselves. We hoped, however, to make at least a closer affair of it than the other was.

" Once more we were off with a mighty clamor from the shore, each boat struggling for the lead. 'Yale' won it. None but a boating man knows the glorious excitement — excitement without wildness—that then leaped through our arms into the oars. Henry Camp himself afterward said that his first battle did not surpass it. Every thing went well with us, and we reached the mile-and-a-half goal, four good lengths ahead ; but the 'Harvard' made a splendid turn, and we darted away on the home stretch, almost bow and bow. The fortune of the day trembled in even balances : less than ten minutes would decide it. ' Pull!' cried our cockswain, as if for his life ; and we heard the Harvard stroke inspiring his fellows with brave words. Then came the hot, momentous work, — the literal agony. Those twelve men will never forget it, though it is doubtful if any can or could recall it in detail, minute by minute, short as it was. There is an indistinctness about it in my memory at least; and the last half-mile is especially cloudy. It would not be easy to describe it. Most accounts of boat-races, like that in 'Tom Brown at Oxford,' are from the standpoint of a looker-on, rather than an actor. The real tragedy is in the boat.

"The near neighborhood of the other contestant, not so much seen as felt; the occasional sidewise gleam of red from the handkerchiefs the Harvard men wore about their heads; the burning exhortations of the cockswain, gradually rising in pitch of intensity, and setting at last upon the formula, 'Pull, if you *die!*' the pain of continued utmost exertion; the various mental phenomena, some of which were strange enough; and, as we neared the goal, the vociferous greetings of the first little groups of spectators,—a vague sound in the ears, we scarcely thought what it was, except a sweet token of the end at hand; then, a little further on, the cry of the great multitude, neutralized as a distraction by the cockswain's deepening passion; the order to quicken the stroke, the final 'Spur!'—all these remain indelible impressions of that fragment of an hour in 1859; but, like the impressions that survive a stormy dream, they are not orderly or clear.

"I doubt if any one remembers the command to stop. For a minute or two, there was utter collapse. Each bowed upon his oar, with every sense suspended through exhaustion: but, thanks to the training, one after another revived, and sat upright, and blessed himself; for all knew, though rather confusedly, that we had done well in entering that race. To our looks of inquiry, the cockswain, whose thun-

der-bolts had suddenly dissolved in sunshine, made this sufficient reply, 'We've got 'em!' It had come at last! Hurrah,.
hurrah for Yale! We wanted the voice of ten thousand
wherewith to vent our hearts, and the shore supplied it. We
looked around: the 'Harvard' was slowly making for the land.
To us it was permitted by custom to go before the spectators, and receive their congratulations. As, with easy oar,
we pulled our proud boat along either border of the lake,
the applause that rose in a great wave to meet us was probably the sweetest taste of glory our lives will have afforded. In our young eyes, nothing could be more magnificent than our victory; and it seemed like an old Olympic
triumph.

" When we landed, the Cambridge crew, though their philosophy was much more grievously taxed than was ours the
day before, gave us honest hands, and made us handsome
speeches, to which we properly responded, or at least wished
we could. Altogether, they took defeat in such a manly
way, that we felt very anxious to refrain from all victorious
airs in their presence, and to conduct ourselves with the utmost magnanimity.

" The telegraph soon sent the news home to *Alma Mater*,
and that night there was jubilee in New Haven; but all of
us, save the cockswain, abode in Worcester till the next morning. Then the Harvard men went north, and the Yale men
south, and fair Quinsigamond was vacant of college keels for
another year. It was commencement day; and, returning
crowned, we were welcomed under the elms in a manner
peculiar to collegians: but from that hour our close alliance

was broken. Two or three went down to put up the boat; but the six never sat together again.

"It is pleasant now to see, that through those youthful rivalries, useful as they were in themselves, God was raising up strength for nobler work than we proposed or could imagine. As we stretched away at our practice down the Bay, we never thought of war, or battle, or the great service of liberty that would soon call for thews of hardy men. Looking back to those warm afternoons when we used to disembark for a respite, and sit upon the ruined wall of old Fort Hale, and wonder how it seemed in those early days when Yalensians were called out from college halls to fight in the field, I cannot realize that then and now are less than six years apart.

"Strange things have happened since. The voice of the cockswain has been heard at the head of his regiment on many a bloody field. The stroke has followed the flag ever since the fall of Sumter, and came very near death on the Peninsula. The iron right arm of No. 2 is maimed for life by a shot through the elbow. No. 5 will likewise carry to his grave the weakness of a wound. But No. 3 fell, and lay dead. Can it be? can it be? This is strangest of all. Yet it is not, perhaps, altogether strange that a sacrifice so fair and so truly consecrated should prove acceptable to God, and be consumed. There is comfort for our grief.

> 'Our Knights are dust;
> Their good swords rust;
> Their souls are with the saints, we trust.'"

Henry Camp thoroughly enjoyed college life. He did

not sever connection with old Yale at his graduation, in July, 1860. He loved always to tell of, and to think over, his experiences there ; and he watched with hearty interest the subsequent career of his classmates. Most warmly he greeted any of those whom he encountered in army service ; and, even while a captive within the enemy's lines, he acknowledged an existing bond between himself and each son of his *Alma Mater*. But a few months before his death, he remarked, that the only public sentiment to which he was ever keenly sensitive was that of college. His intense modesty prevented his ever dreaming how highly he was esteemed, and how warmly he was beloved, by his fellow-students.

The valedictorian of his class writes of him : —

"I had profound respect and admiration for him as a classmate. He was frank, wise, clear and pure minded, changeless in friendship. We his classmates feel deeply the diminution of mental and moral power suffered in his loss. The sum total of the class is less by a vast amount. As a positive power, as a man, as a friend, we esteemed him highly. I almost envy you the task of delineating the character of one so pure, noble, and manly. It is a priceless remembrance, the friendship of such a man."

Says another classmate : —

" A character so noble, a life so pure, a heart so warm with kind impulses, and a manner replete with the gentle courtesies of friendship, could not fail to win the love and esteem of us all."

Yet another, who knew him well, adds : —

"I dare say he had faults; but I never saw them. I know of nothing in his life I would correct."

As showing the power of his Christian example during his college course, one who sat by his side in the chapel and at recitation gives this narration : —

"On entering college, I was wholly without hope and without God in the world. I was beyond the reach of any power except the power of Jesus. I do not know whether I believed the Bible or not. I did not hesitate to ridicule such parts of it as my inclinations, urged on by such a state, prompted. I could sit in a prayer-meeting in the revival of '58, when nearly all my classmates were giving testimony of the power of God to send hope and peace to despairing souls, wholly unmoved. I could even smile at the emotions there expressed. Camp was my companion through college more than any other member of the class. He was by my side at recitation and in the chapel during the entire four years. I saw in him a character and a life I had never seen before. By his life I was forced to admit that his profession was *per se* no libel on the Master in whose service he was.

"I do not recollect what part of our college life it was when he first spoke to me on the subject of my soul's salvation. It was not, however, till after his upright and godly life had forced from me the most profound respect for him and the

Saviour to whom he prayed. He said very little; but he said enough to lead me to think over my past life, and to cast a glance at the future. I shall never forget the impression that first conversation had upon my mind. It was not so much what he said, as the way he said it. He believed he was setting forth God's truth, and spoke as if he knew it was so. I believe that he knew it was true, though unable to explain how he became conscious of it. This I pondered, and felt that he had evidences that had been withheld from me. He spoke with me only a few times on this wise, but every time with telling effect. I could not help thinking of it; and after we were parted, and I had lost his companionship, I made his thoughts the companions of my lonely hours. I began to love him more than ever, and with love for him grew the love of the same Lord whom he loved and served. The conflict to me was a severe one, and how I longed to meet him, and converse with him!

"Passing through New Haven when first on his way to his regiment, he left on my table a line to this effect: —

' DEAR B.:

Sorry to have missed seeing you.

Good-by, God bless you!

HENRY W. CAMP.'

"I would have given a fortune to have seen him for an hour! I had not at that time revealed my feelings to any one, and felt that he alone was fit to receive them. I wrote to him, and his letters supplied in part the loss I felt. Not a day since we parted, I venture to say, has he not been in my mind. I cannot but feel that he was the instrument cho-sen of God to unveil the darkness that shut out the light from my soul. I fear that, had I never known him, I had never known the love of God, nor welcomed the glad enjoy-ment of a Christian experience."

His classmate Holden thus sums up the college estimate of Camp : —

" Those who were members of the class which graduated at Yale college, in the year 1860, can bear ample testimony to that earnest Christian manhood, that sincere and faithful performance of every duty, that quiet, simple, childlike asser-tion of purity of mind, that magnanimity and generosity, and that courtesy of manner, which made Henry Camp a hero at every period and in every position of his life.

" The influence which he exerted in the class by this moral force was most wonderful, and none the less so because he was totally unconscious of its existence. He wielded his scep-tre without displaying it, and (except that he knew on general principles that sincerity of purpose always asserts its prerog-atives) without knowing that he held the sceptre. He was not, at least until his senior year, what is called a 'popular' man. While invariably and impulsively a gentleman, and demonstratively kind in his demeanor toward every person he had to do with, his intimacies were few. Not only were his natural sensitiveness and retiring disposition an obstacle to a free general acquaintance, but his intensity of feeling was doubtless gratified by concentrating his friendship on a few chosen companions. And yet without exertion, and by the unpretending grandeur of his character, he won not only the respect, but the profound love, of his classmates to an extent of which he had no idea. His conscientiousness was never intrusive. No one dreamed of his being a paragon, any more than they dreamed of his being inconsistent, not with his professions (for he never made any), but with his former invariable practice. ' To know him once and under any circumstances,' says an intimate friend, ' was to know him always; for he was always the same.'

" He was not a pretentious scholar. His recitations were not characterized by a flashing repetition of the text, perhaps not always by a *quick* perception of the meaning, but invariably by a quiet self-possession that was evidently founded on a thorough, profound, and solid comprehension of what he had been studying, whether it had been acquired by an intuitive knowledge, or by close and energetic application. Although occupying a fine position on the list of honors, he might have stood much higher had he not deliberately chosen partially to devote himself to other things which he deemed equally useful. Books outside of the prescribed course of study, chess, the gymnasium, and boating, occupied a part of his time and attention. Into all these exercises he threw that same earnest, hearty, untiring energy which he gave to every thing else. Whether in laying his plans for an inevitable check-mate upon his antagonist, or whether laboring at his oar after the hope of triumph had vanished, he displayed the same indomitable and persistent courage with

which he performed every act in life as soon as he had determined that it was right in itself and a part of his duty.
Possessing a splendid, athletic body, he seemed as much in
earnest in developing it by physical exercises as in conning
Greek or obeying a college law, and awakened by his hearti-
ness the enthusiasm of those around him in gymnastic sports
or the contest of shell-boats.

"Prominent among his traits was his absolute, unqualified,
and unmistakable hatred of every thing mean. He could
be silent under an act of injustice, of injury, even of insult,
when he believed it to be the result of thoughtlessness or ig-
norance; but his detestation of meanness begotten of deliberate malice or of littleness of soul was inexpressively withering.
'I never saw him angry on any other account,' writes a classmate who knew him well : ' but a mean act would make his
eyes flash fire ; and his words on such occasions, though few
were emphatic.' He seemed almost to have belonged to an
order of Christian Knighthood whose mission might be to ex-
terminate dastardly and premeditated wickedness. Alas!
that his sword should have dropped so soon from his hand!

"His inflexible resolution always to act with a full understanding of his duty, preliminary to an equally inflexible determination to perform it, cannot perhaps be better illustrated
than by his course relative to his acquiring the elective franchise, which occurred while he was in college. He carefully
made the Constitution of the United States a subject of close
and reflective study, not merely as an intellectual exercise,
but for the purpose of becoming thoroughly acquainted with
the nature of the instrument to which he was about to swear

allegiance. One or two of its provisions were the source of protracted deliberation and discussion, until, in fact, his doubts were removed.

" Of his Christian character in college, little can be said that is not true of it in every situation. His modesty did not obscure it; but it did prevent any ostentatious display of it. A college friend on terms of closest intimacy writes as follows: ' Those who saw his heart in this respect will cherish the revelations made to them as something sacred. I know one who was brought to Christ, who, had it not been for him, for his Christian character as revealed in his conversation, and for the sincerity and whole-heartedness of his trust in Christ, would not, as far as I can see, have ever been a Christian. Others I know who were influenced by him, whom he did not know or dream of, — whom he knows *now.*'

" Undoubtedly there is a cloud of witnesses to the sublimity of that faith, and the simplicity of that piety, which made their lasting impression upon otherwise heedless souls. To those acquainted with or superficially knowing Henry Camp, this sketch may seem only a fulsome panegyric; but it is true (and it can be said of very few men) that no word of praise could be erased without doing him injustice. Indeed, words are worth very little to those who knew him thoroughly. They may perhaps suggest tender memories that will come thronging back, laden with renewed love and respect for him who commanded by his intrinsic worth so much of affection and so much of reverence.

" ' No man despised his youth ;' for he was ' an example of

the believers in word, in conversation, in charity, in spirit, in faith, in purity.'

" The poet of his class, in his valedictory poem, described, as beautifully as he did correctly, such a character as Camp's, in the following verses : —

> " Living well is not mere living
>   In the cultured taste of schools :
> 'Tis not in the knack of business,
>   Or the hoarded gold of fools ;
>
> But an earnest life's deep passion
>   Beating in a kingly heart,
> With the gentle grace of goodness
>   Glorifying every part."

" If ever there was ' a voice from the tomb sweeter than song, and a recollection of the dead to which we turn, even from the charms of the living,' it is when such Christian bravery as his achieves its crowning victory over the grave, and when the homage we pay to his intellectual nobility is sanctified by the blessed memory of those virtues which are ' the native growth of noble mind.' "

CHAPTER III.

TEACHER, LAW STUDENT, SOLDIER.

N September, after leaving college, Camp took charge of the high school at East Hartford, and remained as its principal about six months. He became warmly attached to some who were his pupils there; but teaching was tame business to him, especially in the stirring times then opening before the nation.

Accepting the responsibilities of the elective franchise after his careful study of the Constitution, he cast his first vote, in the spring of 1860, for good Governor Buckingham. In the Presidential election of the November following, he voted for Abraham Lincoln. Of the possible consequences of this vote he was not unmindful, yet he had no hesitation in casting it. Doing what he believed to be right, he was never anxious as to the result. He did not desire war. Brought up in the strictest nonresistant school, he was emphatically a lover of peace. Of gentle, retiring nature, he shrunk instinctively from unpleasant collision with any. He never quarrelled. Up to this time he had never lifted a hand in anger, or even struck a blow in self-defense. He was ready to yield whatever was properly at his disposal, for the good of others, or for the sake of harmony. But, though never obstinate, he was ever firm. He could not concede an iota of principle. It seemed an impossibility for him to swerve a hair, on any inducement, from the path of duty as he saw it. Nothing but a clear change of conviction ever changed a position which he assumed on a moral question. War or no war, he would vote and act as he believed to be right.

In the early spring of 1861, a letter received from a resident of the South, formerly his playfellow and school-mate, while it grieved him by its unprovoked harshness of spirit, aroused his sense of manliness by its contemptuous flings at Northerners, and its defiant threats of resistance to Federal rule. He replied to the letter in calm dignity, avoiding every issue but the simple one of duty to a Government whose beneficent rule its bitterest opposers could not gainsay, while he held to account for all consequences those who arrayed themselves against just authority. In concluding, he said : —

" Should you resist, as you threaten, upon your heads, and yours alone, will rest the fearful responsibility of commencing a civil war. We have planted ourselves upon the foundation of the Constitution and the laws : from it, we shall neither advance to aggression, nor retreat one hair's breadth in concession. Conscious that we have done all in our power for the maintenance of peace and harmo-

ny, loth to encounter in arms those whom we have been
wont to greet as brothers, we shall yet meet unflinchingly
whatever issue may be forced upon us, urged on, not by
impulse or passion, but by a solemn sense of the duty which
we owe to our country. Nor will the men of New England, sons of those who fought at Bunker Hill and Sara-
toga, who defended for the South the soil which her Tories
would not and her patriots could not defend for themselves, be found wanting in the hour of trial. Side by side
with the brave men of the West, we will stand to the last
for the Union, the Constitution, and the Laws, — and may
God defend the right ! "

After leaving his charge in East Hartford, Camp commenced the study of law in the office of John Hooker, Esq.,
reporter of the Supreme Court of Connecticut. What capa-
bilities he showed in the pursuit of this science, his appreci-
ative instructor states in a letter at the close of this volume.

The opening of the war found him thus engaged ; and,
during the first seven months of its progress, he remained
a law student, — yet by no means contentedly.

Had he followed his impulses, he would have sprung
forward at the first call of the President for troops ; for he
was already prepared for the issue, and he was never a
laggard in duty. But there were considerations that held
him back for a time. Those whose judgment he had ever
deferred to, and whom above all others he loved to please,
while as warmly patriotic as himself, were so imbued with

the gentle spirit of Christian charity, of love to all, that they could not, at first, see the justification of war, even under any pressure of wrong from others. They were unwilling that the son of their hearts should be engaged in a work of blood, not because he might lose his own life, but lest he should take the life of others.

If the need of men to defend the Government, had, at that time, been greater, the issue might have been raised, in Camp's mind, between filial and patriotic obligations; but just then more men were offering themselves than could be accepted, and it was rather as a privilege than a duty that any entered the army. Hence, Henry Camp denied himself, and stayed at home; and no sacrifice which he ever made cost him more, or was more purely an act of generous self-abnegation, than to sit down in ease at the North during the earlier months of the nation's struggle for life. But, although at home, he was making ready for the service in which he was yet to bear a part. Joining in April the Hartford City Guard, a fine organization of citizen soldiery, he acquired proficiency in the details of drill and company movements, while making army tactics more or less his study. Sept. 5, 1861, he accompanied, as a member of the City Guard, doing escort duty, the remains of Gen. Lyon to their resting-place in Eastford; and the impressions of that occasion only added fervor to his strong desire to have a part in the contest in which the hero, then buried, had fallen.

His opportunity came at length. In November, a commission was tendered him in the 10th Volunteer Regiment of Connecticut infantry, then at the Annapolis rendezvous of Gen. Burnside's Coast Division. The proffered position was unsought and unexpected. The call to it enabled him to urge anew upon his parents the claims of country on his personal service, and the fresh indication of his duty furnished by this seeming providential summons. While the subject was under deliberation, he prayerfully sought God's counsel, and earnestly searched the Scriptures, as often before, for direction as to the path of right. The consent of his parents was obtained. The way was then clear before him. He signified his readiness to accept an appointment, and received a commission as second lieutenant, dated December 5, 1861. He was commissioned by Gov. Buckingham on the nomination of Col. Charles L. Russell, the gallant and experienced commander of the 10th, whose desire of increasing the number of good officers in the regiment induced him to seek the best material from without to take the place of that sifted out in the process of organization.

Camp entered joyfully upon his new sphere of action. Those who saw and heard him at the Asylum Hill Sabbath school, where he was a faithful and beloved teacher, on the Sabbath before his departure for the army, will not soon forget the impressions of that occasion. Just before the close of the session, the superintendent called the attention of the school to the fact, that another of its valued teachers was to leave for the army in the course of the week, and added, that it would be gratifying to all to listen to his parting words. Thus called upon, Camp rose at his seat, in a far corner of the room, and, modestly declining to step forward to a more prominent place, said in substance, in his quiet, unassuming, yet dignified and impressive manner, " My friends, I have no farewell speech to make to-day, nor would it be becoming in me to attempt one. I am only one more going out to the war, as many, who will be more missed than I shall be, have gone before. Why should this call for special notice? Although I love my home, and love this old school, I can not say that I am sorry I am going away. I can not even say that I leave you all *because* I deem it my duty to go. I rejoice rather, that, at length, I am to have the part I have longed for, but which has been denied me until now, in defending my Government and in serving my country. I go because I want to go; and I give God thanks for the privilege of going." And it was thus that Henry Camp went to war.

Hastening to Annapolis, he joined his regiment, and entered on the performance of a soldier's duty, and the study of his new profession. He was among strangers, and in a strange work. Few men ever left a pleasanter home, or more entirely changed their associates, habits, and surroundings on joining the army, than did Henry Camp. It was impossible that he should feel entirely at ease, and

have no yearnings for the delights he had left behind. Yet he did not repent his decision. Writing home on his first sabbath evening in camp, he said, —

"I have just been to a prayer-meeting, and it really seems good, after such a busy, working week. I shall prize these services, and, I think, enjoy them a great deal better than I did at home. They are held nearly every evening; but our officers' school interferes with my attending them, except on Sunday. To-night, a great fire was built at the foot of one of the company streets, and we gathered around it, standing, of course. There are several Greenwich men here, who have come to see how their boys are getting along, — men who have already done a great deal, and are ready to do more; and one of them spoke very earnestly. Chaplain Hall said a few words: the rest consisted about equally of prayers and singing.

"The only trouble about these meetings is, that they seem so homelike and pleasant, that I believe a few more would make me homesick. I suspect I should be very soon, if every day was Sunday, and I had leisure to write to you, and think about you: yet I have no doubt that it is a hundred times better for me to be here; and I am very glad that I came. I enjoy the idea that I am really at work, though I can't tell yet how much my work will accomplish: something, I believe, for myself, if for nobody else."

Then, in full appreciation of the novelties and incongruities of life in camp, he added : —

4

"There are all sorts of things going on here at once. Anybody that can't suit himself *somewhere* must be hard to suit.   Prayer-meetings at one end of an avenue ; a group swearing till they make every thing blue, at the other ; one set singing, 'Down in Alabam ;' another, hymns ; some reading in their tents ; some chasing each other round, or wrestling ;   bands playing or drums beating somewhere almost all the time ; sentinels calling for the corporal of the guard, and passing the word along the lines ; a little, or rather a good deal, of every thing, — it isn't much like a home Sunday, unless you happen to get into the right spot, and then it is."

He had not been long in the regiment, before he learned that a prejudice existed against himself, and the newly appointed officers who came with him from Connecticut, because they were commissioned from without, and now filled places aspired to by non-commissioned officers, who were in the regiment at its organization.   The discovery of this fact gave Camp scarcely any annoyance.   He merely mentions it incidentally in a home letter.   It does not seem to have caused him an hour's discomfort.   He had not sought the commission : it had been tendered him by those who had the right to give it, and who, being competent judges, and having the interests of the regiment at heart, had thought it best to secure his services.   He had come, not to obtain popularity or advancement, but to serve his country, and perform the duties of his sphere.   What others thought of him, while his conscience was clear, was not a point about which he was anxious. With all his modesty, he had the intuitive consciousness that time would right him as it did most gloriously. Meantime he moved on in the calm dignity of his nobleness, respected ever by all, — as well by those who envied him, and had jealousy of his position, as by those who admired him and were always glad he had entered the regiment.

The 10th was in the brigade of Gen. John G. Foster, which included also the 23d, 24th, 25th, and 27th Massachusetts regiments, — all New-England troops of the very choicest material. The time passed at Annapolis was every hour improved in the perfecting of drill and discipline, and in other preparations for the somewhat delayed move of the expedition.

In a home letter, Camp sent, as a Christmas token of affection, a good sketch, in pencil, of his regimental camp at Annapolis ; an engraving from which is on the opposite page.

About the first of January, 1862, orders were received for the embarkation of the troops of the expedition ; but a delay of several days occurred ere all was ready, and the fleet left Annapolis. Eight companies of the 10th were on the steamer " New Brunswick." Two companies, I and B, were on the schooner " E. W. Farrington." Lieut. Camp was of Co. I. The fleet rendezvoused at Fort Monroe, thence sailed for Hatteras. On his first sabbath at sea, Camp wrote : —

"It hasn't seemed much like sabbath to me. Every thing on shipboard must of course go on as usual, and reading the 'Independent' is almost the only thing that reminds me of home, — by association I mean: there is plenty to do it by contrast. How little I thought a few sabbaths ago, that I should be on the Atlantic to-day, bound for Hatteras, in a little schooner full of soldiers on their way to the battlefield, — and I one of them! *that's* the strangest of it! I can't realize it yet any better than I could at first. I have to stop once in a while, and take a good look at myself, — and that doesn't do much toward it either; and then go back to the time I left home, and think it all over from the beginning, before I can be quite sure that this fellow here isn't somebody else, and that *I* am not back in Hartford, studying law and teaching Sunday school, and living a good-for-nothing lazy life of it generally."

He lived no "good-for-nothing lazy life" in army service. While on the transport, his opportunities to exert himself for others were as few as they could be anywhere; yet even there he proved how ready he was to do his utmost in his sphere. Stormy weather delayed the progress of the fleet. Some of the vessels drew more water than had been agreed upon, and could not pass the shoal across Hatteras Inlet, known as the "Swash." Weeks instead of days went by before all were fairly inside. The quarters of the men were cramped, close, and uncleanly. The drinking water had all been put in filthy casks. Commissary stores were of the poorest kind. Army contractors had proved a curse to the entire expedition. The health and the spirits of officers and men suffered greatly. Drill was out of the question. Discipline could be but partial, at the best. Every thing tended to laxness and demoralization.

Under these circumstances, the pure example of Lieut. Camp was most effective for good. A brother officer tells of sitting by a table with him, in the saloon of the " New Brunswick," one evening, playing chess, when an officer near them indulged in impure language. Camp, he says, fairly blushed like a maiden ; and then, as the same style of remark was repeated, he rose from his seat, saying, " Let us find another place, the air is very foul here." Another officer, who was his companion on the " Farrington," says, that during all those weeks of wearisomeness, with the entire lack of home restraints, with the stern temptation to idle talk, and with the example of so many in coarseness or profanity, no one ever heard Camp utter a single word that might not properly have been spoken in his parlor before his mother and sisters.

Before he had been many days on shipboard, he had an opportunity of proving conspicuously his courage and gallantry. The steamer " City of New York " was wrecked just outside the bar, after the " Farrington " had passed within. The captain of the schooner determined to attempt the rescue of those on the wreck by putting off in his yawl in the

severe storm then raging. Lieut. Camp proposed to accompany him; but the old skipper "disdained him, for he
was but a youth, and ruddy, and of a fair countenance."
"You!" he cried in a contemptuous tone, "why, you
couldn't handle one of those big oars!" On Camp's assur-
ing him that he had had some experience in rowing, and
thought he could get along, the captain hesitatingly accepted his services, taking an extra man in the boat in view of
the lieutenant's probable failure.

The storm was fearful. The little boat which put off
for the wreck was a mere plaything in the boiling surge,
tossed hither and thither by the lashing waves and the
driving gale, shipping more than one sea that seemed sure
to swamp it, and being kept on its way only by the stout-
est hearts, the strongest arms, and the steadiest nerves.
The attempt to reach the steamer proved vain. Human
strength was helpless against the combined power of the
enraged elements. One after another of the boat's crew
gave up in despair, until only a single sailor remained with
Lieut. Camp, self-possessed and undaunted. The order
was given to return to the transport. When again on his
own deck, the captain, whose distrust of the fair-faced
young officer had given place to admiration for the brave-
hearted, unflinching, skilful oarsman, declared, that
"Lieut. Camp was game, and the pluckiest fellow he ever
saw: if he had had a boat's crew like him he could have
gone through to the wreck." Others who watched the scene

were equally impressed in the lieutenant's favor. Said one, " Lieut. Camp would never have given the word to turn back, for fear was no part of his composition." The story of this exploit was often repeated in his praise among the men of his company and throughout the regiment.

CHAPTER IV.

ROANOKE AND NEWBERNE.

AT length there was a break in the long storm. The vessels of the fleet were either over the "Swash," or their troops and freight were transferred to other craft. Early in February, there was an advance up Pamlico Sound toward Roanoke Island.

"It was something of a sight," wrote Camp, "to see so many vessels under headway at once; gunboats leading off, steamers and sailing vessels in tow of them, following on in a procession some four or five miles long, while little tugs and fast propellers dodged about among them in all directions. Gen. Burnside passed us soon after we started, standing on the hurricane-deck of a small steamer, and compelled to keep his head uncovered half the time in acknowledgment of the cheers which went up from every vessel as he came opposite. He and Foster are both of them magnificent-looking men, tall, of commanding presence, and generally quite the article one reads of."

Of his personal feelings on the approach of the battle, Camp wrote, the evening before the landing : —

"I can't realize that I am to have my first experience

of battle to-morrow, — perhaps my last; not fully, at least. I believe that something so entirely out of the range of all one's previous experience needs to be once seen before it can be brought by any effort fairly into the scope of thought. I suppose that is one reason why it affects me so little. I expected to be at least somewhat excited beforehand; but I have been ten times more so the evening before a boat-race. I shall sleep to-night like a top, and don't believe I shall dream about it. I wish I could feel so when the time comes. I shall be excited enough then, I'll venture. If I can keep cool enough to behave myself, it's all I expect."

His farewell letter written on that night of eventful anticipation, to be delivered to his home friends in case of his fall, was touchingly beautiful, so full of tenderness for those whom he addressed, so firm in its assurance of satisfaction with his lot in such a cause, so clear in its expression of faith in Jesus as his sufficient Saviour. It was never forwarded, but destroyed by him long after, when it had been read to the friend in whom he, later, confided so fully.

In the afternoon of February 7th, the troops landed on Roanoke Island under cover of the gunboats' fire. There was a dismal night in a pitiless storm, without shelter for the poor men, who were as yet unused to the exposures of active campaigning. The following morning was the day of battle. To his disappointment and regret, Camp was prevented sharing in all the excitements of the contest by

being ordered to the landing on special duty, just as his
regiment was taking position on the field. His hurried
letter of the following day told the story briefly : —

"I suppose you will hear of the fight, and be anxious.
I am safe and well, — *wasn't in the action*, I'm sorry to
say ; not through any fault of mine, though. Just before
our regiment was ordered to the front, I was sent, by General Foster's orders, on detached service. Ammunition was
needed ; and I was directed to take a steamer, get 140,000
rounds from a vessel that lay two or three miles off shore,
and use my discretion as to the means of bringing it forward as rapidly as possible. I used all speed ; but the
affair was over before I could rejoin the regiment. It was
a hard fight, and a splendid victory. If I only *could* have
been there ! To think that the regiment has been in such
a glorious affair, and I have no part in it ! It was hard
to be the one sent away."

In a subsequent letter, he described vividly the advance
of his regiment to the battle, and the incidents of the
opening fight. Although not actually under fire, he passed
through all the tedious preliminaries of the action, which
every old soldier knows constitute the most trying, even
if not the most perilous, part of such an engagement.
It was of the early morning of February 8th, that he
wrote : —

"The men fell in promptly and coolly, and stood
awaiting orders, — eating their breakfasts, many of them,

in the mean time. The regiments on the right of the brigade took up the march first, the others following in brigade order (we came third), marching in column, four abreast, along a narrow road with dense underbrush on either side; making it very difficult for the skirmishers on the flanks to advance, and furnishing every advantage for an enterprising enemy to annoy us. They didn't, however. . . .

"As we advanced, we could hear the frequent reports of muskets, and the occasional crack of a rifle, sounding some half a mile ahead. It was evident that the skirmishers were at it. Not far beyond the brook, we passed the 21st Mass., who had been at the outposts during the night,— some in line along the roadside, some around fires a little farther in the woods, — a fine-looking set of fellows, who exchanged jokes and greetings with us as we went by. The farther we went, the sharper the firing became; and soon we had to make way for four men who came carrying a litter, heavy, with a blanket thrown over what lay upon it. Men looked at each other, and grew sober. Presently a couple more came with one between them: no wound was visible; but he was ghastly pale, and could scarcely walk with their support. Then we came upon another, lying quite still by the roadside; he had been brought so far and left, the wounded needed attention more than he. There was no blood, or almost none, upon any of them. I looked to see the wounds, and wondered that there

seemed to be none, until I remembered that gunshot
injuries seldom cause any flow of blood which would soak
through the clothing.   Another passed, with one on each
side to help him : he groaned heavily; and his left arm,
what there was of it, hung in rags from its bloody stump :
it had been shattered by the premature discharge of one
of our own field-pieces.

" These things are so different to *see* and to read about,
it strikes one like a new idea to have the sight actually
before his eyes, just as if he hadn't expected that very
thing.   I can't exactly describe the sensation it gave me.
I sha'n't pretend to say that I wasn't at all affected by it ;
indeed, of all the men whom I have heard speak about it
since the time, there was only one who did pretend so, —
he may, perhaps, have told the truth.

" Our march was obstructed by water and thickets;
sometimes we halted to allow those behind to come up,
then started off at double-quick to gain lost distance.
The discharge of cannon and musketry grew constantly
louder and more frequent, until there was an almost
uninterrupted rattle, evidently quite near, but more
apparently to the left than in front.   At length we halted,
and the men rested for a few moments to give the regiment
before us time to get into position before we advanced to
ours.   The wounded were being brought by at short
intervals, and we had nothing to do but watch them as
they passed.

" It was curious to notice the different effect which the first true idea of what battle is produced on different men. I looked at various faces. Some were perfectly natural; a few bright; a large majority exceedingly sober; more than one a little pale. I was wondering whether I looked pale, when Major Pettibone came up and ordered me to the head of the column to tell Colonel Russell that the general's orders were to advance. I delivered the message, and received for reply that General Foster was himself there and in command. So I reported to the major, and took my place again."

It was just then that Lieutenant Camp was ordered back for the ammunition. The task assigned him was a tedious one; and when it was at length accomplished, his regiment, having changed position, was not easily found by him. Although he strained every nerve to be speedily again at the front, it was evening before he was once more with his command.

" Late in the afternoon," he continued, " after I had given up all hopes of rejoining the regiment in season to take any part in the action, General Foster, with a couple of his aides, came riding along. He stopped and told us the news himself. ' They have surrendered! — 2,000 prisoners! They asked what terms I would give them: I said an unconditional surrender, and they accepted!' The men didn't give him time to finish. Up went the caps, and up went the cheers, and up went the men bodily; their loads didn't weigh a feather. He inquired about the ammunition, and passed on."

The part of the Tenth in the engagement had been prominent and honorable, and its losses severe. Gallant Colonel Russell had been killed early in the action. Other brave officers and good men had given the testimony of blood to their patriotism. To one who had so longed for the privilege of an active part in the nation's life-struggle as Henry Camp, the disappointment of being separated from his regiment, at the decisive hour of such a contest, was bitter and enduring. The thrilling narrative of the excitements and perils of the day, to which he listened with profoundest interest by the bivouac fire on the stormy night succeeding, and every repetition of its noteworthy incidents, from brother-officers, on subsequent occasions, only intensified his regret, and deepened his sense of personal loss.

"The more I think of my own absence," he wrote a few days later, "the more it provokes me. Not that I, or any one else, feel as if I was at all to blame for it; but it has drawn a sort of line between me and all the rest. They shared the danger, and, of course, share the exultation of the battle. I can only rejoice as I would over any other victory. They have all been tested, and stood the test. I am still untried. They, in short, are the victors in one of the most glorious battles — perhaps the very most so — that have yet been fought. I had nothing to do with it:

even my wretched ammunition wasn't needed or used. It's very doubtful whether our regiment has another chance. Even if there is another fight at Newberne, the second brigade will probably claim and receive the advance. At the best, I shall always be one behind the rest, —have one less deed to remember and be proud of.

" I don't like to think of all my friends who know that the Tenth Connecticut distinguished itself, inquiring where I was, and what I was about; and what will provoke me most of all will be the attempt I know some of them will make to persuade me they think it was just as well, all the same thing, and all that humbug. Any thing but that! If the war *should* come to an end, as I suppose I ought to hope it will, without my having been in battle, I shall never want to show my face again at home; not that I shall have any thing to be *ashamed* of, but that I sha'n't have any thing else. There's enough of grumbling ! — it's babyish, and does no good : but that's just the way I feel about it ; and now that I've cried my cry out, I'll stop."

The troops remained but a few days on shore at Roanoke Island. Re-embarking, they made several demonstrations up Pamlico Sound; but the advance to Newberne was delayed until the following month. During the weeks of waiting on shipboard, before and after the first landing, Camp's home letters were full and varied, showing him in his true light as the man of cheerfulness, of honor, of courage, of patriotism, of purity, of poetry, and of Christian faith.

"I have just been hearing," he wrote, "part of a letter from the 'New-York Times,' about this expedition, written at Hatteras; very accurate in its statements; but I really hadn't realized before what a hard time we have had of it. It sounds quite formidable, all boiled down and concentrated into the space of one newspaper column; but taken in small doses, as we have had it, at considerable intervals, it hasn't seemed to amount to so much. We have concluded, since reading it, to set up for martyrs: the idea hadn't occurred to us before.

"These things are not half as hard as they sound; they are just what we anticipate, and go prepared for; very different from what they would be to one fresh from home, without the hardening process which we have already undergone in camp."

It was thus that he sought to encourage his friends at home as to his personal trials and privations on the close, cramped, and filthy transport. If he mentioned these at all, it was in a burlesque strain that hardly made an appeal for pitying sympathy. Thus from the "Swash:" —

"The poor fellows down in the hold would be glad to stretch their legs ashore, I know. They are terribly crowded. They are packed so close at night, that, when they have lain long enough on one side, somebody sings out, 'Hard-a-lee,' and over they all go together, just as we used to hoist the signal, ' Leg over,' in the recitation-room at college, and astonish the tutors with a simultaneous whisk from one side to the other. This is a little more practical.

. . . "All our water is brought from Baltimore : it costs seven cents a gallon, delivered at Annapolis. It isn't first-rate, though the barrel we are now on answers well enough. The flavor depends on what the barrel held before. This was a whiskey barrel : those we have had — kerosene and turpentine — were not so good. . . .

" I'll venture to say that there's no spot in the United States where there are more men, boys, negroes, and cockroaches, to the square foot, than in the cabin of the ' E. W. Farrington.' The first three I'm used to, — can stand being crowded by them ; but this having cockroaches hold a door when one tries to open it, and pull his blankets off from him at night, is something new. We have held our own pretty well ; but they are gradually getting the upper hand of us : infantry are no match for them, and we talk of getting a few artillerymen, with their guns, from Fort Hatteras. I thought of putting a few specimens into the box of curiosities I send home, making a regular infernal machine of it ; but, reflecting that you have no arms but the old Revolutionary sword, concluded to wait."

Of the national situation just then, before the brilliant victories on the Western waters had re-assured confidence in the Federal cause, and while enemies at the North were

5

co-operating with enemies beyond the seas to give encouragement and aid to treason and to traitors, he spoke with firmness and courage.

"Things abroad do look pretty dark for us, don't they? if foreign newspapers at all reflect the feelings of their governments. It is a hard fight now: European intervention would make it well-nigh desperate. I *hope* that our Government will stand firm at all hazards, and that the North will sustain such a policy until the last dollar is gone, the last village burned to the ground, and the last able-bodied man has fallen on the battle-field; but I'm afraid they haven't the resolution and the self-denial to hold out to the end. I am afraid that danger and disaster will develop cowardice, as they always do, and we shall be left to the fate we shall then deserve. I haven't really looked upon such a thing as possible, hitherto: it need not be now, if the nation will only put forth its strength; but *will* it? That's the question. I don't see how any man, who *can* do any thing, can be inactive now, when every day of his life is worth a century."

Referring to the advance of the troops up Roanoke Island after the battle, and their visits to the camps and homes of the enemy, he gave expression to his refined sense of honor as a truly chivalrous soldier.

"Besides many other articles taken from the field or from houses, a number of letters were found, curious specimens enough, some of them, in point both of manner and matter, — on all subjects, from love to shoe-pegs. I was almost ashamed of myself for listening while some of them were being read. I don't know what title a victory gives one to pry into other men's private matters in this way, those at least of a domestic or social nature; and it really seems too bad. This letter business strikes me as a very different thing from the transfer of ordinary property, according to the rule which every one recognizes, that to the victors belong the spoils."

Surely a college-mate esteemed him rightly who wrote, on hearing of his death, "I can conceive nothing knightlier than Henry Camp, the soldier. All the graces of valor, loyalty, and generosity must have sat upon him, and made him the very flower of our heroic youth. Great-Heart is the name that became him. Like Bunyan's knight, he has overcome, and passed on and up before us to the better country."

A few nights before the battle of Newberne, he wrote :—

"It has been a beautiful day, and the fleet was a fine sight, at noon, as it stretched in long line from east to west, moving steadily, and with a look of *power* that was magnificent. No land in sight, except a few blue lines at intervals along the horizon; and again at sunset, when the sun, which had been for some hours clouded, came out and lit the whole scene most gorgeously. I climbed the shrouds, and stayed aloft until it began to grow dark. It isn't often, in an ordinary lifetime, that one sees a sight better worth looking at than that was. It's very true that soldiering isn't all poetry, according to some; but neither is it all prose, according to others.

"I wish I was good at description. I'd like to paint you a scene occasionally, so that you could *see* it as you can Scott's or Longfellow's. And that *I,* of all men, who have never pictured to myself, even in imagination, any but the most commonplace, dog-trot sort of a life, should be in the midst of what seems to me, even now, more like romance than fact, — I can't realize it more than half the time."

It was after such an evening of poetic musing that he wrote the following lines, — as stately and as graceful as his own manly form, and as warm as his own loving heart. They shortly after appeared anonymously in the " Hartford Evening Press : " —

BETWEEN ROANOKE AND NEWBERNE.

The swift-winged Northern breezes are blowing fair and free:
I pace by night the spray-wet deck, and watch the rushing sea;
The whistling of the shrill-voiced wind is full of speech to me:
It stretches taut the swelling sail, it crests the wave with foam:
I drink its bracing freshness; it is the breath of home.

From hoary monarch mountains, whose giant cliffs, piled high,
Lift up their snow-crowned foreheads against the clear, cold sky, —
From forests dark with shadow, where pine and cedar fling
Music and fragrance mingled upon the zephyr's wing, —
From leaping white-maned torrents, that thunder on their way,
Cleaving a path of madness through splintered granite gray, —

From every hill and valley, — from every rock and tree, —
New England sends a deep-drawn breath, far o'er the Southern sea.

Slowly the anxious hours passed on in dark suspense
With breathing hushed to silence, and nerve and heartstring tense:
Now swells from heaving bosom the sigh of deep relief,
Too sad for shout of triumph, too proud for sob of grief, —
The banners of our victory wave o'er a fallen chief. *

Yet welcome, at whatever price, the Nation's leap to life:
Rather than deathly stupor, hail to the deadly strife!
From East to West, the solid tramp of armies shakes the ground;
The vibrant clang of ringing steel fills all the air with sound;
The sword, so long uplifted, sweeps down in sudden wrath:
Right through the hosts of treason, it hews its crimson path.

Before its edge of terror, shrinks back the rebel foe,
As leaves that curl before the breath of Etna's fiery flow;
Again is bared the red right arm another blow to smite;
Already blaze the signals that tell of coming fight, —
To-morrow's sun shall set in blood, — Amen! — God speed the right!

On the 13th of March, the troops landed at Slocum's Creek, about fifteen miles below Newberne, and marched some ten miles in a drenching rain toward the city. There was another night of bivouac in a pelting storm, as at Roanoke, to the sore discomfort of all.

"I stood before the fire," wrote Camp, cheerfully, of that night, "until I was tolerably dry; took my blankets, which the india-rubber had kept in good order, for a seat;

---

* Colonel Russell of the Tenth.

leaned my back against a stack of rifles, and slept three or four hours quite comfortably. I believe, with a little practice, I could sleep standing on one foot or on my head : it's all habit, and I'm quite getting over the foolish prejudice in favor of lying down,— especially on any thing soft.''

An early start was made on the morning of the 14th, and an advance toward the enemy's intrenched position. It was not long before Camp had the desired opportunity to test himself in battle.

"I was afraid," he wrote, "we shouldn't reach the front before the affair was over ; but very soon the order came to turn aside from the road, and march through the fields to a position further to the left. We took an oblique direction, and hadn't gone a hundred rods when a loud, swift whiz went through the air, sounding as if some one had torn a thousand yards of canvas from one end to the other at a single pull. Almost everybody involuntarily looked up (I did), as if we could have seen it pass, when it was far beyond us when the sound first struck our ears. Some stooped, — one or two crouching close to the earth, and hardly ready to rise until they were sharply started. A few yards further, and there was another, — this time apparently passing but a little above our heads ; then another, and still more ; some further, and some nearer, — every one causing more or less dodging, and an occasional irregularity in the ranks, promptly checked, as far as possible, by the officers. We passed obliquely into the woods, and were ordered to lie down just behind the crest of a slightly inclining slope. The men were behaving well enough; but they didn't wait to hear the order twice. I never saw a crowd drop quite so suddenly as they did. As we lay on the marshy ground, bullets flew thick; some seeming to pass only two or three feet over us: one entered the ground just at the elbow of one of the men. Occasionally there would be none heard for some little time, then a perfect shower would hiss along, with a sharp 'thud' now and then as one struck a tree close by. Grape rattled through once or twice, generally passing high; though I saw the water dashed up by it, from a pool a little to the right. We had been in this position perhaps twenty or thirty minutes, when an order came for us to march to the front, and open fire immediately. 'Now,' said I, 'it's coming: in about three minutes we shall see who's who, and what's what.' The fire of the enemy, at this time, seemed to be directed elsewhere. We advanced to the edge of the woods, formed line of battle, and prepared to fire, without, I think, their having observed us at all.

"We know that, as soon as we discovered our situation by firing, we should be answered; but, in the mean time, we had opportunity to form and dress the line without disturbance. It had scarcely been done, when our right opened fire; and it passed rapidly down the line toward us. The men were, for the moment, wild with excitement, and waited for no orders, but raised their pieces and fired, —

half of them without taking aim. I checked those who were near me. But soon the order was given, and at it they went again, — loading and firing just as rapidly as they could handle their pieces.

"We could see the puffs of smoke rise from the breast-works in front of us, and once or twice a momentary slack-ening of our own volleys allowed us to hear the whistle of bullets. It didn't need that to make the reports of artillery, and roar of solid shot through the air, audible; but it was some little time before I saw any effects of their reply to us. I had been moving from one to another, rectifying the aim of some who fired high, and seeing to it, that they understood what they were about, when I saw a man who had been lying on the ground a few yards to the left, roll suddenly over. I turned toward him; but some one was already supporting his head, as the blood gushed over his face from a hideous wound: a bullet had entered his eye, and lodged in the lower part of his head. Several of the men gathered around; but I sent them back to their places, and they went without a word. Most of them behaved excellently throughout, listening to orders, and obeying them promptly, after the wild excitement of the first few rounds was over.

"We were still firing rapidly, when cheering rose loud in front; and, in a moment more, our flag appeared, waving from the parapet of the breastwork. They cheered on the right, and they cheered on the left, and they cheered before us, and we cheered; and had hardly finished cheering when the order came to resume our march. The battle was over, and we had only to take possession of Newberne."

Camp had passed bravely the ordeal of battle. So cool was he, seemingly unmoved when the fight was hottest, and those about him most excited, that the men of his company called him their Iron Man, and told how efficient he was, in directing the fire of some, in giving assistance to others whose pieces were out of order, and in speaking encouraging words to all, ever with "the same pleasant look in his face."

"As to my own feelings," he said, in his home letter, "I can't describe them any more than I could when I tried before. They were much the same, only less in degree, as when we were marching into action at Roanoke. I was thoroughly excited internally, and every nerve was tense; but I can't accuse myself of any tendency to avoid the danger I felt, or even of dodging bullets, as I have heard that most men involuntarily do when they are first under fire. This excitement of nerves continued until the action fairly commenced, and then seemed to wear off rapidly, until, after we had been engaged a few minutes. I felt as cool, and, I thought then, as natural as ever. It couldn't have been natural though; for I have been shocked since to think how little I cared for the poor fellows that were wounded. The reason, I suppose, that the danger

ceased to affect me was, that I had something more important to occupy my mind. I thought of it, of course, but
was too busy to pay any attention to it."

In another letter, describing the battle to his friend
Owen, he said, —

"The sensation of coming under fire is, to me, very
much like that I used to feel in boat-racing, — exceedingly
nervous business waiting for the signal to give way, but
comfortable enough as soon as there is an opportunity to
work off the surplus excitement. How a bayonet charge
or a repulse of cavalry might seem, I can not tell; but
there has been nothing in such work as has fallen to us
hitherto, more exciting than there was for the oarsmen in
one of our grand boat-races between Harvard and Yale."

The bridge across the Trent being burned by the rebels,
there was a delay of some hours in transporting the troops
of Foster's brigade, on gunboats, to the city bank of the
river. Late in the afternoon, the 10th marched through
the streets of Newberne to the old Fair Grounds, and,
taking possession of the just deserted camp of the Thirty-
third North-Carolina Regiment, made ready for a night of
rest. Not many officers would speak as cheerfully of a
detail for guard-duty, under such circumstances, as did
Lieutenant Camp when called upon that evening.

"I was too tired," he said, "to spend much time
looking about me, — was reflecting how nicely I should
feel inside my blankets in about five minutes (it was now

two or three hours after dark), and had just pulled off my boots for the first time since I left the vessel, when the adjutant came in. ' You'll have to put them on again,' said he. ' You are detailed, with thirty men from your company, to do provost guard-duty. Can you stand it ? ' It was rather tough after two such days; but I was less tired than most of the rest. I find that my endurance is greater than that of men who consider themselves tough. My old training stands me in good stead, and especially my habits of walking. I haven't yet been so tired by any march as not to feel equal to ten miles more, though I mightn't have been anxious to carry my overcoat and equipments along. But the men, — I really hated to call out some of them, poor fellows, hardly able to drag one foot after the other.''

This considerate regard for the men who were under him, showed itself in all his home-letters, and also — to those who knew him well — in his conversation and actions. His quiet, undemonstrative ways prevented its being fully understood by all. His calm dignity of demeanor was not unfrequently deemed an indication of coldness or hauteur. Never a greater mistake. His heart was far warmer, and his feelings kindlier, than could be judged from his modest reticence and his shrinking reserve of manner.

At Newberne there was a long season of comparative quiet. As the spring months passed away, Camp grew restive.

"Save me," he wrote, "from a summer in Newberne, or any other one place. Our life, except when in active service, is mere machine-work, at best; endurable, even enjoyable, by way of preparation for something better, but, as a 'regular beverage,' altogether insipid and flat. Our wits grow rusty in this tread-mill business, — that's the worst of it. I was beginning a while ago [on the transport] to fear that the result of our campaigning would be in having more brains softened from within than perforated from without."

Yet Newberne life was not without its activities. Picketing in the face of the enemy was something new to the soldiers of the Tenth; and there was an occasional alarm or skirmish on the outer lines, that gave zest to the service. Of the first march to the picket front, Camp wrote : —

"All the negro huts in the outskirts sent out large delegations to the gates to watch us go by, evidently enjoying the sight hugely. One old woman stood in her doorway, beaming upon us most graciously, and addressing us as we came opposite, 'I hopes you is all well, genlin,' getting a volley of answers from our men."

It was on one of the earlier tours of picket-duty, that Camp's coolness and courage stood out prominently in an emergency. Another lieutenant had taken out a scouting-party of a dozen men, beyond the lines, to obtain information, and, if possible, to pick up a prisoner or two; having been told by the negroes that small squads of the enemy

sometimes came down to within a short distance of the
Union position. While this party was out, Captain Otis
and Lieutenant Camp were eating dinner in a cabin near
the picket-reserve, " when suddenly," as Camp described
it, " while we were enjoying our hoe-cake and bacon, two
or three of the negroes in the cabin exclaimed in a low
tone, ' De Southerners comin'! de Southerners comin'!'
We seized our swords, which we had laid aside so as to eat
with more comfort, and stepped to the door just as one of
the cavalrymen dismounted from a horse, panting and
covered with sweat. ' Every one of your men,' said he,
' is killed or taken prisoner!' A glance showed that he
did not refer, as one would naturally think, to our reserve
across the way; and we knew he must be speaking of the
scouting-party. The affair had taken place, he said, a few
minutes before, at a distance of two or three miles. The
enemy were still advancing, — a large force of cavalry.
He and two others had put their horses to speed, and
escaped; but all those on foot, and one or two of the
mounted men, were either shot or taken. By this time,
the other two came in sight, their horses on the full run.
I half expected to see the rebels on their heels; but
they drew rein, and came up to report. Their story was
less alarming than that of the first, — who was, I think,
the most frightened fellow I ever saw. They said our
men had been surprised by a party of cavalry, and had
taken to the woods. They had seen none killed or taken,

though several volleys were fired, — couldn't be sure, however, being hard pressed themselves, and only saved by the speed of their horses and the poor aim of the enemy. We saw that we ourselves were in no danger; and the reserve, which had been called to arms, was dismissed."

It was no slight evidence of character, for a young lieutenant, inexperienced in border warfare, to rise at once above the influences of a picket alarm, at that stage of the war, and propose to go out, in the face of the enemy, to the rescue of his endangered comrades. Lieutenant Camp's impulse prompted him to an instant suggestion of this kind.

"I thought," he wrote, "that a party ought to be sent out immediately to find our men, who were probably in the woods, not daring to retake the road until they were certain that the enemy had retired. Captain Otis finally said, that, if the men chose to volunteer, he wouldn't object."

Volunteers being called for, eight men of the Tenth came promptly forward. Besides these, four of the horsemen — artillerymen acting as cavalry — were induced to go along as advance skirmishers; and Camp started at once on his scout. His cavalry did not please him. "Their failing, certainly, wasn't lack of vigilance. They walked their horses, with revolvers drawn, and one eye cocked over the shoulder, ready to run. My men," he added, with pride in the brave fellows, "would have marched straight upon Goldsborough, if I had only asked them to." The enterprise was entirely successful. The scattered party were found, a few at a time, until there was but one missing and unaccounted for. "As there then was no more than time to go back before sunset, it seemed unwise to wait any longer; and we returned, having at length accomplished what we went out for. It was dark when we reached the reserve; and they had begun to grow anxious about us, having expected us back hours before. The other man came in the next morning, having spent the night in the woods. The whole thing ended much better than any of us anticipated."

In the full and free sketches of such exploits as this, in his home-letters, never a boastful word is found of his own performance, although praise is given heartily to all who were with him, and did well. His modesty equaled his courage and his nobleness.

Each new call upon his energies seemed to give Camp fresh satisfaction in his work. "I am contented now," he wrote, "for the first time in three years. It doesn't seem as if the old fret ever need come back, — perhaps it will." Then, as showing that his heart was in no degree weaned from the loved ones at home, he added, "I never realized before, as I do now, the difference between a dear old New-England home and the rest of the world. I long to see you all, — you know how, — but not enough to wish to leave unfinished that which we came to do. I want to

see a workmanlike job made of it, — no botch-work.
I want to help put in the last touches, and then won't we
all be glad to come back? You know how I felt about it
when I left home: I feel just so now. I have always
been glad that I came, and think, whether I return or not,
that I always shall be."

In response to the suggestion from home, that he ought
to be satisfied with going into danger when he was *ordered*
there, he wrote : —

"As to volunteering, its being my duty simply to
obey orders, &c., — I am sure, when you think of it, that
you would have me do as much, not as little, as possible.
I certainly won't run any unnecessary risks, — risks which
it is not necessary that *somebody* should run ; but, when
there is work to be done, I want to do it. That, you
know, was the idea with which I started, and the more
opportunity I have to carry it into practice, the more I
shall feel as though I were accomplishing my object. If
men are sent where they should not be, the more need
they have of officers to lead them through with as little
loss as possible, and neutralize a blunder, if it is a blunder,
by all the means which can be used. For my own sake,
as well as for yours, — and that I may accomplish the more,
— I intend to be prudent, and do nothing fool-hardy, or
that my calm judgment doesn't approve. What it does,
I know you would not have me avoid."

Henry Camp wished to live to a purpose, and if he

must die, to die to a purpose. His desire was to be where he could accomplish most for the cause that had his heart. He did not seek his own advancement. He did not crave a place of danger. But he was never content, except at the post of duty; and he longed for that to be just where his every blow would be most effective for the right. Referring to unimportant scouts from Newberne, and to trifling engagements on the picket-line, he said, —

"There would be no satisfaction at all in being shot or captured in one of these miserable little skirmishes where neither side could possibly gain any thing worth a single life, — a very different thing from falling in battle."

Again he wrote : —

"I should like to have a share in the grand blows of the Army of the East. Our out-of-the-way performances, down here, don't seem to amount to much by themselves; and yet we've had sharp work, — it's no exaggeration to say so. The list of casualities looks small alongside of what you read of in the great battles of the West; yet, when you come to compare the numbers engaged, we lost as many in four hours at Newberne as they did in two days at Pittsburg Landing, or in three at Fort Donelson, — as large a percentage, I mean, of course."

Later, when the Peninsular campaign was at its hight, he wrote in the same strain : —

"We groan in spirit at having to stay here idle while the fight at Richmond is so fierce, every man needed, —

6

every man there worth a hundred elsewhere. Nothing else that the war can bring forth will furnish cause for so proud a satisfaction as to have thrown one's weight into the scale while the balance yet trembled. What is left to do will be boy's play in comparison, — as has been all before on this side the Alleghanies. When the race is won, there's nothing like feeling that you pulled a good oar on the home stretch." Then, as showing his real interest in hard service, he added, "I don't want to fight for the sake of fighting, but for the sake of accomplishing something that will tell upon the grand result." For that grand result, he was ready to toil or to suffer, or willing, if need be, to wait. "I have chosen," he said, "the sphere in which I think I can work most efficiently for God and my country; and, if we have thirty-years' war instead of three, I expect to see it through, — or as much of it as comes in my lifetime."

CHAPTER V.

CAMP LIFE AND CAMPAIGNING.

OME of Camp's experiences with the liberated slaves in Newberne were recounted by him in an interesting manner : —

" Did I tell you," he wrote home, " about the family of fugitives that came in while we were out on picket? I was on duty at the time. One of the men called me, saying that some one wished to pass our lines. I came to the post where they had been stopped, and there were two negro women with a swarm of little things, — one or two in their arms; one or two, hardly big enough to walk, carrying others. They had come five miles that night; their masters intended to send them up country the next day; they had got wind of it, and seized the only chance of escape. I asked how many children they had. ' She have four head, and I four.' (So many *head*, — that's the way these darkies talk.) I don't see how they could have done it; little barefooted toddlers! — some of them, trotting along in their nightgowns as if they had just come out of a warm bed, instead of having tramped five miles in the cold and dark; but there wasn't one of them whimpering, or making the least fuss about it, — poor little things! I didn't keep them long with questions, — passed them, of course; but advised them, now that they were safe within our lines, to spend the rest of the night in a deserted house near by, and so they did. Their mistress, a widow of strong secesh sympathies, came into town next day. 'She wanted to see General Foster.' I don't know what was the object or result of the interview; but I think it safe to say, she didn't get back the runaways."

Another of his stories concerning this class of people was published at the time in the "Hartford Press," and copied widely : —

"I was in a negro house yesterday, and had some conversation with the inmates. I asked one gray-headed old negress if she had ever had children sold away from her. 'Sold! dey *all* sold! chil'en an' gran'chil'en an' great gran'chil'en, — dey sell ebry one!' She clasped her bony hands over her head, and looked up at me as she spoke, 'Dere was one — de lass one — de on'y gran'chile I did hab lef'. He neber knowed his mammy. I took him when he *dat* little. I bringed him up to massa, an' I say, "Massa, dis my little gran'chile : may I keep him 'bout heah?" An' he say, "I don' care what you do wid him." So I take him; he *dat* little. Den one mornin', when he all rolled up in blanket 'tween my knees, Massa Green

com'd in, an' say, " Dis boy sold ; " and *dey take him 'way!*
O Lord Jesus, help me pray ! '

" I can't begin to do justice to the way in which she
told me this, nor describe the earnestness of voice and
gesture, which made it impressive. I wish some of our
Northern editors, who cringe just as abjectly as ever
before their old masters, and howl in such consternation
whenever it seems likely that the war may interfere,
directly or indirectly, with their pet deviltry, — I wish
some of them could have heard and seen her.

" I made further inquiries about the old woman's grand‐
child. He is now, it seems, somewhere near Raleigh.
She seemed wonderfully comforted when I told her that
we meant to go up there by and by, and I hoped we
should find him. She seemed to take it in the light of a
promise; and I heard her, just before I went out, saying
to herself, ' Bress de Lord ! — bress de Lord ! I shall
see my gran'chile again ! ' Poor old creature ! I hope
she won't be disappointed."

Then, as expressive of his own views of the " pet
deviltry " of the South, he added : —

" It *can't be* but that this war will kill slavery ; and
if it does, cost what it will of our blood, and your tears,
and every man's money, it won't be too much. Don't
you think so ? I *know* you do. Not that I've changed
my ideas as to the ultimate object of the war ; but I
am more firmly convinced than ever that the destruc-

tion of slavery is one of the means indispensable to the end."

His "ideas as to the ultimate *object* of the war" were fully set forth on a later occasion. He longed and hoped and prayed for the end of slavery. He *fought* for government as a divinely ordained power. His sympathies were with the cause of universal freedom. His work of war was for the maintenance of law and order. "Work," he said, "which I am as sure that God approves as I am sure that he designs to have order and law prevail throughout the universe over chaos and anarchy.

"What on earth have I said to give you the idea that I am fighting, not for the Government, but the abolition of slavery? Exactly the reverse. It is the maintenance of the Government that I consider the object, and the *only* object of the war; abolition, one of the means, but no more. I think as ill of slavery as you do : I believe, with you, that it is the cause of the Rebellion, and that it must be crushed wherever rebellion exists; but I fight for the preservation of the republic, not for the abolition of slavery, because I consider the former the nobler and more important object, — *the* object for which the latter is but a means. Strike at the root, you say. Yes; but why? Because the poisonous growth is killing that which it is my highest aim to keep alive and flourishing. It is not always the cause of an evil that must be made the great object of an attack in remedying its effects.

"Government is the human embodiment of law, and law is the central idea of the universe. 'Liberty for ever and for all,' is a taking watchword; and a thousand will catch it up as the expression of their highest aim, where one will adopt the far higher and nobler one of universal law. Among free moral agents, perfect liberty involves inevitable abuse, incalculable sin and suffering. Perfect law would be the acquiescence of all in God's plans, — the unquestioned supremacy of his will. Of the two abstractions, therefore, I choose the latter; and, when they become embodied in material forms for which a man can fight, I will fight for the republic — which is the concrete expression, however imperfect, of the higher — rather than for the emancipation of four million negroes, which is the corresponding outgrowth of the lower.

"As to the soundness or unsoundness of the Administration, my action is independent of it. Government and the ideas behind it, — the nation and its republican institutions, — are what I fight for, not Abraham Lincoln or his advisers. There's nobody that I dislike more than a young old fogy. I don't think I'm in any danger of being generally so considered; but, if public opinion *does* run wild, I shan't try to keep up with it. It will settle back again by and by. We shall see whether I am behind it ten years from now."

Writing, after one of the many changes of camp at Newberne, of the absolute necessity of one's looking out for himself in army life, especially at a time of breaking camp, or otherwise changing quarters, Camp said, jocosely, " The only way to get what belongs to you, down here, is to *take* it, and put in a claim to half your neighbor's property to balance what he demands of yours. When everybody is at hand to do their own fighting and stealing, the system works very fairly : nobody suffers, unless it is some modest, honest greenhorn, who deserves it for not learning, when he is at the South, to do as the Southerners do ; but, when two or three are absent, the rest of the rogues make short work with their share of the plunder." In pleasant irony, he added, in comment on the grasping spirit he had seen displayed, " But it takes time to learn to steal as well as to acquire any other useful art, — especially when one's early education has been neglected. Can't you find somebody like Fagin to apprentice Charley to ? You've no idea how much it will be worth to him if we happen to get into war with England or France by and by, when he is old enough to have a finger and thumb in the pie."

It was during the spring and summer in Newberne, that Camp wrote most of those letters to his college classmate, which are referred to, in the earlier pages of this volume, as being so richly blessed to their recipient. There is, perhaps, nothing remaining of his writings, more clearly expressive of his religious views and convictions than the subjoined extracts from those letters : —

" I am glad to hear from you, which is the next best

thing to seeing you," he wrote, in his first of the series, " and still more glad to hear that your interest in religious subjects still continues. You know I never could say what I wanted to say. I am afraid I shall find it even more difficult to write what I want to write. I am rejoiced that you find yourself making progress, — that you have conquered the theoretical difficulties which formerly troubled you; and yet, I can not but fear, from what you say, that you have paused before still more serious obstacles. As far as intellectual conviction of the truth and excellence of Christianity goes, a man can carry himself, — though I think I can see the hand of God leading you, unconsciously, perhaps, to yourself, even there; but, beyond that, comes a barrier which can not be passed without one's earnest call for, and acceptance of, help from above, *voluntarily* sought, and freely given.

"I think I know exactly what you mean when you say you have not interest enough in the matter to pray. I used to feel the same. I do still, far oftener than I ought, or wish to ; but there are other times when I wonder at myself, when I seem to realize, in some faint degree, the real and infinite importance of these things, and when it seems to me strange that I can take any interest, comparatively, in other matters. I wish I knew how to present the motives to a Christian life as they appear to me then. Passing by, for the present, those of reward and punishment, considered merely as such, let us look for a moment at another, — one which has often struck me with great force, and must, I think, have weight with a mind constituted like your own.

" We are just at the commencement of a life with which this one compares only as time compares with eternity; whose interests are to those of the present as the infinite to the finite. Admitting the truth of the Christian religion, its hearty and thorough acceptance is the only preparation we can now make for this future; and the entrance upon a real Christian life is the entrance upon the first stage of progress toward all that is worthy to be made an end to a reasoning and immortal being, — all, in short, that is worthy of a *man.* It is at this point that we must, at some time, start, if we are ever to take up earnestly the pursuit of the highest good, if we are ever to enter upon the life of truest manliness. Until we have reached this, we are living to no real purpose; we have not commenced the work which is to be the work of our existence. Is it worth while to live for any thing less? Are not our energies, in effect, wasted, unless we devote them, not only to that which is noble and excellent, but to that which is noblest and most excellent? And is not every day lost until we begin to act up to this belief?

" Surely there is no ideal which one can set before himself higher than that of a life whose mainspring is *duty,* — with all that seems hard and cold in that word softened and warmed by a love that turns trial and difficulty into joy: the same feeling which makes pleasant a service rendered to a dear earthly friend intensified, as is fitting, toward him who has done and suffered more for us than we can ever comprehend, until we see him face to face and know him even as we are known. Is there not something in this to rouse an earnest man to vigorous effort? something worth striving for with the whole soul? Then, why wait for feeling? It will not come at the bidding of the will. Why not enter at once upon the course which understanding and conscience approve? Why not obey them in this, as you would in any thing else?

"Just here comes a difficulty. He who resolves to do this just as he may have resolved to carry out former purposes, — by the force of his own determination, relying upon that and that alone, — inevitably fails. He may live a moral life, a philanthropic life, one which gains for him the highest respect and esteem of his fellow-men; but when he comes to compare it with the strict requirements of God's law, he finds the standard too high, hopelessly beyond his reach, though he spends life in the efforts to attain it. The longer he tries in this way, the lower he falls. There is nothing left but an utter abandonment of trust in one's own exertions, and a simple leaning on Christ for his support, his aid in living a life of obedience to his will, and his pardon for all its thousand imperfections. He stands ready; only '*knock*, and it shall be opened unto you.'

"I think you strike the key-note of your difficulties, when you say, 'I have hitherto relied solely upon myself.' That is what keeps you at a stand-still, the effort ' to solve the problem ' for yourself. It is hard to give it up, — hard to bend one's pride to the acknowledgment of weakness and dependence. The way is narrow; but unless we become as little children in our humility, there is no entrance for us into the kingdom of heaven. So far from being really a degradation, it is the highest test of true nobility of soul, that it should be willing to take the place which God created it for, — the highest privilege to come into harmony with his great system, to enjoy his direct and conscious personal influence, to feel the joy of his approval.

"I am afraid I have preached you more of a sermon than you will care to read; but I have spoken plainly and earnestly, because it is to a dear friend. How I should rejoice to know that you had at length found what you have sought and your friends have sought for you! It is now some years that I have remembered you in my prayers; with such encouragement, I certainly shall not now forget you: but do pray for yourself. Don't fall into the mistake of thinking that you must wait for a certain degree of *feeling*. If you feel that you need God's help, and are willing to ask for it, that is enough. He is more willing to give than you to receive, if you will only be persuaded to prove for yourself the truth of all these things."

Again Camp wrote: "It is encouraging to know that you feel a growth in your moral nature, come in what shape it will; but I can not judge from what you say whether you have reached, or are still on this side of, the point which must be passed before any radical and permanent change for the better can fairly commence. One may stroll for ever on the ground outside the narrow gate, — receding or advancing, — even till his hand is upon the latch; but, until he enters, his journey along the true path is yet to begin.

"I want to believe that your decision has been made, not merely to experiment a while, but, relying upon God's help, to make your life henceforth no longer your own, but his. Then, however feeble your faith, it will increase; however slowly you move, it will be in the right direction. Love, as you say, will grow with time and the experience of God's goodness; culture will produce its effects. I do hope that it is so with you; and that the doubts and misgivings of which you speak will vanish with the steady increase of light in your soul. But don't think, though you should remain stationary, or even go backward, that you have proved whether there is 'any thing in it.' Be sure that the difficulty is in yourself, and that it is as impossible that God should refuse to hear and help one who comes to him in sincerity and humility, as that he should cease to exist. The universe shall sink into annihilation before his word shall fail."

When, at length, came a letter giving full assurance of faith, on the part of the one in whom he had been so deeply interested, Camp replied : —

"So you have finally entered upon a Christian life. You do not know, my dear fellow, how glad I am to hear it, both on your own account, and my own, if I have been, in any degree, of assistance to you. You will know, I hope, some time, when one for whom you have so sincere a friendship takes the same step which you have taken, — one which I am sure you will rejoice in, more and more, the longer you live."

It is noteworthy evidence of his rarest humility and modesty, that Camp, in writing to his home of the coming to Christ of this friend whom he had been leading with such fidelity and prayerfulness, mentions several who might have had an influence for good over his classmate, without saying a word of his own agency in the matter; but the record is on high, and all the world shall know it, "when the dead, small and great, stand before God, and the books are opened."

Exposure, on guard and picket, to the malarial atmosphere of the North Carolina nights brought Camp down with chills and fever during the summer months; and again an attack of jaundice confined him in the hospital. His sole anxiety seems then to have been lest he should miss some active service with his regiment, or disturb his friends at home by fears as to his condition. "I went down to the hospital," he wrote, "partly to consult Dr. Douglass, and partly to see if they had any cherries left, — no more idea of staying there than of cutting up any other foolish caper; but once there, and they had me. Dr. Douglass said stay, and stay it was. So I am luxuriating again on a mattress, between cotton sheets. I tell you about my playing sick, because I suppose I must, to fulfil literally my part of our compact; but you mustn't suppose there is any thing to speak of the matter with me, because there isn't."

His stay in hospital was, however, for several weeks, and the confinement was irksome to him. "It is quiet enough, up at camp," he said; "but you know that, there, there are drills, though you may not go out to them; and there are forty little things to discuss, — whether the colonel was exactly right in the order he gave, and whose fault this or that blunder was, and how this or that little matter of company business is to be settled. Here it is, 'How do you feel this morning?' 'Anybody die last night?' 'Doctor been around yet?' And after he has, and prescribed the dose for the day, that is about all, until night, when bedtime comes."

Speaking of reported orders for a move of the regiment, he added, "Wouldn't I be provoked to have to stay here, and have them leave me? It would be worse than Roanoke." To his bitter sorrow, the orders came; and the surgeon positively forbade his accompanying the expedition, telling him he could not go five miles before he would have to be brought back. In his disappointment, he said, " Here I have been impatient to get away, and do something, fretting at long idleness, ready for a start any day until now; and now the time comes, the move is made, and I am fast. If I was really sick, down with a fever, laid up with a broken leg, or any thing of that sort, there would be some satisfaction in it : I should know I was helpless, and make up my mind to it. But to be tied down by this miserable little bilious difficulty, — to be upset by such a thing as this, — I feel like some great lubber who has been thrashed by a youngster half his size, and sneaks off into a corner to hide himself. It s more of a disappointment to me than you will probably imagine."

But the orders for his regiment were countermanded. General Burnside left for the Army of the Potomac, taking with him Generals Rake and Reno, and their commands, constituting the newly-formed Ninth Army Corps; while General Foster remained in command of the district of North Carolina, retaining his old brigade, with some additions to it. In the re-organization of the troops, the Tenth was brigaded with the 24th Massachusetts, the 9th New Jersey, and the 5th Rhode Island regiments, under gallant Colonel (afterwards General) Stevenson, of the 24th Massachusetts.

In one of Camp's letters from the hospital is a paragraph worthy of special note in this Memoir, prepared by one subsequently intimate with him, but not his army comrade until some months later. "I have been reading Captain Vickars's Life this afternoon, for the first time. He was the right man in the right place,—just such a one as one or two whom I know could be, and only one or two. Memoirs like his, and others of his stamp, don't affect me as they ought to. Such men are too far out of common sight: I am wretchedly uncomfortable when I read of them, — that is all. I wish I could get hold of a life of some fellow like myself, if there ever was one, — which I honestly don't believe, — and see how he turned out. But no, — catch any such memoir as that being given to the public!

"One of the chief, perhaps *the* chief, privations of being away from home, is the having no intimate friend, —no one with whom to talk freely; being shut up within one's self. There are few who would allow themselves to be so, but you know I have no social qualities about me. I am very particular: there are only one or two in a hundred whom I would have for friends anyhow, and those one or two I haven't the faculty of gaining; and the result is that I am as solitary as the sphynx. How I should enjoy the right fellow for a chum!" Why this connection of thought? Did he know instinctively, that, if he had an intimate friend who should outlive him, that friend would give his memoir to the public?

In July, 1862, Camp was advanced to a first lieutenancy,

7

and put in command of Company D, which he greatly
improved by his firm and judicious discipline, during the
few weeks he had charge of it.   August 5, he was promoted to the adjutancy of the regiment; a position more
congenial to his tastes and acquirements than that of sub-
altern in the line.   His first experience with a consolidated
report will be appreciated by any one who has had the
responsibility of such a mass of perplexing figures : —

  " I finished a copy of the consolidated monthly return,
— the principal one, — Tuesday afternoon, and carried it
down to headquarters, immensely rejoiced to have it done
with.   About an hour afterward, up came an orderly to
my tent, ' Adjutant Camp's report is respectfully returned
for correction.'   I was thunderstruck, to speak moderately.
Hadn't I added those figures lengthwise and crosswise,
vertically, horizontally, diagonally, spherically, and miscel-
laneously? — got 'em at length so that it would have done
old Daboll good to look over the columns ?   I thought so;
but, come to examine the work again, there were two mis-
takes for which the serjeant-major, at whose dictation I had
copied, was responsible, and one of my own.   It didn't
take fifteen minutes to straighten them out; but I was
vexed to think that my first performance should have
been a boggle.   However, it did me good to find out
that the adjutants of the 25th and 27th, both old hands
at the business, had blundered in theirs too; so I wasn't
alone.   I don't intend to be caught again, though."

A week after Camp was appointed adjutant, Chaplain Hall — his friend and college classmate — resigned, and left the regiment. It was thus that Camp wrote home of Hall's successor : —

"I wonder if you know, by this time, whom we are probably going to have as chaplain. If you don't, you'll be very glad to hear it, though you'd never guess in the world, — Henry Clay Trumbull. I can't think of any man I ever knew, whom I should be so well pleased to have accept it. . . . I am selfish about it, too : the chaplain and I, both being members of the staff, will see a great deal of each other, and be thrown much together."

Chaplain Trumbull, whose coming was so pleasantly anticipated by Adjutant Camp, reached the regiment early in October. The two comrades, ordinary friends before, were speedily drawn into closest intimacy. Away from home, they craved personal sympathy. Their tastes were similar. Their characters were sufficiently unlike to be in harmony. The training of each was such that he possessed what the other deemed his lack. One had a finely cultured, richly stored mind ; the other a fund of personal experience. The opinions of the one were all formed from the study of underlying principles ; the judgments of the other were based upon practical observations. Their regimental duties kept them near each other. Their home friends being side by side, they were linked in every interest.

It was after a sacred communion service in the Presby-

terian Church at Newberne, at which Adjutant Camp was
the only officer present with the chaplain from their regiment, that, in a midnight talk, they opened their hearts
to each other, and entered upon that life of peculiar oneness
which was so marked to all who, thenceforward, saw them
together. Like Jonathan and David, when they "had
made an end of speaking," at that time, "the soul of
the one was knit with the soul of the other." They
"made a covenant, because each loved the other as his
own soul."

During the month of October, 1862, General Foster
was largely reinforced by nine-months' regiments from
Massachusetts. Of these, the 44th was added to Colonel
Stevenson's brigade, and soon became a favorite with
the old troops of the command. It was composed of
choice material, including many students from Harvard.
Pleasant acquaintances were made among the officers and
men of the newly associated battalions.

October 30th, Stevenson's brigade left Newberne on
transports for Little Washington, the 10th accompanying General Foster, on his own boat, the "Pilot Boy."
At the same time, a column moved overland to Washington, whence an expedition set out for Tarborough on
Sunday morning, November 2, the 10th leading, for
the day, the infantry advance. Before night had fairly
shut in, the enemy was found posted in the woods, just
beyond a troublesome ford at Little Creek, a short distance

below Williamston, opening fire on the approaching skirmishers of the 10th. The latter, reinforced by a portion of the 44th, charged across the stream, and drove out the rebels, capturing several prisoners of the 26th North Carolina Regiment, of which Governor Vance was the first colonel.

This was the first engagement in which Camp had acted as adjutant, and thus been brought into prominence before all the regiment. His courageous bearing won warm praise from the men, as, by the side of brave Colonel Pettibone, he pressed forward in the charge over the creek, through the shower of bullets and the sweep of grape from the foe of unknown strength in the thicket beyond. "I never knew what Adjutant Camp was until that night," said a sergeant, long afterward. "I saw his face was pale, as if he understood the danger" (the soldier knows the difference between the bloodless cheek of determination and the pallor of cowardice); "and he looked just as if *he was ready to go anywhere*, as he ran along on that log foot-bridge, and cheered on the men, while they splashed through the water, with the bullets all about them. I always liked him after that."

The enemy was pursued rapidly to Rawl's Mills, where, at midnight, General Foster brought up heavy batteries of artillery to a commanding hill-crest, and rained shot and shell upon the retreating column. After an exhausting day of twenty-two hours of activity, the troops bivouacked that night in the clear moonlight, on the soft clay of the captured line of works. The next morning, Williamston was entered without opposition, the enemy having evacuated it during the night, and most of the citizens having fled, terror-stricken, from their homes. As the head of the incoming column reached a principal street-corner of the well-nigh deserted town, a party of Jack-tars from the Union gunboats which had just ascended the Roanoke River gave an unexpected greeting to the army, by singing the stirring song, "We'll rally round the flag, boys!" and roused the enthusiasm of the soldiers to the highest pitch. During the halt of several hours in the village, there was, in spite of every effort to prevent it, much of reckless pillaging and wanton destruction of private property by the troops. Every thing eatable was, of course, seized at once; and at each street-corner, and in each back-yard, pork, poultry, and beef were being cooked in the most primitive style, at fires kindled from the convenient fence-palings, or articles of household furniture. The few families who remained seemed doubtful if even their lives were to be spared by the bloodthirsty and relentless Yankees; and it was with difficulty that some, whose homes were, from the first, specially guarded against intrusion, could be induced to refrain from loud shrieks for mercy, or made to believe that no harm was intended

them, or injury to be done their property. The empty
cradle from which a sick child had been hurried away at
the risk of its life, and the cot from which a consumptive
patient had been borne out beyond the limits of the town,
in the cold night air, at his own earnest request, as pointed
out by those who knew the story of both, touched the
hearts of the Union officers, and showed to all how thoroughly misunderstood in the Southern community was the
purpose of the Federal army.

Passing on from Williamston, the column rested for the
night in an extensive cornfield of hundreds of broad acres,
presenting a scene of peculiar picturesqueness, — a fire-
lit bivouac of thousands of armed men, with no seeming
limit to the stretch of blazing piles and clustered groups
and flashing weapons and moving forms, all overhung by
the illumined smoke-clouds, with the glimmering stars
beyond.

The next day, the column pressed on to Rainbow Fort,
a strong work on a high bluff above Roanoke River, and
flanked the position, so that it was evacuated in hot haste.
Thence to Hamilton, and across the country to Tar River,
to the suburbs of Tarborough. Returning to Hamilton, and
again to Williamston, it moved down to Janesville, and on
to Plymouth, where it took transports to Newberne; reaching its old base after an absence of two weeks, having
marched more than one hundred miles, and moved more
than four hundred by water.

In illustration of the truth, familiar to every soldier, that inaction causes far more complaint and discontent than the severest service in campaigning, Camp wrote, in one of his letters from Little Washington, on this expedition, —

"We are all enjoying the return to active service. Officers and men alike are more cheerful than for a long time past. More enthusiasm has lain concealed beneath a crust of grumbling complaints and talk of resignation than I had any idea of. We need work, — that's all, — to keep us good-natured. Ice freezes thick over most men's patriotism when it is dammed up, so that it seems to have utterly vanished. Only open the sluiceways once in a while, and the current, deep as ever, sweeps it away in a twinkling, and again runs free and strong."

The expedition to Tarborough was novel in its nature, partaking, in many features, of the general character of Sherman's grand march through Georgia. There was the same cutting loose from the base of supplies, the depending on the surrounding country for subsistence, the moving through a tract hitherto unreached by the devastations of war, the entering one town after another and quartering, on its inhabitants, the visiting and emptying of richly stored plantations and elegantly furnished private dwellings, the seizure of horses and cattle for Government use, and the gathering of slaves to give them freedom in a new home. And there was the same inevitable lawlessness

among the men having part in such a work. Passing a
farm-house, they would dart from the ranks to seize a fowl
or to gather a cap full of eggs, to bring back a pail of
sugar or of the demoralizing apple-brandy, or to bear off a
well-filled hive, with "two bees to one honey," as they
facetiously expressed it; and in a twinkling they would
ransack the dwelling from garret to cellar, making as great
havoc with those things utterly useless to themselves as
with that which their appetites or personal comfort demanded.

Camp entered heartily into all the legitimate excitements
and enjoyments of the expedition. No one was more
ready than he to have a run for live pork or poultry for
the field and staff mess, or for company cooks, while all
were dependent on what could thus be secured; and no
one took more delight than he in all that was picturesque
or delightful in the surrounding country.

But he never forgot the dictates of honor or humanity.
He aided in soothing alarmed households; he spoke kind
words to the sorrowing; and, on one occasion, when he
saw officers making sport of neatly-tied locks of hair and
other mementoes of the loved ones of a scattered family,
preserved in a quarto dictionary, he watched his opportunity, and, securing the volume with its precious contents,
hid it in a remote cupboard of the house, where probably
it would not again be seen until the proper inmates
returned to their home.

The experiences of the expedition were widely varied, — in weather, face of country, and duties of the hour. There were fair, bright days, and days and nights of cheerless storm, cold drenching rain, and even frost and a fall of snow. There were the low sand plains of the Southern coast, and, inland, hills almost like New England, and dense woods, and fertile fields, and even clear purling brooks, as well as chocolate-colored rivers; then there were North-Carolina swamps. Who, that has ever passed through one of these, will fail to recognize the truthfulness of Camp's description of it? —

"Perhaps mother knows what a Southern swamp is. I am sure the rest of you don't. You'll find a better description of it in 'Dred,' than I can give you; but you can't realize the dismal abominations of it until you see them. For all that, it is pleasant enough to ride through them on a bright, cool morning There is something grand in the dark impenetrability, and the huge pines that lift themselves out of it and seem as if they could look down into all manner of inaccessible recesses and secret hiding places, open only toward the sky. There is a great deal that is beautiful, even in the midst of the swamp. Trees have a luxuriance of growth, and density of cool, fleshy, solid foliage, that you don't see at home. Even the same varieties have a larger leaf and thicker twigs, so that at first one hardly recognizes them. There are thousands of unfamiliar vegetable shapes, — vines, and shrubs, and bushes, with odd and beautiful leaves and flowers. I think, if I were a botanist (or still more, if I were an entomologist, though I haven't enlarged upon that subject), I shouldn't ask for any thing more than a square rod of Southern swamp, to give me occupation for a year."

One sunny morning, the road traveled by the column wound down a hill, through the woods, across a wide brook spanned by a rustic bridge. An old mill showed itself among the trees at the left. A gum-canoe floated near the bridge. The morning light struggled down through the branches of pine and cypress and moss-hung oaks. The bracing air of the morning was very exhilarating to the refreshed soldiers. The unusual beauty of the spot and the influences of the hour impressed every beholder; and, as the head of the first brigade reached the bridge, a Massachusetts regiment started the "John Brown" chorus. The next regiment at once caught up the strain, and it passed rapidly along the column, until the rich melody rolled up from thousands of glad voices, far up and down the winding road, thrilling the nerves and stirring the soul of every participant and listener. Beyond the woods the country opened into immense plains, showing the yellow corn, the rank sorghum, and the snow-flecked cotton-fields; while the plantation-house was in view, with its broad piazzas, its rear rows of negro shanties, its cotton-press and gin-house. At this point there was a halt; and the joyous singing was changed to no less universal and hearty cheering, as Major-General Foster, — the admired and beloved commander, — with his staff, rode through the open ranks to the extreme front.

Camp enjoyed such an hour as that, as he did, also, the hour of social worship, when, around the blazing fire, officers and men of the regiment gathered at evening in the open field to sing and to pray, and to listen to God's word. One evening, at a bivouac near Plymouth, when the chaplain missed the adjutant for an hour, he ascertained that the latter, in crossing the field, had found a prayer-meeting of another regiment, and had stopped to enjoy its privileges and be refreshed by its influence. And at many a point, the quiet woods could tell how earnestly he pleaded with God in the morning and evening hour of private devotion.

On the return of the troops from the Tarborough Scout, Colonel Pettibone resigned command of the 10th, and left for the North, Adjutant Camp accompanying him on a brief leave of absence. The delights of that first visit home, after a year of separation, could not be better described than in the few telling lines which he wrote concerning it to his friend in camp : —

"Once on the train which was to carry me straight home, steam seemed very slow. There was a constantly growing thrill of excitement, pleasant, yet with a dash of anxious pain. If *then* I were to meet or find any thing amiss! I was driven from the depot as near the house as I ventured to allow a carriage, lest its sound should betray my coming; walked softly, with feet that hardly felt the ground, past the cheerfully shining windows, to the rear entrance; noiselessly stepped along to the library door, and threw it open. There they were! What was said or done I hardly know. Oh, the joy of that evening, and of every moment since! I wonder if you have ever been long enough away from those you loved to know it thoroughly."

It was while Camp was at home at this time that General Foster made his celebrated Goldsborough Raid from Newberne, in conjunction with Burnside's advance on Fredericksburg, fighting the battles of South-west Creek, Kinston, Whitehall, and Goldsborough. On this expedition, the 10th Regiment performed hard service, and won dearly bought distinction, losing in twenty minutes more than one hundred men, with some of its best and bravest officers, in the fight at Kinston.

Again Camp was deeply grieved at his loss of a share in the work of his regiment. Nothing had seemed more unlikely than such an expedition, at the time he went North; and his surprise was as great as his disappointment, on returning to Newberne, to find that his regiment had been some ten days away. He was at once in the saddle and on his way to overtake his command; but the column was already returning, and he met it but a few miles from the city.

" So I am about a week too late," he wrote. " I would give more than that of life to have been in that bayonet charge. My absence from it, like that from the battle of Roanoke, — much more, even, — will be a life-long disappointment and regret. When the war is over, what shall *I* have done? It is hard. . . . I have nothing to *reproach* myself with, only I feel like a man who has unfortunately lost a magnificent opportunity."

So keenly did he feel this disappointment, that when, shortly after, unusual promotion was tendered him, he positively refused it, preferring that it should advantage some one who had shared the perils of the recent expedition.

Burnside's Fredericksburg defeat depressed many in the army, as out of it; but Henry Camp never despaired of the cause which had his heart; nor did he admit the possibility of any course but one for Government or people.

" *Has* the North pluck enough to try it once more?" he wrote after his return to Newberne. " Now is the time to try men. I am astonished at the way some of them talk. A man can not help it if things look dark to him, — they do to me; but he can help slackening effort, or talking in a way to slacken others. If every man would set his teeth, and walk straight up to meet the ruin which he sees coming, it would vanish before he came within striking distance ; and, let worst come to worst, the nation could at least die with all its wounds in front. Better so than to sneak into its grave a few years later with scars on its back."

CHAPTER VI.

THE FIRST CHARLESTON EXPEDITION.

 NEW expedition was talked of. Troops were coming from Suffolk to Newberne, and a naval fleet was gathering at Beaufort. Wilmington was aimed at. The division to which the 10th belonged was to remain behind. Adjutant Camp was so anxious to atone for what he deemed his recent loss of service, that he proposed to accompany the expedition on the staff of a commander of another division. But, at the last hour, the 10th was ordered to move also, and Camp gladly remained with his regiment.

The 10th left Newberne by railroad for Morehead City, Monday, Jan. 26, 1863, and went on board a transport in Beaufort Harbor the same day. The expedition planned for Wilmington was, on account of the loss of the original " Monitor " and from other causes, turned to the department of the South. Its destination was known only to the commanding general, until the sailing orders were opened, after leaving the harbor, Saturday the 31st. The trip to Port Royal was quickly and pleasantly made.

The satisfaction on finding that Charleston was the point aimed at was general among the troops of the expedition; and Camp expressed his unfeigned delight at the prospect of immediate . participation in a movement against the nursery of treason.

The unfortunate collision between Generals Hunter and Foster, resulting in the return of the latter to North Carolina without his troops, was a cause of sad disappointment to those who were thus parted from the commander whom they loved and trusted without measure or doubt. The officers and men of the 10th were peculiarly tried; for they had been ordered off only at the last moment, with the assurance that they were to be away from camp not more than ten days, or at the outside a fortnight. They had left behind all camp and garrison equipage, regimental and company papers, personal baggage beyond what was necessary for a short tour of field-service, and even those officers and men who were not strong enough for a march and an immediate fight. The order to land on St. Helena Island, opposite Hilton Head, and go into camp while thus circumstanced, was exceedingly unsatisfactory; and it was by no means easy for them to have a home feeling, even as soldiers, while lacking so much that they had hitherto deemed essential to enjoyable camp life. But they adapted themselves as best they could to their situation; and with the shelter-tents, of which they then first had experience, supplemented by the broad leaves of the palmetto, soon had an attractive army settlement, with its embowered chapel, its hedged streets, and its neatly finished and ornamented quarters for officers and men.

The long delay in waiting, with anxious and often deferred hope for active operations in the department, was not lost time to the troops of the expedition. They improved the passing days in perfecting their drill and discipline. Indeed, the 10th Regiment never appeared better in drill, or on parade and review, than at St. Helena. It won the highest commendations from commanders who visited or reviewed it. Adjutant Camp did much, even in the subordinate position he then held, to maintain its character and advance its highest interests. Many who were there remember how he was called on by Lieutenant-Colonel Leggett one afternoon to conduct the battalion-drill, and how he performed his task. He had never before taken the battalion in hand. He had not for weeks even attended drill, — his services not being essential there, and neither field nor staff having horses with them, — nor had he five minutes' notice that he was to be pressed into the service. He said aside to his friend that he should have liked ten minutes to refresh his mind as to a few movements; but he made no excuse to his commander. Stepping out to the parade-ground, he relieved his seniors, the captains, and then for an hour and a half handled the regiment so easily and correctly, that the lieutenant-colonel — enthusiastic and accomplished soldier as he was — said to him, in the presence of others that evening, that it was the finest battalion-drill that had been held on the island.

Moreover, Camp was rarely absent from a religious service in the regiment; and, although always loth at home to have his voice heard in public, he was now ready to share with the chaplain in the exercises of the camp prayer-meeting or sabbath school, and even to assume the conduct of either, in case of the illness of his friend, or when the latter was unavoidably kept away. His sabbath-school experiences, as he then described them, will not be deemed by all peculiar to himself alone : —

" I don't know how to interest a class. I have improved somewhat in the ability to talk against time, though it horrifies me sometimes to take out my watch and find that I've got to make two verses last twenty minutes. But when it comes to drawing out others, getting them to interest themselves and to talk themselves on the subject in question, I'm stumped."

Again he wrote, when called to act as both superintendent and teacher, —

" Sabbath school was in the morning instead of the afternoon. I had to take charge again. Teachers as well as scholars are irregular. To-day, after the opening exercises, Captain Atherton and I divided the school between us. I became thoroughly interested in the lesson before we were through, as I often do, and enjoyed it, but sha'n't dread it a particle less for next time."

Those whom he taught would have a different story to tell of his ability to interest a class. Few of them imagined that he so dreaded the duty he performed so well.

Of the South-Carolina coast-scenery he wrote, after a visit to a neighboring island to St. Helena, —

" I stood a few hundred yards from the beach, and looked seaward through a grove of palmetto-trees, with their tufted tops and strangely figured trunks. The sun beat down hot on the yellow sands; there was a warm haze over the blue water, dimming the nearer shore, and hiding the distant horizon; and the scene was so thoroughly oriental, that I could as easily fancy myself on the shores of Palestine as realize that I was on those of Port Royal, and shouldn't have been at all surprised to see a camelopard stalk up, and commence browsing on the palm-shoots."

The intimacy of the adjutant and the chaplain grew closer day by day. After leaving Newberne they were seldom separated from each other for many minutes at a time. They had the same tent and blankets, and shared all their army possessions. They came to be known widely as " the twins," from being always seen together. Their free interchange of sentiment modified the views of each on many points concerning which his opinions had before been positive. Camp's calm, reliable judgment many times held in check the chaplain's nervous impulsiveness; his

stores of information proved the other often in error as to
facts bearing on a question at issue ; his uniform fairness —
liberalized some sentiments of his friend as to men and
measures ; and his remarkable purity of mind and consis-
tency of adherence to his conscientious views of right could
not fail to be elevating and ennobling to one closely associated with him.   On the other hand, Camp had been so
accustomed to examine every question in its purely logical
bearings, as sometimes to overlook its practical relations to
every-day life in the world as it is.   The chaplain's experience among men furnished his friend with new elements
of thought in some discussions, and those elements he
always accepted at their fullest weight.

His change of sentiment as to the propriety of card-
playing and wine-drinking should not be passed over without
mention in the record of Camp's army-life.   As neither
of these practices was viewed by him as in the abstract
sinful, he could not join in sweepingly condemning them.
Although personally abstemious, he recognized no positive
duty of abstinence, hence would not have hesitated to drink
a glass of wine had he wished it, and as readily before
others as by himself; for what he considered right in his
practice he was willing to have as an example to those
about him.   Of card-playing, in the light in which he saw
it, he said at one time that he should no more shrink from
the thought of being killed while thus engaged than while
reading the daily paper.

The abstinence question he discussed with his friend while they were making a passage on an army-transport. The two stood or sat together on the deck during nearly all of one night in the final argument. Camp's clear head made the discussion most searching and thorough; and no reason that could be adduced in defense of alcohol as a beverage, or the propriety of its use by any, was overlooked. It was after mature deliberation upon the discussion of that night, that Camp expressed his conviction that total abstinence was a duty, in view of the evils of intemperance, the weakness of tempted human nature, and the responsibility of every man for his personal example. Thenceforward, until the day of his death, only on one occasion, did a drop of alcoholic liquor pass his lips; and that was during his week of escape from prison, after such a soaking in the cold river, on a wintry night, as required an immediate stimulant to arouse sufficient nervous action to sustain life. He more than once refused its use, even when advised as a medicine by the very friend whose words had led him to renounce it.

Of the other mooted theme, he wrote from St. Helena, —

"Last evening we discussed card-playing. You know how I have thought and talked on that subject for the last five or six years. Three-quarters of an hour brought me to his side of the question, — no point of abstract right or of absolute duty, but of practical expediency. That is what I have all my life neglected sufficiently to consider. I have failed both in theory and action to give it due weight. A thing of such universal application too; there is no point which it doesn't touch. I am beginning to realize this as I never have before, and my views are being modified to an extent, that, if carried out in practice, will affect my life both for the present and the future."

Never afterward, even in all the lonely prison-hours at Charleston, Columbia, and Richmond, where at times he was the only officer thus strict in his views, did he indulge in a single game of cards. Thus true was he ever to his convictions of duty, whether they coincided with popular opinion or were peculiarly his own.

General Stevenson's brigade left St. Helena March 27, and the following day proceeded on transports to North Edisto Inlet, as the advance of Hunter and Dupont's expedition against Charleston; having in view the occupation of Seabrook Island to protect its harbor as a rendezvous for the iron-clads and army-transports. That island was then in the enemy's possession, patroled by his cavalry. General Stevenson's command having reached the inlet soon after noon of the 28th, the 10th landed first, while the navy vigorously shelled the woods of the island. With the knowledge that resistance, if made at all, would most likely be offered while the troops were landing, the debarkation was exciting. Five huge launches, containing about one hundred men each, pushed off from the steamer

"Cahawba," which brought the 10th from Hilton Head, and were slowly pulled to the shore; the men meantime singing cheerily the "John Brown" chorus. Soon as the first prow struck the beach, there was a scramble for the land, officers and men vying with each other in endeavors to be first on the island. Many plunged to their waists into water and mud in their haste to be foremost. Then, as Camp wrote, —

"We formed line with all speed, ready to repel attack; and when all had landed, and piled their knapsacks so as to march with ease and rapidity, started along a road which skirted the beach and led toward the upper end of the island, — Captains Goodyear and Atherton deploying skirmishers in advance of the regiment. General Stevenson, Colonel Otis, Lieutenant-Colonel Leggett, Trumbull, and myself walked at the head of the column, within a few yards of Captain Goodyear's men. It was somewhat exciting to advance thus through an enemy's country, doubtful whether it was occupied by them at the time, and uncertain at what moment we might meet sudden opposition. T. and I enjoyed it exceedingly together."

Two miles up the island the regiment halted for the night, on the Seabrook Plantation, darkness having already shut in. The 24th Massachusetts and the 56th New-York State Volunteers were in close support of the 10th. Soon after the halt, the rebel cavalry made a dash upon the picket-reserves; and, in the skirmish which followed, a sergeant of the 10th was carried off a prisoner, mortally wounded. "He is the first man," wrote Camp, "ever taken forcibly prisoner from the regiment. It would have been better to lose a dozen in action."

The following morning the 10th was relieved from picket, and returned in a drenching rain-storm to the lower end of the island to find itself quarters in a comfortless swamp.

"It isn't particularly cheerful, after a stormy march," wrote Camp, "to halt in the midst of dripping trees and bushes, look about one, and consider that his home for the next few days is to be right there; that he'll have just as much comfort as he can get out of those surroundings, and no more. Walk out to Talcott Mountain (though that is altogether too pleasant a place) next time there's a good heavy storm fairly in progress, and see how it seems."

The 10th was soon, in spite of this unpromising location, in a comfortable camp, from which it thenceforward alternated with the other regiments of the command in three-day tours of outpost duty, anticipating hopefully an order to advance to a more active part in the opening campaign. As the enemy held the upper part of Seabrook Island, and the opposing pickets were in sight of each other (the enemy often firing upon the "intruding Yankees," or coming down in the night to feel their strength, and in the hope of capturing a few prisoners), outpost service was there sufficiently exciting to render it attractive.

General Stevenson wishing to know more of the topography of the island, of its approaches from the main land, and of the location of the enemy's reserves, small scouting parties went out beyond his lines from time to time to obtain the desired information. Such undertakings were peculiarly in keeping with the tastes and impulses of Adjutant Camp. Rarely, if ever, did he fail to make one of the party so advancing; and in more instances than one he and his friend were alone on such a scout. Describing some of these adventures in his home-letters, he said of his enjoyment in them, —

"The necessity of constant watchfulness, of having an eye for every sight and an ear for every sound; the consciousness of what you are staking upon every movement you make, and the uncertainty, once advanced to a dangerous position, whether even the utmost prudence and courage may not fail to extricate you, bring into play every faculty a man possesses, and put a tension upon every nerve. The enjoyment is intense; and I think any man who is thoroughly *ennuyé*, and has worn out the round of civilized amusements, would find there was one thrill of untried excitement and pleasure left for him if he would go with us on a little excursion outside the lines. Nothing but an actual brush with the enemy, which we are provoked to have missed after having once or twice offered them so fair an opportunity, has been wanting to make all complete.

Trumbull and I have been together each time, and enjoyed each other's presence exceedingly."

When finally the navy was ready for a move, the troops on Seabrook Island found no part assigned them in a further advance. This was to Camp a sore disappointment. It was with longing eyes that he watched from a high sand-bluff, on the morning of Easter Sabbath, April 4th, the great fleet of iron-clads and wooden gunboats sail out of Edisto Inlet, and up toward Stono, to commence the attack. Two days later, writing from his little " A " tent, at the picket reserve, he said, —

" As I write this, the thunder of heavy guns to the northward is almost incessant. The attack on Charleston has commenced. I counted ten reports in a minute a little while ago, and the fire seems to be growing hotter and hotter. We chafe and fret at our distance from the fight ; but there's nothing for us but a masterly inactivity. It is terribly provoking to sit here and listen, guarding a few miserable old schooners from an attack which would never be made in any event, —and to think that this is our share in the great Charleston expedition ! "

A few hours' cannonading ended the great enterprise, which had been so many weeks preparing. Camp listened in vain for a resumption of the attack after the first intermission in the firing ; and, as he listened, he wrote thus of his outpost-home with its attractions and annoyances : —

"I have hardly seen a prettier spot than this island since leaving home, Beaufort, perhaps, excepted. Our field and staff tents are by themselves in a quiet, shady spot, a little retired from the main road up the island. The high sand-bluff upon the beach, used as a lookout, is directly opposite us, — a quarter of a mile distant through the woods; and we are lulled to sleep at night by the roar of the surf at its base. To-night, perhaps, it will be a sterner thunder than that of ocean storms; a fiercer crash than that of waves along the shore.

"But the gnats, and the ants, and the spiders, and the lizards, and the scorpions, and the moccasins, and the alligators, and the rebels (most harmless to us of any), are the slight drawbacks upon our enjoyment."

Of another drawback upon enjoyment on the Southern coast, he humorously added, in another letter, —

"When you hear of mosquitoes, you think of a small brown insect, don't you? with legs and wings almost invisible, and a hum audible some inches from the ear. I wish you could see the animal that goes by the same name here. When *I* speak of a mosquito, I mean something that stands a little less than fourteen hands high (can't give the weight, because we have no platform-scales); whose wings are like Apollyon's in the 'Pilgrim's Progress;' whose muscular legs are horribly striped with black and white; whose sting is like the dragon's which St. George slew, and whose voice is as the sound of many

waters. I think of writing an article for the 'New-Eng-
lander,' settling the question what beast Job described
under the name of Behemoth, by demonstrating that it
was a Carolina mosquito or a woodtick, — either of them
would furnish a more plausible theory than some I have
read."

The stay of the 10th at Seabrook Island was prolonged; and, in spite of the chafing desire to be in more
active service, Camp enjoyed his life there. The island
was a good specimen of the cotton-growing ones of the
South-Carolina coast. There were rich plantation-plains,
malaria-breeding marshes, "wild swamps, dense thickets of
the tangled Southern undergrowth, lonely palmetto-jungles,
and groves of low branching live-oaks, deeply fringed with
long gray moss." Alligators moved lazily through the
sluggish waters of the gloomy lagoon, and poisonous rep-
tiles glided through the rank grass before the tread of the
passing soldier. Game was plenty, — deer and raccoons
and opossums in the forests, and wild fowl in the creeks
and inlets, while the waters adjacent furnished a rich variety of fish, from the mammoth sturgeon to the small and
palatable mullet.

Here is one of many incidents of army-life on the
island : —

"Coming back just after dark from the picket-reserve
to camp, we heard distant singing, which proved, as we
came near, to be a group of the 97th Pennsylvania

singing hymns.   We stopped to listen; and finally T.
determined to say a few words to them, and did it as
he knows how to do such a thing, interesting every man
of them, from beginning to end, and concluding with
prayer.   I liked the men's appearance, — the way in
which every cap came off when T. entered the group,
and the respectful attention they paid.   Their manners
were real Western, — free and easy, without the slightest intentional disrespect.   The moment the meeting
was over, they crowded around, asked T. if I was a
Christian man; and every one of them wanted to shake
hands with us, and have a good sociable talk.   Cordial, open-hearted fellows, — it was very pleasant, if not
quite military.   The last thing our men would think of
would be offering to shake hands with an officer.   The
97th have no chaplain; but there is a strong religious
element in the regiment, and quite a number they say
have been converted since joining the army.   .   .   .

"Returning to picket at dusk that evening, the air was
one blaze of fire-flies.   I never saw any pyrotechny to
equal it.   There are many beautiful things at the South;
but nothing under heaven would ever tempt me to spend
my life here.   I should die for pure air and clear streams,
and rocks and hills.   I wouldn't exchange our home-lot
for the whole State of South Carolina."

About the first of May, while the work of intrenching

was going on at Seabrook Island, Chaplain Trumbull left for a brief visit to Newberne and the North, on business for the regiment. The parting of the two friends, intimate as they had become, and in view of the possibilities of war, was trying to both.

Writing to his friend, during that separation, of his loneliness, Camp expressively declared it to be "as if the air were deprived of one-half of its oxygen;" and then added, —

"I used to think, a year ago, that a single wall-tent furnished very narrow accommodations for an officer, — mine was not large enough. But ours seems very lonely and empty this evening: there is a great vacancy here, and it remains unfilled, no matter how many come in. I could not fully realize, before we were separated, how thoroughly our lives had become blended, how sadly I should miss you every hour of the day, how anxiously I should await the time of your return. . . .

" There is a constant sense of want while you are absent, — not at all times making itself distinctly intelligible, but ever recurring and still unsatisfied. Wherever I turn, there is a great vacuum before me. I want it filled. What do you suppose would do it?"

In the chaplain's absence, the adjutant assumed the conduct of the regimental prayer-meetings and Sabbath school. He re-organized the latter, secured additional teachers, assembled them with their associates for an examination of the lesson at his own tent on Saturday evenings, and canvassed the regiment for scholars. In all respects, the school was better managed than while the chaplain was with it ; and the prayer-meetings of the regiment were never warmer or seemingly more truly profitable than then. As in every thing else to which he set his hand and heart, he filled the place better than it could be filled by another.

Gen. Terry assumed command, in May, of the troops in North Edisto Inlet, including those on Seabrook and Botany Bay islands. Two members of his staff, Capt. Ives and Lieut. Johnson, were college comrades — the latter a fellow-oarsman in the Worcester regatta — of Henry Camp, who enjoyed having near him those with whom he had been before so pleasantly associated. Occasional excursions were made by officers and men of the 10th to neighboring islands patrolled by the enemy, to make observations, and to obtain furniture and building-materials for their camp from deserted plantation-houses. Of an excursion to Edisto Island, with two companies as escort of the party of officers, Camp wrote, in description of the approach to the Seabrook place : —

" Beyond the bridge we moved with great caution ; the skirmishers widely deployed, and keenly observant of the house and shrubbery, from which, as we were now within rifle-range, we half expected to be fired upon. Standing still for a moment, Dr. Newton saw a crow perched upon the cupola of the house. ' All right ! ' he exclaimed :

'there wouldn't be a crow there if there were fire-arms near by.' That crow was worth to us, in the way of evidence, as much as a whole battalion of skirmishers. It was a very short time before we were in possession of the establishment. . . .

" It is strange what a tendency there is, after once taking possession of a place and becoming convinced that no enemy is actually on the premises, to settle down into a feeling of security. No matter how nervously it may have been approached, perhaps all the more for the very reasons that the first apprehensions proved groundless, no matter how clear a knowledge of the danger still existing men may have, — they will yet act as if there were none ; and it is often impossible, without a distinct effort of the reason, to realize it. Every thing looks so peaceful and quiet, — and, then, there is the guard (seldom in fact adequate to cover half the approaches), who would probably give the alarm in time enough, unless they were surprised. So, arms are stacked, and we wander over the estate as carelessly as if it was on the shores of Long-Island Sound, instead of Edisto Inlet. Still there is an almost unconscious watchfulness of the senses, the ear is wide awake for the sound of a rifle-shot, no matter what the head may be thinking of ; the eye, when not otherwise employed, is very apt to sweep the circuit of surrounding woods, or glance down the road ; and the crash of a breaking window, the fall of a heavy timber, or the sight of an animal moving among the distant

9

bushes, arrests the blackberry half way between the vine
and one's mouth, or saves the flower for which his hand
was stretched out, and puts him in readiness, on the slightest confirmation of his suspicion, to make quick time to the
rendezvous. . . .

" The grounds about the place were very pleasant, only
needing care. There were paths winding through dense
shrubbery and passing by ornamental bridges over a little
stream ; there were arbors and walks shaded by foliage too
close and thick to give passage to a single ray of sunlight;
there were enormous rose-trees lifting far above my head
such masses of gold and crimson as I had never seen, —
cloth-of-gold roses, do you know them ? — each as large as
half a dozen of any ordinary variety, crowded with petals
of golden velvet, so rich and thick, and of a color so soft,
that you can compare them with nothing but bits of sunset
cloud : a single one is a magnificent bouquet. There was
a grove of orange-trees, some of them in blossom ; the pure
white buds bursting out of glossy deep-green leaves, and
filling all the air around with perfume almost too rich and
overpowering. There were strange century-plants like
mighty cactuses, and unfamiliar tropical-looking growths
to which I could give no name. The luxuriance and fullness of vegetation is wonderful : every plant seems to feel
itself at home, and abandons itself to utter dissipation and
wantonness of unrestrained development. A Southern
April has more of glowing bloom, fierce intensity of color

and brilliancy, in contrast with more of somber shade, density of massive growth, and depth of green gloom beneath, than Northern midsummer. I have spoken of this before; but it was peculiarly noticeable in this garden where cultivation had done its utmost, and then left Nature to work its own will. . . .

"We marched back along the sea-beach, almost every man with some article of comfort or convenience for his tent, scarcely one without a huge bunch of these gorgeous flowers in the muzzle of his rifle or in his hand; so that, marching at will, we looked more like a procession of Italian peasants returning from a festival than a battalion of Connecticut Yankees coming back from a hazardous reconnoissance."

About the first of June, the chaplain returned to the regiment, and the friends were again as one. Not many days after their re-union, they accompanied Gen. Stevenson, with several companies of the 10th, beyond the picket-lines on a reconnoissance to the extreme upper end of the island to examine its approaches from John's Island. The rebel pickets fell back on the approach of the general's party, and retired over a broken causeway to a collection of buildings, including an old sugar-house on the John's-Island side of the little creek which bounded Seabrook Island in that direction. There were indications that they had a strong reserve in the rear of those buildings; but, it not being the general's purpose to go beyond the island, he ordered a return by another path than that which had just been passed over. Up to this time, he had met with no resistance.

"Retiring, the skirmishers, deployed in open line, marched in the rear. Within a dozen paces were the general, with two or three of his friends, — Colonel Otis, Lieutenant-Colonel Leggett, Dr. Newton, T., and myself. Captain White, who commanded the skirmishers, was close by. We had gone some little distance, supposing that the affair was over, and half grumbling that it had amounted to no more, when we were startled by a report behind us, followed instantly by the sharp hiss of a bullet close past our heads. The skirmishers — to say nothing of any others — were a trifle surprised. Every man of them ducked his head; and we found ourselves suddenly just about in line with them. Then another report and another bullet; this time a few feet over us, and a little one side. Shot followed shot in quick succession; now two or three almost together, then an interval of quiet.

"We walked slowly along, not altering our pace, — sometimes stooping at the sound of the explosion, and sometimes not. I was surprised to find that there was abundant time for this before the arrival of the bullet, — a distinct interval, — showing that its velocity and that of sound differ more than I had supposed. It must have been long range; but the marksmanship was excellent. Bullets struck among us, passed over us, by us, between us,

everywhere but through us. We were undoubtedly made
special targets. The group walking together was an
excellent mark, and the distance was short enough; so that,
with a glass at least, badges of rank must have been easily
distinguishable. Dr. Newton had on a white Panama hat,
— just the thing at which to aim. Colonel Leggett was
just in front of T. and myself, a little one side. He looked
around once, saw the smoke curl from the muzzle of a piece,
and instinctively stepped to the left. In a second more
the bullet whistled between us and him, passing directly
where he had stood, and striking the ground within a few
inches of his foot.

" The difference in sound between different bullets was
marked. Some had the fierce whizz of the spinning rifle-
ball, some the sharp hiss of the smooth-bore missile, and
some a fainter and less vicious ' whssh,' as if they were
almost spent, and had lost half their venom. Some were
more distant; some seemed close to our ears: but there
was hardly one ill aimed, and it was really strange — providential, I should say — that none of us were hit. . . .
The most tantalizing thing all this time was that the enemy
kept closely under cover. We didn't catch sight of a man
after fire was opened. Our men were told not to return
it unless they could see their mark; and the result was
that not a shot was fired from our side. They did not
keep it up long, — probably kept near the bridge, — and
we were soon out of range."

The enemy seemed provoked at the escape of the venturesome party, and, soon after the latter had reached its former lines, came down with cavalry, artillery, and infantry, and opened with a section of a light battery from the front yard of the Seabrook House, on the woods which shielded the Union pickets. General Stevenson ordered up two guns to reply; and a brisk artillery duel followed, with a few casualties on both sides. "We enjoyed intensely the exciting sport," wrote Camp to his home, in description of this afternoon's experiences : then, in defense of the sentiment thus expressed, he said in a subsequent letter, —

"No motive that is not positively wrong can, I think, be spared. There is lack, rather than excess, with most. Whatever may be the underlying principle of action which is really at the basis of all else, I am inclined to believe that that which is usually uppermost in the mind, as immediately affecting the conduct in time of danger and trial, is the excitement of the struggle, positively; negatively, the shame of misconduct or failure. As long as men are mere men, I don't see how it can be otherwise. If the higher inducements to duty were the only ones, I should fear for results. What will be the effect upon character, we can judge better, perhaps, when the war is over. It does not seem to me that they will be otherwise than beneficial; belief which is, of course, the necessary sequence of a belief in the motives themselves as being — in ultimate subordination to nobler ones — justifiable and right."

The fleet-captain of the iron-clads in the waters of Edisto was Commander George W. Rodgers of the "Cattskill," a Christian officer of rare worth and attainments, whom the two friends found congenial in tastes and sympathy. They visited him in his vessel, and he was frequently in their tent. It was Captain Rodgers's custom to conduct a religious service among his men each sabbath, and he was glad to have the chaplain preach for him occasionally; while he always came to the shore for the camp service on the sabbath, when he could do so. He greatly admired Adjutant Camp, saying to his friend that he deemed him the most attractive volunteer officer he had ever met.

The adjutant was detailed as judge-advocate of a general court-martial on Seabrook Island; and although, with his accustomed distrust of himself and his relentless self-censure, he wrote, "I was careless and clumsy, made omissions and blunders, and did myself very little credit," he won warm praise from the officers composing the court; and one of the most prominent of them remarked afterward, that every member of it became attached to him, although but one or two had known him before.

The power of his personal presence was remarkable. Few ever saw him without being impressed with a sense of his superiority. The impulse to lift a hat to him, as a tribute to his dignified manliness, was often manifested even by those above him in official rank. Said one who was always his superior officer, " I was never very intimate with Camp, for I always had too much respect for him." The better he was known, the more he was esteemed and beloved.

CHAPTER VII.

JAMES ISLAND AND FORT WAGNER.

ON the evening of Monday, July 6, 1863, a pleasant party sat at dinner in the field and staff mess-tent of the 10th C. V. on Seabrook Island. An old-fashioned New-England chowder had been prepared, and General Stevenson and Commander Rodgers invited to share it. Besides their guests, there were present Colonel Otis, Lieutenant-Colonel Leggett, Major Greeley, Surgeon Newton, and Assistant-Surgeon Hart, together with the adjutant and the chaplain. While the dinner was in progress, and all were enjoying themselves, with hardly a thought of severe service as a possibility for the season, word came that a steamer was crossing the bar at the mouth of the inlet; and at once the party was broken up, never to be re-united on earth. Within a fortnight from that evening, Adjutant Camp and his friend were prisoners in a Charleston jail. The brave Lieutenant-Colonel Leggett lost a leg in the trenches of Morris Island, and good Commander Rodgers yielded his life in the bombardment of Wagner. Later, gallant General Stevenson was

137

killed at Spottsylvania Court House, and Major Camp
fell before Richmond; while Colonel Otis and Surgeon
Newton left the service, after prolonged and arduous campaigning.   At the time of the writing of this memorial,
only Major (now Colonel) Greeley, Surgeon Hart, and
Chaplain Trumbull, remain in service of the nine who then
arose from the table.

" Orders had come to go aboard the 'Ben de Ford' (a
large ocean steamer) as soon as she arrived, which would
be during the night. 'Light marching order, forty rounds
of ammunition in the cartridge-boxes, ten days' rations,
shelter-tents for the men.'   I carried the order round to
company commanders.   It is curious to see how men will
take a bit of news that has somewhat of the startling in it.
I like to take one, and watch ; see with what an utterly
matter-of-course air they listen ; ask a question that may
be of life or death as unconcernedly as they would ask
whether you liked your beefsteak rare or well done; and see
behind it all the intense interest and curiosity with which
the smallest item of information in reference to the affair is
caught at and treasured up.   I was amused last night at
a lieutenant, who heard what I had to say to him as quietly
as if it hardly paid him for taking his eyes off his newspaper.   I left the tent, but had occasion to repass it immediately.   There he was, performing the wildest kind of
a Pawnee war-dance ; just about half crazy with delight
and excitement at the prospect of work ahead.   News

went before me as I passed down the line; and, in ten minutes, preparations were under full headway."

General Stevenson's troops, with the exception of enough for guard duty, left Seabrook Island on the early morning of July 7. Only the effective men of the command went along, and the officers took merely such personal baggage as could be carried in a haversack or light valise. The understanding was that they were to return in a few days; but, as in the leaving of Newberne, the event proved that they were not to go back. Sailing to Port-Royal Harbor, they waited the perfection of arrangements for General Gillmore's attack on Morris Island. The 56th New-York regiment, under Colonel Van Wyck, was with the 10th on the "Ben de Ford." On the evening of the 9th, there was a delightfully impressive prayer-meeting on the after-deck of the steamer, attended largely by the officers and men of both regiments, which will not soon be forgotten by any who participated in it. Soldiers love to pray before they fight. Those who trust in Jesus draw closer to him then, and the roughest are reverent at such a time. The voices of prayer were subdued, yet earnest; and the songs of praise were mellow with deep feeling.

The morning of July 10 found the troops of General Terry — under whom General Stevenson was commanding his brigade — landing at the lower end of James Island, in conjunction with General Strong's advance from Folly

to Morris Island.   The former's move was unopposed,
and he chose his first position a short distance up the
island.   From the roof of the River House, a full view
was obtained of Charleston and its harbor; and the friends
watched with deepest interest the firing from Sumter and
Moultrie and the Morris-Island batteries, and from the
iron-clad fleet in the offing, and speculated on the progress
and prospects of the battle as reports came over from the
forces of General Gillmore in that direction.

On Saturday evening, just before sundown, a demonstration was made toward the works at Secessionville.

"The 24th Massachusetts, 97th Pennsylvania, and ourselves, advanced; formed line of battle in a large open
field, while the gunboats shelled the ground in front; and
at dusk we threw out pickets a few hundred yards, and
bivouacked for the night.   All our men, except one company, were posted on picket, and covered a very long
front.   Henry went in one direction, and I in another,
along the line, to carry orders.   (Henry I always call
him here; and I'm going to quit insulting him as 'T.'
in my letters to you; and here is a commencement.)
Darkness coming on rapidly, I lost my way in endeavoring to gain the reserve.   The field had been plowed in
deep furrows; was overgrown with rank weeds, breast-
high; was broken up by thorny, impenetrable hedges, and
miry, impassable ditches; and was in all respects about as
undesirable a place for an evening ramble as could be got

up to order. Every other step among the irregular furrows pitched one unexpectedly forward, jarring every bone in his body, or brought him up standing against an ascending slope. Every few rods brought him to a chasm, invisible in the darkness, until his foot was on its edge. Every few hundred yards plunged him into briers and bushes, where he would do well if he could retrace his steps to the entrance with any considerable remnant of clothes or skin. Then there was the more than even chance of being shot by our own pickets, who, so near the enemy's works, stand upon very little ceremony, and give their single challenge in scarcely audible tones, lest they should be heard too far. Twice I but just distinguished it among the crackling underbrush; and often I halted abruptly, doubting whether I had heard it or not. Ordinarily, having found the picket-line, it would be easy to reach the reserve: but here, the pickets, having been moved after dark, gave the most contrary directions; and repeated attempts to follow their advice only bewildered me the more by want of success in ascertaining where they had brought me.''

A spot is seldom found more perplexing for a night tramp than that seemingly boundless field, with its furrows and ditches and entangling weeds, and the enemy so near at hand. Men who were then on post tell to this day of the many bewildered wanderers who came prowling along the line that night in search of the reserve, and of the confusing whistling and signal-calling at right and left and rear, kept up for hours by the lost ones, or by those who were searching for them. Hardly an officer left his position but he had difficulty in finding his way back to it. It was near midnight before Camp and his friend were again together at the reserve, both by that time well-nigh exhausted from their exertions in the suffocating air of a South-Carolina July night.

"We spread Henry's buffalo and my blankets," wrote Camp the next day, "over an India-rubber, across the furrows, our heads resting on one ridge, our feet over another; and composed ourselves for a capital sleep, tired enough. Never were poor fellows worse disappointed. Mosquitoes attacked us in a style to which rebels wouldn't have been a circumstance. I suppose we did sleep during the night; but we didn't know it. We seemed to spend every moment in writhing into new positions of defense or suffering. I was driven up at daylight. Having accomplished that, the enemy retired, and now seem to be waiting until we try to sleep again at night."

Camp omitted in that letter to tell of an act of generous self-forgetfulness of his that morning. The chaplain, who had left Seabrook Island in poor health, and had no surplus strength to expend, suffered acutely during that night of torment; tossing restlessly; unable to sleep, yet unable to fully awake; at times pulling the blanket as a mosquito-bar over his face and hands, to swelter under its oppressive weight; then throwing it off only to be bitten at every exposed atom as before; and thus until nearly morning, when there came to him in his half-consciousness a sense of exquisite relief in the drawing-away of the heavy blanket, the wiping of the soaked face, the fanning of the heated brow, the keeping-back of the persecuting swarm, followed by such delightful, refreshing, satisfying repose, as he scarce ever knew before or since. Understanding his friend's condition from his own experience, Camp had risen to care for him with affectionate tenderness: and there he sat, for nearly two hours, to secure sleep to the one of whose comfort he was ever thus considerate; waking him, finally, only to give him a cup of fresh and invigorating army coffee which he had had prepared. Such evidences of his warmth of heart and nobleness of nature were by no means rare toward the one blessed with his friendship.

"There is no probability," Camp added, "that we shall do any fighting here, though we expected to come under fire when we marched yesterday afternoon.

"The most uncomfortable sensations connected with a fight are those of immediate anticipation, without the excitement of action. Such we experienced then, but army life has rendered them quite familiar.

"Give me a short march to the field, fight or no fight."

The advanced position taken on Saturday night by General Terry's troops was held for several days, the different regiments alternating in picketing its front. During the afternoon of Wednesday the 15th, while the 10th was on outpost, the enemy made a demonstration on the line for the purpose of ascertaining its location and strength, but retired without making an attack. Of what followed, Camp thus wrote : —

" During the night, there were occasional shots along the line of outposts. We had had a booth constructed, open on all four sides, but covered at the top. Under this, dry grass was thickly spread. Our buffalo and blankets laid upon this made the most luxurious bed we had enjoyed since leaving Seabrook Island ; and, after being disturbed once or twice in the evening by slight showers, I was taking the comfort of it, when, just about daylight, I was aroused by the bustle about me. ' What does this mean?' said I to a man near me. ' There's so much firing,' said he, ' that the colonel has ordered the tents struck ; ' (shelter tents, of course). I opened my ears : there was the popping of not very distant musketry, growing, every instant that I listened, louder and more rapid. There was no time for delay. Henry and I dressed ourselves by putting on our coats and boots, rolled up our blankets, and slung our haversacks. As we did so, a messenger came to say that the 54th Massachusetts (colored), who were picketed on our right, were falling back, and the enemy following close upon them. This was serious news; for, being on the extreme left, with a swamp behind us, our communications with the supports in the rear were endangered. Almost at the same moment, the boom of artillery came to our ears from the left; and a glance showed us that the enemy had opened upon the 'Pawnee,' which lay nearly opposite us in the river. A second shot followed almost immediately upon the first, and the shriek of the shell through the air ended with a heavy crash as it tore its way through the vessel's timbers. The rebel artillerists already had the range; and two batteries at once opened, keeping up an almost incessant roar of explosions, while the frequent sound of splintering wood-work showed how effective was their fire.

" A cloud of smoke, lit up with constant flashes, marked their position within easy range of our own; and the plan seemed evident, — to drive in the center of our picket-line, depriving us of all chance of support; to cripple the vessel by whose guns we were covered, and thus render us helpless against the attack of the vastly superior force which could easily be brought down upon us. Under this fire, — wonderful for its precision and rapidity, — the 'Pawnee' at first seemed to show no signs of life. Shot after shot apparently raked her from stem to stern: still no answer. At length came the deep thunder of her huge Parrott gun; compared with which, the voices of the rebel field-pieces were like the barking of a pack of curs against a mastiff. But the wildness of her fire contrasted sadly

10

with the accuracy of the enemy. Her gunners were evidently taken by surprise; and shell after shell burst wide of the mark, while with tedious slowness she swung gradually broadside on. The sight was a beautiful and exciting one, rarely witnessed to such advantage as now.

"Meantime we were not idle. Our pickets had been sent for, with orders to make all haste; and from every part of the line we could see them across the wide plain coming in on the double-quick, while the sound of musketry upon the right grew continually more distinct and frequent. As the pickets reached the reserve, they formed line. The last-comers reported that the enemy were plainly to be seen near at hand from the outposts, a few hundred yards distant. Had we been in any other position along the line, it would have been our duty to resist their advance; and we should have retired slowly, if we had retired at all, fighting as we went. Here it would have been the useless and inevitable sacrifice of the whole regiment by isolation from the rest of the command. Colonel Leggett had received orders with reference to this contingency, and acted upon them, as it proved, not a moment too soon.

"The order was given to march. As we started, heavy discharges of artillery sounded from the right: at least a section or two of a rebel battery had taken possession not far from us in that direction. In reply to these, our own field-guns soon opened, and were served with a rapidity and accuracy which spoke well for our friend Captain Rock-well (of the 1st Connecticut light-battery), and compared favorably with the rebel fire. So, to the music of cannon on the right and left, and musketry in the rear, we took up our unaccustomed movement away from the front. The rebels and ourselves were marching upon converging lines, and their distance from the point of intersection was but slightly greater than our own. It became an interesting question, how much before them we should reach it. Thickets and hedges for the first few minutes prevented our seeing them, and we moved in ordinary quick time. Coming at length to a point whence we could obtain a view of the wide plain, the sight that disclosed itself was a startling one. Large bodies of gray-coated men, plainly visible, and already within rifle-range, were rapidly and steadily moving down toward the path along which we must march; their advance and ours very nearly upon the same line. 'Double-quick' was the word; and we increased our gait to a trot. Cut off by such a force as that, our case was hopeless: it was life or death, captivity or free-dom. Few words were spoken: each man saved his breath and strength for the time of greatest need, kept his place in the ranks, and moved steadily forward, only now and then turning his head to see what was gained or lost. The dusk of morning had not yet changed to full day-light. The bushes by the roadside partially concealed us, and we were probably still unseen. Looking back toward the place we had left, a long line of cavalry could be seen advancing in open order; the enemy's skirmishers feeling their way toward the position, which, as far as they knew, we still occupied, closing about it from all sides.

" Five minutes later that morning, and I should be writing to you, if writing at all, from a Charleston prison." [He was there before this letter reached his home.]

" The sight was a fine one : an outside spectator, at least, would have considered it so. It is seldom that one sees simultaneous operations of artillery, cavalry, and infantry upon the same field. We were naturally more interested in results than appearances. Had fire then been opened upon us, it would have put the soldierly discipline and steadiness which our men were proving so well to a severer test than I should have wished to see. It was not done. We soon reached and passed the point of greatest danger, and, leaving the road as soon as the nature of the ground made it practicable, made our way through the woods to our camp, and took our position in the line of battle upon which several regiments were already formed.

" Great as was our relief at escaping the more immediate danger, the excitement of the day was by no means over. The rebel forces which had so nearly intercepted us were soon in line before us. Their flag, with its white field and red union, transversely crossed with blue, floated at intervals along the front, showing the space occupied by each regiment. Mounted officers galloped along their ranks;

and it looked as if for once we were to have a fair field-
fight. So we stood for a little time, watching for the ball
to open. Then, instead of the advance which we expected,
they faced to the right, and passed at a double-quick along
our front, and out of sight behind the woods. This might
be a movement more threatening than a direct one. Our
left was greatly exposed. Should their battery flank and
enfilade us, our own regiment and the 56th would be in a
very critical position, unable to resist an attack to any advantage. Meantime the artillery and gunboats kept up a
constant roar. A shell, which probably came from the
latter, exploded in the woods, half a dozen rods behind us;
and their fire repeatedly endangered our skirmishers more
than that of the enemy. For half an hour, we were in suspense : then came word that they had retired. The artillery fire ceased, and we were dismissed from our position."

The loss in the engagement was exclusively to the 54th
Massachusetts, Colonel Shaw's regiment, which had fought
so bravely, in retiring from the picket line under overwhelm-
ing pressure, as to win respect from all other troops of the
command.

The night after the battle, James Island was quietly
evacuated by our troops ; the purpose of its occupancy, in
drawing forces from the direction of Morris Island while
Gen. Gillmore obtained a foothold there, being successfully
accomplished. The march in darkness and rain across the

marshes and over the rickety causeways toward Cole Island was tedious and perplexing; and a brief rest during the next day, on Cole Island, was most grateful to the weary men of Stevenson's brigade. Yet another night called for a new move. Hours of waiting on the beach for the rising tide were followed by hours of cramped confinement on a crowded barge in a drenching rain.

The morning of Saturday, July 18, brought the troops to the shore of Folly Island. Marching to its upper end, they were ferried thence across Lighthouse Creek to Morris Island, just as the heavy bombardment of Fort Wagner was commenced by the land batteries and the fleet of ironclads and wooden gunboats. The tired troops from James Island had but little time for rest.

"About five P.M.," wrote Camp, "came the order to fall in, and march down to the shore. We were not the only troops, it seemed, who had received the same instructions. Far up the beach stretched the long column, of which Stevenson's entire brigade formed less than a third part. There was little doubt as to the work before us, and that little was speedily set at rest by word from the general himself. We were to storm the fort. Our hearts beat high and fast. Our men were faint and weary with days and nights of sleeplessness and toil. Scarcely three hours' rest, and now work to which all else had been as play was set before them; but the announcement sent new strength through each vein. To storm the fort — that was a new and untried task. On the open field, and before rifle-pits and field-works, they had more than once already marched through the rain of bullets, and over captured batteries. But now it was to wade the ditch, to clamber with hand and foot up the steep slope beyond, while grape and canister would pour forth with the very blaze of the powder in their faces from the huge siege-guns, into whose muzzles they must look, to meet at the parapet's edge the bayonets of its defenders, and force the foe upward and backward over his own vantage-ground. The feeling was not of doubt or shrinking, but of curiosity mingled with firm resolve, be the untried struggle what it might, — wonder with fierce excitement. Among the groups of officers, as we stood at a halt and along the ranks, some faces glowed with the strange joy of combat; but most had the fixed look of determination, swallowing up every trace of emotion.

"We anticipated, at first, the leading place in the assault; but, when the column finally moved forward, we were some distance from its head. As we advanced, the bombardment grew hotter and hotter; while the enemy, on their part, sent only an occasional shot or shell, — sometimes from the Cummings-Point Battery, sometimes even from distant Sumter, — whizzing by in front of us, or passing overhead, and dashing up the water a little distance from the shore. Reaching at length the outermost range of sand hills, from which level marshy ground stretches away toward the fort some twelve or fourteen hundred yards distant, our brigade was detached from the column, and sent into the trenches, to remain under cover until re-enforcements should be needed at the front. It was a disappointment not to be allowed to participate in the first attack; but the decision was probably made in view of the physical exhaustion of the men after their recent hardships.

"For a few moments we stood still in the shelter thus afforded, and listened with a feeling of comparative security to the howl of shot and shell over us, as the fire of the enemy increased in rapidity and frequency. But the desire to see the progress of the movement conquered all else; and Henry and I speedily mounted the bank, and looked out before us, — taking, a few minutes afterward, still another position, partially covered, and yet able to command a view of the entire field. Our column was still moving on in silence, the rapidly advancing darkness almost hiding them from our sight. On our left, within a few yards of us, stood General Gillmore and his staff, watching intently from a slight elevation all that lay beneath, regardless of the no inconsiderable danger to which we were all exposed. The intervals were short between the discharges of the enemy's artillery. We could see the burning fuze describe its curve through the air, unable sometimes to determine whether from a piece of theirs or of our own, — now diverging widely to the right or left, now seeming to come directly toward us; then, as we stooped behind our defences, the swift rush of the shell and the loud report of its explosion, — harmless if in front, dangerous if overhead or within short distance to the rear. One, bursting a few yards behind Henry and myself, sprinkled us with the earth which it threw up.

"Night was soon fairly upon us, and the scene became one of absolute magnificence. The firing of the fleet was almost incessant, — twenty or thirty discharges in a minute, — keeping up one uninterrupted peal of thunder; while each flash lighted up the vessel from which it came, the smoke which rolled upward, and the water beneath, with vivid brilliance. Nothing in the way of pyrotechnics could equal in effect a broadside from the 'Ironsides;' its swift tongues of flame piercing deep into the darkness, and bringing out into momentary distinctness the immense hull from which they sprung, and the heavy boom of the discharges coming over the water after long apparent delay; while the fancy followed into the dark fort the fourteen hundred pounds of solid iron which flew meantime, and wondered if they did their work.

"When a small boat put off from the shore toward the fleet, and when shortly afterward the firing from the vessels grew slack, and then ceased altogether, we knew what it must mean, and looked still more anxiously over the plain. A few minutes of comparative silence, and then a burst of flame from the walls of the fort, — otherwise undistinguishable in the darkness, — and the sharp crackle of musketry told us that the assault had commenced. Heavy discharges of artillery followed in rapid succession, flashing like heat-lightning; while the little jets of fire from the rifles made a sparkling frieze along the dark parapet. Ah! how men were falling there!—mowed down by whole companies, as grape-shot and bullets tore through their ranks. Nothing but flash and report was to be seen or heard. We could only fancy the fearful work that was going on, and hope that the result would compensate for it all. Now the fire seemed to be growing less hot; occasionally almost ceasing for a brief space, then bursting out again with new fury.

" We watched eagerly and waited, but no news came back to us; nor did General Gillmore himself seem to receive any information from the front. Finally, as if impatient of the delay, and anxious that no time should be lost when help was called for, he ordered our brigade forward to the outermost lines,—a mere sand-bag breast-work, where a few pieces of artillery had lately been put in position. We advanced in line of battle irregularly enough over the marshy, uneven ground, in darkness so thick that but a small part of the line could be seen at once. Shell flew thickly over and around us, exploding on all sides; but we were unharmed, and soon found ourselves again under shelter, such as it was, several hundred yards further to the front than before.

" The fight was still raging, but with less intensity than an hour previous. Again we watched its varying aspect, until at length a messenger came. ' Our forces were within

the fort, but needed support : Stevenson's brigade would
go forward.' Gladly we obeyed the summons; but the
execution of the order had been hardly commenced when
it was countermanded, and another of ill-boding significance
substituted. We were again to form line, and stop all
stragglers who might endeavor to pass us. Few came.
Once or twice in the darkness, I saw a man moving toward
the rear. ' What are you doing here ?' said I to one poor
fellow as I stopped him. ' I'm wounded,' said he, and,
knowing that I would not accept the threadbare excuse of
every straggler without proof, took my hand, and laid it
into the gory furrow plowed upon his head by some
fragment of shell. I didn't keep him long waiting.
Another was wounded in the leg, but still able to walk.
And so they came ; though most of those who could make
their own way back to hospital followed the beach down,
and we saw nothing of them. Once a horrible chorus of
groans and shrieks rose from the direction of the water,
and then all was silent again. We were told afterward
that the ambulances, in the darkness, ran over some
wounded men.

"About eleven o'clock, a report was brought that we had
been successful ; and it was later than that before the firing
altogether ceased ; but by midnight there was very little
doubt that the result had been unfavorable. Once or twice
we were roused by the report of the sentries that movements were to be seen upon the plain in front ; but we

were exceedingly weary, and I, at least, lost hardly a moment after each story was pronounced false, before sinking back into sound sleep."

The 10th not being engaged, the chaplain had turned aside from his regiment, when the earliest wounded came back from the assaulting column, to aid in caring for them; and he was separated from his friend until the dawning of the gloomy sabbath morning which succeeded that night of carnage and defeat. Their regiment holding the outermost lines of defense, the friends could then see distinctly the entire battle-field, with its scores of dead and wounded yet uncared for, — the rising tide actually drowning some of the poor fellows who were unable to crawl away to higher ground than the sand-hollows in which they lay; but they could do nothing for the relief of any beyond their lines. When, about noon, they were told by their commanding officer that a flag of truce which they had seen pass out had secured a brief armistice, that the dead might be buried and the wounded removed, the chaplain was glad of an opportunity to go and minister to those who so sadly needed help; and Camp was ready to accompany him, as always,— not only, in this instance, that he might be of service, but in the hope of hearing of some college classmates, who were from the vicinity of Charleston.

The friends went out, with the full approbation of their superior officers, for a work, which, as the mission of one, was the duty of both. They had no reason to anticipate exposure to capture, or deem their movement in any sense venturesome. Passing a few rods beyond their pickets, they met a Confederate sergeant with a squad of men, who neither halted them nor seemed surprised at their advance. Of him they inquired if the armistice still held. "I believe so," was his reply. To make the matter sure, they asked for his officers. He pointed to a group close at hand; and, as the friends moved thither, one of the officers stepped forward quickly with the remark, "Prisoners! gentlemen." A statement being made as to the understood arrangement and the object of the visit, the officer claimed that the agreement covered only a cessation of hostilities, for attention to dead and wounded by each party, within their own lines, and insisted on considering the friends as prisoners. They protested against being held under such circumstances, while engaged in a humane work, at a time of admitted amity, especially as the sergeant on what was now claimed as the line had freely permitted them to pass. One of the Charleston officers of the party was evidently unwilling to have them detained; but the captain on General Haygood's staff, who had first stopped them, being a renegade Northerner, had less of fairness, and refused to release them until their case was laid before his general, then in command of Fort Wagner. After considerable delay, word came back, that, while General Haygood did not wish to take any advantage of a misunderstanding in such a matter, he could not assume the responsibility of releasing the friends now that they were held, without special authority from General Ripley, at Charleston, to whom he would submit their case. After two or three more hours of anxious waiting, the friends were led blindfold along the beach, past Fort Wagner, to Cummings's Point, where they remained until sundown; being told all the while that the question as to their release was yet undecided. In the evening, they, with other prisoners, including many wounded, were taken up to Charleston by steamer, stopping for awhile at Fort Sumter; being probably the last Union officers at that world-renowned fortress before its destruction, a few weeks later. Reaching the city, they were marched with the colored privates of the Massachusetts 54th Regiment, amid the jeers of the populace, through the streets, to the provost-marshal's. Thence they were taken to the gloomy jail, and at ten o'clock at night thrust — twenty in all — into a small and filthy room, without furniture, and not large enough for all to find a place on the floor, without overlapping one another. By special order from General Ripley, the friends were to pass the night with the colored privates, instead of with white officers; but that was the least annoyance which made their first night in prison so sad and gloomy.

CHAPTER VIII.

PRISON LIFE AND ESCAPE.

STRANGE sensations," wrote Camp, "are those which a man experiences during his first hours in prison. The consciousness of helplessness under restraint produces a feeling of absolute suffocation, a nightmare oppression, with a nervousness that makes it impossible to sit or stand still, to concentrate the thoughts on any subject, or to do any thing but pace up and down the longest possible beat which the narrow limits of confinement will afford.

"We were allowed in the morning to purchase some bread, and a decoction of rye or barley as a substitute for coffee. Early in the forenoon, Henry and I were removed from the room in which we had slept, taken through long corridors with their grated iron doors, up flight after flight of massive stone stairs, to a room in one of the upper stories,— the quarters of imprisoned officers. Here we found the officers taken on Saturday night in the assault. . . .

"Henry and I had been congratulating one another that we were together, speaking of how much harder to endure all this would be but for our mutual help and sympathy;

when, about the middle of the forenoon, an order came detailing the captured chaplain and nineteen men to assist in caring for the wounded at the hospital. It was a heavy blow for us both. I would gladly have gone as one of the nineteen; but orders were strict that no officer should be included in the number. We parted sadly enough, more so than on the eve of battle; for we had more apprehensions for the future. Up to this hour, matters had not worn so gloomy an aspect. Together, we had felt comparatively strong; in the prospect of separation, despondent enough. The day dragged heavily along. . . . At evening, the non-commissioned officers and privates were taken down into the prison-yard, paroled not to bear arms again until exchanged, and returned to their cells. These were in the same corridor with our own: all the doors within it were kept open; and we could pass freely among them. It was rumored that they were to go to Columbia in the morning; whether we should accompany them we did not hear. Even when we were all ordered down to the yard at five o'clock the next morning, we thought it was only that our quarters might be cleaned. The roll was called, and we were formed in line for a march. It was hard thus to be separated so much further from Henry, without the opportunity of exchanging a word with him, so much as to say good-by. Parting thus in an enemy's country, a hundred miles and more of distance to be placed between us, the prospect of our ever meeting again seemed doubtful and distant. He would not even know of my going until I was far away : it was the climax of all I had dreaded. We were marched to the depot, put on board the cars, and the train started almost immediately.''

The party reached Columbia that night, and were taken at once to Richland Jail, where they found the officers captured in the first assault on Wagner.

" We and our new fellow-prisoners introduced ourselves to one another,'' wrote Camp, " talked over, as in the Charleston prison, all the news we brought; and we speedily began to feel ourselves comparatively at home in accommodations far superior to those we had left. At three-quarters past eight, the bell in the tower of the town-hall, only a few rods distant, rung rapidly for a few minutes, — the signal, we were told, for negroes to leave the streets. As the clock struck the last stroke of nine, the watchman in the balcony beneath it called aloud, with curious inflection of tone, ' Past nine o'clock ! ' We took the hint and retired. At quarter past nine, the watchman's voice sounded again, 'All's well ! ' In fifteen minutes more, ' Half-past nine o'clock! ' Again, 'All's well ! ' Then, ' Past ten o'clock,' and so through the night, — though for my part I hardly heard him once.

" The next day passed slowly. I was still exceedingly nervous, and full of anxiety on account of my separation from Henry. I spent a large part of the time pacing up and down the room, and fancying what might be, and

11

might have been, until I was tired enough to sit down upon the floor, and rest. I wrote to Henry that afternoon, giving the letter to the captain of the guard, with that which I wrote home."

In that letter to his friend, Camp said hopefully, —

" No one here seems to know of or believe in any interruption of the arrangements for exchange. The Charleston papers mention recent exchanges at the West, and I hope we may be put rapidly around the track. Wouldn't it be pleasant to meet on our own side of the lines within two or three weeks? I do not flatter myself that this is certainly to be. I know that months of imprisonment and separation may be before us; but I try to look, as far as it is reasonable to do so, upon the bright side, and succeed in this much better than at first. But for my anxiety on your account I should be in good spirits: even as it is, I do not call myself blue. We are both in God's hands. He has dealt with us very kindly hitherto : let us trust him for the future. I do believe that he will permit us again to stand side by side in our country's service ; and, whatever else may be his decree, that we shall see by and by that all was for the best. I have been wont so to lean upon you, that I feel sadly the loss of your support ; but our attachment to one another grows stronger through trial, and there are bright days yet in store for us. Meantime, take courage. There is much to be done. I know you will not break down, however hard the struggle. I trust I shall not until we come 'out of the shadow into the sun.'

"By Thursday," continued Camp in his home-narrative, "I had begun to settle down somewhat more into my position. I contrived to find occupation for most of my time; and made up my mind that, if Henry and I were only here together, we could not merely endure, but enjoy, the life. I thought it all over: it was utterly impossible that his services at the hospital would be dispensed with until all the wounded were dead or convalescent. That would be months, and the trial would be more than he could endure: how doubtful the prospect of our ever meeting again! That doubt, and nothing else, made the future too dark to bear anticipation. Friday morning, about ten o'clock, the door opened, and he came in. Oh, what a meeting for us that was! I sha'n't try to tell you any thing about it. The day was gone before we knew it, and all that have followed have flown like it. Imprisonment is not tedious with him for a companion. I lean upon him as everywhere, and he so much more than doubles my strength! We read together, write together, whittle together, talk together, do every thing together. The value of our friendship could hardly appear elsewhere as it does here; nowhere else could we be so thoroughly inseparable or so greatly dependent upon one another.

"Our life is so different from that of those around us! The *ennui* which oppresses them we know nothing about:

so far from it, we have not time for all that we would do ;
and unfinished work accumulates from day to day. The
hardships we must undergo are so far lightened, that we
can fairly say that we enjoy prison-life. It won't do, here
in prison, to give even thought free scope, — not that
others attempt to limit it ; but we ourselves, for our own
sakes, must do so. I say we enjoy prison-life : it is because we *will not* think. If we allowed ourselves to
imagine what we are losing by absence from our regiment
at such a time as this, — the time and occasion to which we
have been looking forward for tedious months of inactivity, — the prospect of which has kept us cheerful and hopeful through many perplexities and disappointments (and
you know how bitter to me already is the thought of
Roanoke, Goldsborough, Whitehall, and Kinston) ; if we
dwelt upon the difficulty, perhaps impossibility, of com-
municating with you ; our anxiety in regard to your health
and welfare, and that which we know you must be feeling
for us ; the loss we are sustaining in property, which none
in the regiment can attend to as is needful ; the doubtful
prospect of release in the unfortunate condition of affairs
between our own authorities and the Confederate, in regard to prisoners-of-war ; the possibility of months or
even years of close confinement, — if we brooded over all
these, and the multitude of other subjects for sad thought,
we should drive ourselves crazy in twenty-four hours. It
took us some little time to learn this ; but now we under-

stand it, and manage to busy our thoughts in great measure with the trivial matters of every-day life in prison.
What is the quality of the corn-bread this morning? who
shall go after the pail of water? how long the sergeant
will allow us to stay in the yard for air and exercise? —
these are the questions to which we give our attention.
When the mind craves more than this, we sit down to
write or talk on miscellaneous subjects. Nine or ten
hours for sleep, and so we live."

Henry Camp was a man of mark in prison as elsewhere.
The most haughty Southern officer with whom he came in
contact recognized his true nobility, and gave him defer-
ence; while the more brutal of his guards were softened
into respectful treatment of him by the irresistible power
of his commanding presence. His fellow-prisoners respected and esteemed him. The treasures of his stored and
well-trained intellect were much in demand. In the lack
of books during the early prison months, frequent questions
of dispute arose as to points of fact, principles of science,
or subjects of general reading; and he was rarely referred
to in vain for authority as to the truth. German officers
were there; and, when their language was undertaken as a
study, they were surprised at his knowledge of its structure
and the rules governing its use, especially as he disavowed
any claim to be called a German scholar. He played chess,
and, although pitted against some skillful antagonists,
proved himself more thoroughly the master of the game

than any of his opponents; being often successful, single-handed, against several of the best players in consultation.

His intimacy with the chaplain was closer, and, if possible, more noticeable, in prison than elsewhere. Outside, the two had been called the "twins." In confinement, the old negro woman who daily brought in rations spoke of them uniformly as "de mates;" and they were thenceforward thus designated by their companions. The guards spoke to others by name, but to these as, "you two;" always allowing them liberty together, as if they had but one existence. The chaplain was permitted to go out on the sabbath into the yard, or up-stairs, to preach to the Union privates. The officers, except Adjutant Camp, were not at first allowed to attend these services. "You two can go, nobody else," was the usual announcement. The friends were rarely an arm's-length from each other in all their months of confinement together. And while for weary weeks the chaplain was low with jail-fever, as also when he was disheartened and depressed with long confinement, he owed, under God, his life and renewed strength to the gentle and faithful ministry, and the inspiring words and brave example, of his peerless friend.

But few Union officers have been confined in Columbia Jail. Not more than about thirty were together there at any time during the stay of the two friends. At first, there were only those captured in the two assaults on Wagner. Then Captain, now Lieutenant-Colonel Payne, of the 100th New-York State Volunteers, was brought in from the hospital; being wounded and taken in one of his daring scouts up Charleston Harbor. Then came the naval officers of the unsuccessful assaulting party against Sumter, including Lieutenants S. W. Preston and B. H. Porter, who lost their lives at Fort Fisher so soon after their release. Chaplain Fowler, of Colonel Higginson's First South - Carolina Regiment, was the next new-comer. Few besides these have been there within the past two years. The extensive prison-pens outside the city were of later origin. The enlisted men taken at Wagner, and the sailors and marines taken at Sumter, remained but a short time at Columbia before being forwarded to Belle Island to starve and freeze.

The rations furnished the officers were, at first, cooked by colored women, coming in from outside by permission of the guard; then, as money grew scarce, the officers cooked for themselves, taking turns in the kitchen a week at a time. United-States treasury-notes were easily exchanged for Confederate currency, at the rate of one to four or five, notwithstanding the rigid orders against such barter. Newspapers were contraband for several months; but they could usually be obtained, in spite of official commands to the contrary. Finally, permission was granted for their daily purchase.

For awhile, there was a prospect of exchanges being resumed; but, as the chances of that diminished, plans of escape were talked over. Camp chafed under a sense of confinement, and in view of his loss of active service. "I have put to you," he wrote home, "that side of prison-life which is least dark; but how gladly would I exchange for this any imaginable privation or suffering in freedom! My experience in or out of the army has never as yet furnished any thing resembling it. God grant it never again may if the end of this finds me still living! Not that I am especially blue just now: far more cheerful than a great part of the time hitherto. I fully realize how much worse off I might and may be; but this is *captivity*, — a word whose meaning I have but lately learned. . . . Just now, it is not so much the mere fact of confinement, as the knowledge that we are losing opportunities that life can never replace. A day of freedom and activity in times like these is worth a year of the old inaction which used, you know, so to discontent me. But this is just the one thing which it won't do for me to think or write of."

He determined to risk every thing in an attempt to rejoin his regiment. The chaplain's sickness at first interfered with the project: then the announcement that the latter was to be released induced its postponement until he should pass the lines, and send back certain desired information.

Early in November, the two friends were separated by the removal of the chaplain to Richmond for release. The parting was a sad one to both, — scarcely less so to the one who was to regain liberty by the change than to the other who was to remain a prisoner. The hours would have dragged even yet more wearily to the chaplain but for his hope to secure, by untiring endeavor, his friend's release on special parole.

On the sabbath evening before Thanksgiving, Camp wrote in his one-page home-letter: "Sabbath hours drag even more slowly than those of the other days of the week. To-day has been long: it is almost bed-time now. We had singing earlier in the evening, — old familiar hymns and tunes; and I wondered if you were not singing at the same time, as we used to, gathered around the piano in the east room. You have gas there now: it wouldn't look quite natural to me. I would like to sit in the sofa-corner, almost in the dark, and hear Nellie and Kate in that duet I always liked so much, — 'Far o'er the wave;' and then join, all of us together, in 'Lenox,' or 'Coronation,' or some of those stirring old Methodist melodies, winding up with 'Homeward bound.' Do you remember our singing 'When shall we meet again?' the last sabbath evening that I was at home? How little we imagined then that Thanksgiving-week of this year would find us separated by any such cause as now! Thank God that it is not death, which would have seemed so much more probable; and that we may yet hope another Thanksgiving will find us together in an unbroken circle!" [That next Thanksgiving he passed in heaven.]

While the chaplain was laboring for his friend's release, the latter was perfecting his plans of escape ; and, in a little more than a month after the separation of the two, he left the jail with a comrade : but, after a week in the woods, both were recaptured, and remanded to their former quarters. From Camp's full record of that exciting adventure, written out in the leisure of later days in jail, the following extracts are made : —

" The possibility of escape was a subject of thought and conversation among us quite early in our imprisonment. After Henry's departure, I made up my mind to try the experiment as soon as matters seemed ripe for it. The reports of exchange just at hand, which coaxed us into hope from week to week, for four months, no longer tantalized us. I was exceedingly restless and impatient. There was scarcely a day of which I did not spend more than one hour in thinking of the possibilities and probabilities of the attempt ; and many a night did my bedfellow and I lie awake after others had gone to sleep, and discuss the merits of various plans. I used to pace our empty front-room, and think of the sluggish wretchedness of our life here, and the joy of freedom gained by our own efforts, — the same round of thought over and over again, — until I was half wild with the sense of restraint and of suffocation.

" Our plan, as finally agreed upon, was simple. Twice during the day we were allowed half an hour in the yard for exercise; being counted when we came in, or soon after, to assure the sergeant of the guard that we were all present. In this yard was a small brick building * consisting of two rooms used as kitchens, — one by ourselves, the other by the naval officers. The latter of these had a window opening into a woodshed; from which, part of the side being torn away, there was access to a narrow space between another small building and the jail-fence. Our intention was to enter this kitchen during our half-hour of liberty, as we were frequently in the habit of doing; to talk with those who were on duty for the day; remain there after the cooks had gone in, leaving lay-figures to be counted in our stead by the sergeant; thence through the woodshed, and, by removing a board of the high fence already loosened for the purpose, into the adjoining premises, from which we could easily gain the street. The latter part of the movement — all of it, indeed, except the entrance into the kitchen, where we were to remain quiet for several hours — was to be executed after dark.

"The street once gained, my comrade and I intended to take the railroad running northward along the banks of the Broad River, follow it during the first night, while our escape was still undiscovered, then strike as direct a course as possible for the North-Carolina line. Through the latter State, we hoped to make our way westward

* Shown in the engraving on the opposite page.

across the mountains, where we should find friends as well as enemies, ultimately reaching Burnside's lines in East Tennessee. The distance to be passed over we estimated at about three hundred miles; the time which it would occupy, at from twenty to thirty days. The difficulties in our way were very great, the chances for and against us we considered certainly no better than equal. What would be the results of failure we could not anticipate : loss of life certainly was not the least likely of them.

"Our preparations for such a trip were, of necessity, few. We manufactured a couple of stout cloth haversacks, in which, though hardly as large as the army pattern, we were to carry ten days' provision, — each of us two dozen hard-boiled eggs, and about six quarts of what we found described in 'Marcy's Prairie Traveler' as the most nutritious and portable of all food, — corn parched and ground, — just what we children used to call 'rokeeg.' Besides a rubber-blanket to each, we concluded, for the sake of light traveling, to carry but a single woolen one. This, with one or two other articles of some bulk, we placed in a wash-tub and covered with soiled clothes, in order to convey them, without exciting suspicion, to the kitchen. My baggage for the journey, besides what has already been referred to, consisted of an extra pair of cotton socks, a comb, toothbrush, and piece of soap, needle and thread, a piece of stout cloth, a flask about one-third full of excellent brandy, a piece of lard, a paper of salt, pencil and paper, and my home-photographs.

" Two dummies (or lay-figures) were to be made. The first was a mere pile of blankets; but its position in the second story of our double-tier bedstead protected it from close observation. For the second, I borrowed a pair of pants, and for one foot found a cast-off shoe. The upper part of the figures was covered with a blanket; and the face, with a silk handkerchief: attitude was carefully attended to. I flattered myself that the man was enough of a man for pretty sharp eyes, and was satisfied when Lieutenant B. came in, and unsuspectingly addressed him by the name of the officer whose pants he wore. . . .

" After the last thing was done which could be done in the way of preparation, time passed very slowly. I was impatiently nervous, and spent the hours in pacing the rooms and watching the sluggish clock-hands. The excitement of anticipation was hardly less than that which I have felt before an expected fight. The personal stake at issue was little different."

Camp's comrade in this move was Captain V. B. Chamberlain, of the 7th Connecticut Volunteers. " Well-informed (an ex - editor), plucky, and of excellent physique, well calculated to endure hardship, and a good swimmer. He was that day on duty in the kitchen. At four, P.M., we went out as usual for exercise. Entering the kitchen a few minutes before our half-hour had expired, I concealed myself in a snug corner, before which one or two towels, a huge tin boiler, and other convenient articles, were so disposed as to render the shelter complete should so unusual an event occur as a visit from the guard after that hour. Here, like another Ivanhoe in the beleagured castle, I received a running report of the course of events outside from the culinary gentlemen, who had, in their present costume and occupation, about as little resemblance to United-States officers as to the fair Jewess of the story.

"It was but a few minutes before the corporal, acting for the day as sergeant, was seen to enter the room to which all but the cooks and myself had returned. It was Corporal Addison, alias 'Bull-Head,'—a lubberly English clodhopper, looking just like the men in the illustrations to Miss Hannah More's stories. Our confidence that all would go well was based in great measure upon his stupidity; and it was with greatly increased apprehensions that I heard that he was accompanied to-night by Captain Senn.

"Rather than pass the ordeal of a visit from him, had we anticipated it, we should probably have deferred our attempt another day, even at the risk of losing our chance altogether. He opened the door and went in. I waited anxiously to hear what would follow. He seemed to stay longer than usual. Was there any thing wrong? Suspense lengthened the minutes; but it was of no use to question those who could see, while the door remained closed, no more than myself. Presently I was told that the door was open; he was coming out; there seemed to be no alarm; he was stepping briskly toward the yard. We breathed more freely. A moment more, and he was going back, evidently dissatisfied with something. He re-entered the room. 'It's all up,' said my reporter. I thought myself that there was little doubt of it, and prepared, the moment any sign of alarm appeared, to come from my retreat, which I preferred to leave voluntarily rather than with the assistance of a file of men. Too bad to be caught at the very outset, without so much as a whiff of the air of freedom to compensate us for the results of detection! But no: Captain Senn comes quietly out, walks leisurely through the hall; and his pipe is lit,—best evidence in the world that all is tranquil, his mind undisturbed by any thing startling or unexpected.

"But it was too soon to exult: congratulations were cut short by sudden silence on the part of my friends. I listened: it was broken by a step on the threshold, and the voice of the captain close beside me. I didn't hold my breath according to the established precedent in all such cases; but I sat for a little while as still as I did the first time that ever my daguerreotype was taken; then, cautiously moving my head, I caught a view of the visitor as he stood hardly more than at arm's-length from me. He was merely on a tour of inspection; asked a few unimportant questions of the cooks, and, after a brief call, took his leave. It was with more than mere physical relief that I stretched myself, and took a new position in my somewhat cramped quarters. Immediate danger was over: we had nothing more to fear until the cooks went in. We listened anxiously, until it seemed certain that all danger from another visit and the discovery of Captain Chamberlain's absence was over; then sat down to wait for a later hour. . . .

"After perhaps an hour of quiet, we set about what little was to be done before we were ready to leave the building, — the rolling of our blankets, not yet taken from the tub in which they had been brought out, the filling of our haversacks, &c. To do this in perfect silence was no easy task. Any noise made was easily audible outside: the window looking toward the jail had no sash, and the blinds which closed it failed to meet in the center. A sentry stood not far distant. More than once, startled by the loud rattling of the paper which we were unwrapping from our provisions, or the clatter of some dish inadvertently touched in the darkness, we paused, and anxiously peeped through the blinds to see if the sentry had noticed it. The possibility of any one's being in the kitchen at that hour was probably the last thought to enter his mind. Many times we carefully felt our way around the room, — stocking-foot and tip-toe, — searching for some article laid down perhaps but a moment before, lost, without the aid

of eyesight to recover it, until at length we thought ourselves ready to pass into the adjoining room, whose window
opened upon the woodshed.

"The only communication between these rooms was by
a small hole broken through the chimney-back, scarcely
large enough to admit the body, and with the passage
further embarrassed by the stoves on either side, so placed
that it was necessary to lie down, and move serpent-wise
for a considerable distance. Captain Chamberlain made the
first attempt, and discovered that the door of the stove on
the opposite side had been left open, and wedged in that
position by the wood, crowded in for the morning's fire; so
that the passage was effectually obstructed. The hole had
to be enlarged by the tearing-away of more bricks, which,
as fast as removed, he handed to me to be laid on one side.
Patient labor at length made a sufficient opening, and he
passed through. I handed to him the blankets, haversacks,
and shoes, and with some difficulty followed."

The woodshed gained, the loosened board was removed
from the fence, and replaced after they had passed through.
Across a kitchen-garden they hurried to the open street
beyond, and then, without meeting any person, through
Columbia to the railroad.

"Reaching the iron track, we turned northward, and were
speedily out of sight of houses, fairly started upon our
journey through the country. I wish I could describe the
sensation of pleasure that thrilled through every fiber of
12

our frames with an exhilaration like that of wine ! After
five months of confinement, of constant and unavailing
chafing under the galling consciousness of restraint and of
helplessness, we could hardly realize that we were free ;
that we should not wake in the morning to find ourselves
within the narrow jail-limits, under the eyes and the orders
of our old sentries. To be again the masters of our own
acts was like being endowed with a new faculty. We
breathed deep and long. We could have shouted with the
excitement of each free step upon solid earth, each draught
of free air under the open sky. That first hour of liberty
would alone have paid for all the hardships we were to encounter. I shall have pleasant memory of it as long as I
live. Our path led us along the banks of Broad River,
the dash of whose waters was constantly in our ears, and
whose swift current we could often see in the clear star-
light, rushing down in rapids, or foaming around huge
rocks. Such sights and sounds we had not known since
we left our New-England homes ; and we enjoyed to the
full, not only these, but each bush that we passed, each
little stream that flowed across the way, each thicket of
dark undergrowth, or hillside covered with forest, that lifted itself beyond ; all was fresh to us.

" It was a cold night, just the temperature, however, for
walking ; and upon a good path we should have made rapid
progress. But the ties were laid upon the surface of the
ground, instead of being sunk, and were at the most incon-

venient distance possible from one another. This was not
the worst. Before we had gone two miles, we came to
what seemed to be a stream of some size, crossed by a tres-
tle-work bridge. We must pass it by stepping from tie
to tie. It was difficult to see in the darkness how far
beneath us the water flowed, but it was evidently at no inconsiderable depth ; and the light was none too strong to
enable us to plant our footsteps with a feeling of security.
We supposed, however, that a short distance would place
us again upon solid ground, and pushed on slowly and carefully. We were disappointed. Beyond the current of the
stream was a wide marsh, stretching as far as we could
see ; and across this lay our road : it was many minutes of
tedious traveling before we again reached firm footing.
While we were congratulating ourselves that our trouble
was over, we were cut short by a second bridge, of similar
structure, but higher, if any thing, than the first, and certainly longer. Beneath us, we could scarcely see any thing
save a black gulf, — before us the track vanishing at a few
rods' distance into darkness. To add to the difficulty, many
of the ties were rotten to such a degree that we dared not
trust our weight upon the center of them, many displaced
so that it was not easy to pass the chasm created by their
absence.

" We walked on and on, expecting every minute to see
the end ; but no end came in sight : the distance seemed in-
terminable. I might overstate if I should attempt to esti-

mate accurately the length and number of these bridges over which we passed during the night, the nervousness of the task being increased toward morning by a heavy white-frost, which made the footing still more uncertain ; but I am sure that I am within bounds in reckoning them by miles. . . . As morning drew near, we were, of course, far more fatigued than by any ordinary eight hours of walking ; and had made much less progress than we hoped to make before daylight should render it necessary to take shelter in the woods.   We were both thoroughly exhausted with long-unaccustomed exercise, and could scarcely walk without staggering.   We looked at one another, and were astonished at the haggard faces and weary forms which we saw."

After some difficulty in finding a sufficiently secluded place for a rest, they at length reached a spot which seemed to answer their purpose.

" The roots of an uptorn tree upon one side, the trunk of a fallen one upon another, with a sheltering hillock and surrounding undergrowth, furnished us with such protection, that a passer-by, even within a few paces, would not have been likely to see us.   We were too tired to eat.   We spread a rubber-blanket upon the ground, a woolen one over us, and, with our haversacks for pillows, were speedily sleeping as we had not done before since we left Morris Island, and exchanged a life of hard work for a harder one of inaction.   How long we had slept when I awoke I could not tell; but I was too thoroughly chilled to rest longer. I listened before I raised my head, lest there might be some one near. What was that crackling of the dry leaves at a little distance? I closed my eyes again and lay still. Surely those were cautious footsteps that seemed to draw near and halt, and then retreat again. Then all was quiet. I woke Captain Chamberlain, telling him I feared we were discovered, and perhaps at that moment watched. Even if we were, however, it was of no use to wait; and we rose. No one in sight. We searched the bushes in the direction of the sound. No sign of any one's having been there; and, after a few minutes, we convinced ourselves that it was a false alarm. It was not the only one which we raised for one another during the day, nervously suspicious as we were of every cracking bough, every moving object. Once Captain Chamberlain pointed out to me a soldier in gray uniform behind some bushes only a few rods distant, evidently watching us. But, before I could make him out, he resolved himself into his harmless components of tree-trunk and branch.

"We rolled our blankets in convenient form to sling across the shoulder, and, much refreshed, although with joints somewhat stiff and lame, started again northward, intending to halt for breakfast as soon as sunshine and exercise should warm our blood a little. It was not long before circulation was brisk again; and a sunny hillside furnished us with a breakfast-room, which, to say the least of it, compared favorably with that we had occupied the morning before.   Then we made the first trial of our patent provisions.   The eggs, with salt for seasoning, were capital ; but our stock was limited.   We allowed ourselves one each,—the bulk of our meal consisting of the rokeeg. Palatable enough we found it, albeit somewhat dry ; and it proved exceedingly nutritious.   A day or two later, after it had been dampened and dried again, partially at least, it was almost entirely tasteless, and had no more relish or even food-flavor than so much sawdust.   We could only tell when we had eaten enough by estimating the quantity which had vanished or the time consumed in the operation. Still it supported our strength as hardly any thing else in the same quantity could have done ; and we were ready to indorse Captain Marcy's recommendation of it.

" Rest and food had made new men of us : we pushed cheerily along through wood, over hill, and across field. The traveling was neither very difficult, nor easy enough to admit of rapid progress.   The woods were quite open, and we frequently crossed cultivated land.   Houses frequently interrupted us ; and much time was consumed in the long circuit we had to make to pass them without danger of being observed.   The country was altogether too thickly settled for our convenience.   About two, P.M., we found ourselves fairly brought to a stand-still,— open country before us with houses in sight, and no way of getting through under cover.

" We found an excellent shelter, well protected, although near a road; lay down behind an old long-neglected wood-pile and slept again, woke, dined, and waited for dark. As soon as it was fairly dusk, we started once more upon our course. We soon reached a road, upon which, during the afternoon, we had observed a rider moving along at some distance, — the first man we had seen since leaving jail. We hesitated whether to follow this route, or attempt to push through the woods in the dark. We had not intended to venture upon the roads after the first night, but considering the chance that our escape was still undiscovered, and the difficulty of making any progress otherwise, we concluded to run the risk, exercising the utmost possible caution with reference to avoiding any whom we might meet."

Having a narrow escape from detection by a passing horseman, they pressed on, until, across a curve in the road, they saw the lights of a house, and their quick ears caught the sound of steps and voices from within or near it.

" Approaching this place, in addition to the voices so distinctly heard through the quiet night air, we could see near it the bright glare of a fire kindled out of doors, — perhaps a tar-kiln or a coal-pit blazing up. This we must avoid, and we turned aside accordingly into the woods. It was a tedious circuit that we had to make before we could leave them safely. We stumbled over rock and fallen tree, in the darkness of the dense undergrowth; plunged into brook and swamp; tore our way through wildernesses of briers, from which we came out with bleeding hands and tattered clothing, making so slow and so difficult progress, that we were more than ever disposed, in the absence of any positive evidence of danger, to keep the traveled route whenever it was possible.''

Thenceforward they followed the woods by day, and the road by night. At the close of their second day's journey, to their regret, it commenced to rain.

" At four, P.M., the first drops fell. Darkness came on almost immediately, and we took an oblique direction which we thought would bring us in a few minutes back to the road which we had crossed shortly before dinner, and parallel to which we had been traveling for several hours. But either the road curved sharply from us, or we had wandered further from it than we thought. We reached a swamp, which certainly, from what we remembered of the conformation of the land, ought not to lie between us and the line which we wished to strike. There was no passage but to wade through. Dense thickets obstructed our way; rain and darkness made each obstacle more serious; and we were additionally puzzled by the possibility that a traveled path which we had crossed some time before, thinking it from its appearance a by-way, might have been the road itself, and that we were now only plunging ourselves deeper and deeper into the woods. Still we pushed on, unwilling to believe ourselves lost, and were greatly relieved, after a tedious and discouraging tramp, in coming out at length upon what was unmistakably the track for which we had been so long searching.

"The rain had not yet injured the walking, and we made for a while rapid progress. Just after descending a gentle hill, while crossing a stretch of low ground, we heard what seemed to be the rattle of a cart on the slope behind us, and the loud and distinct voice of a man calling to his oxen. We made all haste to shelter ourselves; and, having done so by lying down behind some logs near the roadside, waited for the passage of the team. All was still: not a sound of life anywhere to be heard. We were almost ready to rise, thinking, in spite of our ears, that we must have been mistaken; when the voice, full and clear, came once more down the road apparently close at hand. We lay quiet: there were no indications of its owner's approach. We waited patiently: nothing broke the silence of the night, except the patter of the rain, and the sighing of a low wind which accompanied it. Convinced, at length, that it was useless to remain longer concealed, we rose, and went on our way. It would be hardly more than a fair exercise of the privilege belonging to every chronicler of his own travels, to give to this Southern Sleepy Hollow its spectral darkey and fractious yoke of goblin two-year-olds, which it deserves, and for which the time and circumstances were fitting. I certainly know of no other way of accounting for the facts just set forth.

" The roads were well furnished with guide-posts ; but they were tall, and the pitchy darkness of the night made it impossible to read their directions from the ground. Half a dozen of these, with the assistance of a lift from Captain Chamberlain's broad shoulders, I climbed during the night, — awkward business enough, with their sharp angles and smooth wet sides ; but the information they gave us was invaluable."

Two or three times in the course of the evening or night, they were seen by passers on the road, without special notice being taken of them.   After more than twenty miles of travel since the morning, they stopped in the rain for greatly needed rest.

"At the division of two plantations, near a gateway, we found at length a fence-angle, where, by laying across it two or three rails, and bending down a couple of saplings, we made for ourselves a seat, and a support upon which we could rest our heads.   Wrapping the woolen blanket about us, throwing one of the rubbers across our shoulders, and drawing the other over our heads, we were tolerably protected from the rain, though not from the wind. In this way, too, we could keep our provisions dry : had we attempted to lie down, ourselves and our haversacks would speedily have been drenched together.

" We dropped asleep, in spite of the cold, in a very few minutes, and slept soundly for some time.   Waking again about two o'clock in the morning, we found ourselves chilled to the bone, and suffering from a species of cramp that made it impossible for us to remain longer in the position where we were. There was no prospect, however, of altering our situation for the better if we should move, since it had been with difficulty that we had found even our present resting-place. We opened our haversacks, and food restored the blood in some degree to its circulation. With this relief we contented ourselves as best we could, and succeeded in falling asleep again. When we woke once more, it was about four o'clock, still pitchy dark, and still raining; but we determined to move on, — any thing rather than remain where we were. We could hardly rise from the rails on which we were sitting; and, when we attempted to walk, so cramped and numb was every muscle, that it was with difficulty we could drag one foot after the other. It was not my first experience of bivouacking under a winter's storm. Our North-Carolina campaigns were in cold weather; and some of the nights then spent we thought at the time sufficiently hard : but none of them compared with this. Exercise suppled our joints somewhat ; but we had gained very little of strength or rest during our halt, and we made our way slowly along the road through mud deeper and more tenacious than it had been at midnight. After a mile or two of this, we were glad to find another resting-place, — a fence-corner, much like that we had left; and here we rested until it began to grow light.

"Taking the path again, we came before long to a large barn-yard, where one or two cows stood patiently waiting for the morning milking. It seemed a pity that they should be compelled to wait longer for the lazy farmer whose duty it was to attend to them. The natural kindness of our dispositions prompted us at once to relieve them, and save him from the disagreeable task, which he was doubtless postponing, this rainy morning, later than usual. With these benevolent motives, we began to climb the barn-yard fence. But alas for our hopes of warm milk! Just at that moment the farmer vindicated his character for early rising by coming in sight, dimly visible through the mist, from behind a neighboring building. We did not wait to explain our intentions, or to apologize for the injustice we had done him, but executed a prompt movement to the rear."

Finding a comfortable resting-place on a vine-shaded offset, half-way down the steep side of a dense-wooded ravine, above a small brook, they stopped, exhausted after their wearisome night, to wait until the storm abated. They built a fire, warmed their chilled limbs, partially dried their blanket and clothing, and at the brook washed their mire-coated stockings and shoes. Just before night, the storm, which had slackened during the day, resumed its force ; and soon the rain poured in such torrents as to swell the brook to a sudden freshet. Again they were drenched to the skin, and their haversack of provisions was thoroughly soaked. Later, the violence of the storm subsided; and they laid themselves down for the sleep which they must have, rain or no rain. They slept ten hours; and woke to find the sun shining in their faces through the tree-tops, and a clear sky overhead. They "were thoroughly rested and in good condition for travel." The storm had cost them just one day, aside from the delay growing out of the condition of the roads and streams.

Pressing on, they were seen by two negro-boys, who were apparently afraid of them, and hurried off. In the afternoon, as they were concealed near a dwelling they could not pass until night, a private coach was driven by, then a country wagon; and, later, a drover with cattle went along the road near them.

At night they took in preference a by-road toward Baton Rouge, to avoid the larger towns on the main route northward; but this involved the dispensing with bridges across streams. One stream they bridged with delay and difficulty; a second was not to be crossed in this way.

" In vain we wearied ourselves tramping up and down the half-liquid banks above and below; it ran in a wide turbid flood which it was useless to think of bridging. It was a frosty December night; the ground was beginning to stiffen with the cold. We hesitated. Had there been any available resting-place near by, I fear we should have been found upon the wrong side of the stream when morning dawned; but we saw none, and that decided us. Making the necessary preparations, with much shivering we plunged in. After all, it was not so fearfully cold, nor was the water deep, save in a couple of holes, one near either bank. More than one trip was necessary to transport clothing, blankets, and provisions; but it was soon over, and glad enough we were that we had not postponed the ugly job as we were tempted to. We were pretty thoroughly benumbed; but a little brandy (the only time during our journey we had occasion to use it) assisted exercise in restoring the circulation, and in half an hour we were as warm as ever. We traveled briskly that night, and had accomplished a good distance when we turned aside into the pine-woods on the left, built for ourselves a booth of pine and cedar boughs, quite a luxurious lodging-place, and slept till morning."

Passing Baton Rouge, they took the Pinckneyville Road, and later turned toward Yorkville. The following night, they crossed Turkey Creek, and were disposed to attempt the passage of Broad River near Pinckneyville, but, becoming confused as to the route in the darkness, waited until morning. The weather grew colder, and they suffered from its severity.

"Our morning wakenings were the most cheerless moments of a day's experience. We woke, without the rest which came only after exercise had brought us warmth, numb and shivering; so that we could hardly roll our blankets or take the first few steps upon our journey. There was not a night during our trip in which we did not suffer from cold. This morning (sabbath) was the coldest we had encountered."

They traveled until nearly noon, before finding just the place for a safe rest. Then they slept several hours. Resuming their journey soon after dark they hoped within forty-eight hours to be beyond the limits of South Carolina, and in a region of comparative safety.

" We had been walking an hour or two along an unfrequented road, when a negro rose apparently from a fence-corner, and followed us at a distance of a few paces. We slackened our gait to allow him to pass; but he preserved the same interval whether we moved fast or slow. While we were still in doubt as to the meaning of these proceedings, a horseman rode up in front, making his appearance so suddenly, that even in the absence of our unwelcome attendant we should hardly have had time to conceal ourselves. He addressed us politely; and, after a few embarrassing questions which indicated his suspicion of us, he rode off at a gallop in the direction whence he had come. We looked at one another in dismay. That he suspected us and would soon return we had no doubt; but there were no woods at hand; and, if there had been, it would have been useless to enter them while dogged by our persevering follower. We were now opposite a graveyard of some size; and it was evident from surrounding indications that we had come directly upon a village whose existence we had not suspected.

"We had little time to consider : the sound of clattering hoofs came down the road behind us, and our former friend rode up with two companions. A few more questions were asked, a footman coming up meantime to join the party; and the horsemen rode on, leaving their companion to walk behind us. We knew that our journey was at an end. They were waiting for us at the gate of a house a few hundred yards beyond; reaching which, we were politely invited to walk in and exhibit our papers, with the assurance that they had authority for the request they made. ' Did we know any thing of some Yankee officers who had recently escaped from Columbia?' We told them they need trouble themselves no further : we were the men for whom they were looking."

The recaptured officers were taken into the house, and given seats before the fire. They found that hounds were out in pursuit of them, and that the roads in every direction beyond were closely watched and guarded.

"The report of the capture of Yankee officers spread like wildfire, and men gathered in for a look at the strange sight, until the room was nearly filled. It was amusing to see the curiosity manifested, and we felt specially complimented by a remark of Mr. McNeil's little girl, who had evidently been on the lookout for horns and hoofs. Finding us apparently harmless, she ventured timidly to the other side of the fireplace, and finally, after some coaxing, came across and stood shyly by my side, while I told her of my little sister at home, and astonished her with a small coin, the only specie, I will venture to say, that had been seen for a long time in that part of the Confederacy. She talked, like most Southern children, an unmitigated negro dialect. ' What sort of men did you think Yankees were?' asked I. ' I didn't tink,' said she, ' dey was dat good-lookin' ! '

" The conversation turned upon politics; and the whole question of the war was discussed with perfect freedom on both sides. We talked with the utmost plainness, and were listened to courteously, though with a good deal of surprise and some incredulity. In the graveyard of this little hamlet, too small to occupy a place upon the map, were the bodies of twenty-two Confederate soldiers; and there was hardly a man there but that either belonged to the army or had a son or brother connected with it. Mr. McNeil, our host, — for we were treated rather as guests than as prisoners, — was an elder of the Methodist Church. Few of those who talked with us took a sanguine view of their prospects; and there were even indications that not all would consider failure the worst of calamities. Most, however, were thoroughly in earnest for continued resistance; nor, believing as they believed, should I have felt differently. They appreciated our desire for freedom, and were by no means disposed to blame us for attempting to escape. Even our captors, in their sympathy for us, seemed almost to regret that their duty compelled them to put an end to our hopes of regaining liberty.

"After about an hour of conversation came the welcome invitation to walk out to supper. This was served in a small room upon the opposite side of the entry, warmed only—since there was neither stove nor fireplace—by the heat of the smoking dishes which stood upon the table. A most attractive sight it was to us after months of prison-fare, and a week of sawdust. Beefsteak, ham and eggs, griddle-cakes, hot biscuit and fresh butter, wheat-coffee, &c., a clean white table-cloth, and a servant to wait upon table, seemed more homelike than any thing we had seen for many a day. We had hardly known how cold and hungry we were until we came within reach of warm fire and appetizing food. Mr. McNeil's table looked as if it were spread for half a dozen men; and it looked, when we left it, as if the half dozen had been there.

"Among other visitors to the house was a woman, who, surveying us with a severe countenance, sharply inquired of Captain Chamberlain, 'what kind of weather he called that for gathering broom-straws?' Captain Chamberlain, to whom the drift of the question was not obvious, mildly and with some wonderment replied, that it appeared to him somewhat cold weather for any branch of out-door industry. With a manner indicative of the utmost animosity, she proceeded to observe, that 'she would have us to know that gathering broom-straw was something she never had done, and, what was more, never would do ; not if she lived to be a hundred years old, she wouldn't !' Against an attack so vigorous and so mysterious, we were incapable of defense ; and, after one or two remarks equally indignant and equally incomprehensible, our assailant retired, evidently much relieved in mind. It turned out that a party of five, to which we were supposed to belong, had met her servant in the field gathering broom-straw, and had taken it into their heads to send her home, with a message to her mistress, that, if she wanted the article, she might come and collect it herself. Their sins had been visited upon our heads.

" We were assigned quarters for sleeping in the huge feather-bed in the corner, while four men sat up through the night as guard. Our couch was most luxurious, and I was asleep before my head had been ten minutes on the pillow. Captain Chamberlain, whose readiness and force in argument had much impressed our listeners, and had been repeatedly complimented during the evening, lay awake long enough to hear some interesting remarks upon the discussion, and their expression of wonder that men in our circumstances could rest as quietly as we seemed to be doing. For what reason I do not know, but it was not for some time after our capture, even after our return to Columbia, that the bitterness of disappointment came in full force upon us.

" After an excellent breakfast, preparations were made
to take us to Chesterville, sixteen miles distant, the nearest place upon the railroad. We were between sixty and
seventy miles from Columbia, though we had traveled,
probably, about one hundred to reach the place of our
capture. We were accompanied by a guard of four men ;
so that we made quite a little cavalcade, mounted, some
upon horses and some upon mules. For security, Captain
Chamberlain and myself were each lashed by one ankle to
the stirrup-leather,—a precaution which had nearly resulted
seriously. Captain Chamberlain's horse taking sudden
fright simultaneously with another, both riders were thrown.
I thought for a moment that it was all up with my friend ;
but, happily, his saddle-girth had been broken, and tied
up, in true Southern style, with a cotton string. This
gave way as he fell, and freed him, saddle and all, from
the plunging horse. Not caring to run any further risk,
I had my saddle-girth unbuckled, and met the mishap I
might have expected. We stopped at a stream for a drink
of water. I forgot the insecurity of my seat, and, leaning
forward to receive a cup of water, threw my weight too
far to one side. The saddle slipped ; once displaced, it
was in vain that I attempted to regain balance. Slowly, if
not gracefully, we slid off to the ground ; and the lashing
had to be unloosed before I could remount. Our route
led through a thickly settled region ; and we were objects

of no little curiosity to those who saw us as we passed, or met us upon the road."

Reaching Chesterville, they were taken to the jail, followed by a constantly increasing crowd of townspeople. A cell was assigned them.

"It was exceedingly filthy and repulsive in its appearance. Upon the floor lay a tumbled heap of rags, scraps of carpeting, torn bagging, &c., which had evidently formed the bedding of the last inmate. An old pitcher stood in one corner. Of furniture, there was none whatever. The walls upon three sides were of heavy planking, well whittled, and ornamented with every variety of illustrations in charcoal, with now and then a long tally where some wretched occupant had kept weary account of the days of his imprisonment. The fourth side, opposite the door, was composed entirely of iron grating; so that every corner of the room could be inspected from the passage which ran around each tier of cells. We hoped that here we should at least have refuge from the not uniformly courteous curiosity of the crowd which had gathered around us; whose persistent gaze, as they followed us up stairs, and peeped through the small aperture in the door, we endeavored to avoid by stepping out of the range of vision which it afforded. But they were not to be balked in that way; and, in a moment more, were rushing into the passage-way, outside the grating, with looks and words of exultation that we could no longer evade them. We were fairly on exhibition. There they stood, and gazed through the bars, as at the wild animals in a menagerie; while we paced up and down our narrow limits with a restlessness which did not impair the likeness. The unwillingness we had shown to gratify them, no doubt, increased their natural good-will toward Yankees; and questions and comments were by no means as few as the answers they received. At length the jail was cleared, and we were left to our-selves." . . .

A better room was assigned them.

"McDonnell the jailer, and one of his neighbors, a physician, spent the evening with us. The former was confident that, if he could have a few days' opportunity for discussion, he could turn us from the error of our ways, and convince us of the justice of the Confederate cause. We expressed some doubt on the subject; but he *knew* there was no question about it. Just let him explain the cause to us, and we couldn't *help* seeing that we were all wrong. He labored with us faithfully, albeit with a very misty comprehension of the theories he was endeavoring to establish, and a very slender knowledge of the facts at their basis; was in no whit discouraged by our flat denial of his premises or disproval of his conclusions; and we left him, at our departure, in the full belief, that, if he could only have had a little more time, he should infallibly have made sound rebels of us.

" Blankets were sent to us in the course of the evening ; and we slept very comfortably upon the floor before the fire. We had seen during the afternoon and evening most of the members of McDonnell's family. His eldest son, just below conscript age, but expecting to be drafted as soon as his birth-day came, was a very kind-hearted fellow. He executed commissions in town for us ; lent us books ; and, in every way, exerted himself to oblige us. He was entirely free from the boisterous bluster so apt to characterize those of his class and age, nor did we hear an oath from his lips. In both respects, he was a marked contrast to his little brother of six or seven years, who, hardly able to speak plainly, lisped out torrents of profanity ; and was, in every thing but size, a well-developed bully. The mother, who had brought up the former, died in the latter's infancy. Miss McDonnell, a young woman of seventeen or eighteen, did not pay us the compliment of a call in person, but sent up by a negro girl a piece of pine, with a message, rather a command than a request, that she desired some crosses, or other specimens of carving, — an art at which she evidently supposed every Yankee an expert by birth. Regretting to disappoint a lady, we sent back word that we were not mechanics.

" There was a little girl of eight or nine years, who, when she heard that we belonged to the Northern army, came to our door to inquire, with touching anxiety, if we knew any thing of her brother, — one of the missing at the battle of Malvern Hill. He had been, it seemed, among those whom Magruder sent to that desperate charge upon the batteries manned by the First Connecticut Artillery, — repulsed with the most terrible slaughter of all that bloody campaign. He was seen lying wounded upon the ground; beyond that, all inquiries as to his fate had been in vain. . . .

" I called McDonnell good-natured, and so he showed himself uniformly toward us; but it was the good-nature of a beast, needing only provocation to turn it into ferocity. He was telling us of various attempts to escape from jail; among others, one of a negro, who, in so doing, broke or otherwise injured some of the jail property. 'I gin that nigger,' said he, 'rather a light floggin'. Cut him up some; but he didn't think as 'twas anyways different from a common floggin'. But when I came to wash him down, instead of brine, I washed him down with red pepper; poured it right on to the raw, good and strong. Then he knew what I meant. Pretty nigh killed the old nigger!' This story he related without the slightest apparent idea that it was otherwise than creditable to him. We had been rather amused with the man hitherto; but this was enough for us.

" During the next day, we received a call from two or three gentlemen, — one of them a graduate of Princeton; another, the editor of the ' Chesterville Standard.' They were curious, they said, to see some Northerners who were

not tired of the war; and wished to learn something of the state of public sentiment among us. A lively discussion followed, conducted with the same freedom as those in which we had engaged before. These, however, were different antagonists from our country friends, familiar with the North and its people, and well-informed upon the questions at issue. Bitter almost to desperation in their hostility to Government, men of influence and standing, they were fair samples of the class which keeps South Carolina in her present position. Our Princeton friend became somewhat excited by the plainness with which we laid down the programme of subjugation, and our confidence in its success, though he did not allow himself to be led into discourtesy, and finally left the room in advance of his friends."

In the afternoon, Lieutenant Belcher of the Columbia Post-Guard arrived with a guard to escort the prisoners to their old place of confinement. He bound the elbows of both, and then tied them together. Thus secured, they journeyed by cars to Columbia, and were marched from the depot through the streets of that city.

" Fifteen or twenty minutes' walk brought us to familiar places. There was the market-house, at which we had so often gazed from our barred windows; the street through which we had passed in going for water; then the old jail, upon which we had hoped never again to look. We entered its door, and our journeyings were at an end. We were ushered into a room which had been used for the confinement of conscripts, adjoining that which we had previously occupied. Here we were unbound for the first time since leaving Chesterville, and left to ourselves. Captain Senn soon called upon us. He was in a state of considerable excitement. Our escape, he said, had nearly ruined him; and he accused us of having abused the privileges which had been granted us. We regretted having caused him inconvenience; but the charge we, of course, most emphatically repelled. Calming down, he expressed much curiosity, as Lieutenant Belcher had before, to know how we had contrived to escape. He had counted us himself the evening before; and how we could have left the building between that time and the next morning he could not imagine. The confidence with which he spoke of our presence at the evening count, when we were so snugly ensconced in the cook-room, was amusing enough; but we declined to enter into any explanations. . .

" We entered our new quarters upon the 23d of December, having been absent from Columbia a little more than eight days. But one of us at a time was permitted to pass the threshold; and then under charge of an armed guard, who was responsible for us until we were again locked up. It was now that we began to realize the disappointment of our failure. Time dragged heavily: release seemed more distant than ever before. Yet there was not that restless torture of impatience which had before taken such complete possession of me. There was no longer an untried possibility to mock me with hope. There was a satisfaction in feeling that I had done my utmost; and I could bend my mind to the thought of patient endurance, as it was impossible for me to do while it seemed that effort might yet accomplish something. . . . On the last day of the old year came an order for us to return to our old quarters to make room for Lieutenant-Commander Williams and Ensign Porter of the navy [the gallant officer afterward killed in the assault on Fort Fisher], consigned to close confinement in irons as hostages for the treatment of certain Confederate prisoners in the hands of the United-States authorities. We regretted to owe our advantage to their misfortune; but, fortunately for us, this arrangement of rooms was the only one practicable; and, after eight days of seclusion, we rejoined our companions, and entered upon the year 1864 in circumstances almost precisely the same as those of the period preceding our escape.

"The whole affair, though it resulted in failure, was one which I by no means regret. So far from considering the attempt rash or hopeless, I was, as you know, on the point of repeating it a few days since, and with excellent prospects, as I think, of success. It broke the monotony of my imprisonment with a week of stirring excitement. The exhilaration of freedom and activity amply repaid the accompanying hardships; and I have an experience upon which I shall always look back with pleasure in its contrast with the dreary months which preceded and followed it."

It was not long after his return to confinement that Camp received a large box of home-comforts, — clothing, books, provisions, cooking utensils, &c.,— sent to him immediately after the chaplain's release. Besides all that was apparent to the eye, the box contained letters, maps, a compass, and other things desirable to a prisoner, so concealed as to escape the rigid scrutiny of the Confederate officials. The arrival of the box — the first from home, and so long on its passage that it had been almost despaired of — was quite an event to the lonely prisoner. His words of grateful joy in acknowledging it indicate more clearly by contrast the gloom and sadness of ordinary prison-life than any thing he wrote of his trials and discomforts. To his home-friends he said, "It has come! of course I mean the box, — and what a box! Like Blitz's bottle, every thing that any one could ask for or think of came out of it, and a thousand things beside of which I never should have thought,— yet not one superfluous. If I should take up the contents in detail, they would furnish me with more really new subject-matter than all that I've written about hitherto since last July: its arrival is the great event of the season. Soberly, you can hardly imagine the importance which such an affair assumes in such a life as this we lead here, so utterly monotonous and destitute of interest. And that box would have been no trifle anywhere to any one away from home and friends. I *fussed* over it and what it contained for two entire days, attending to hardly any thing else, and only began yesterday to settle down again into routine. Indeed, for a little while, thoroughly as I enjoyed the surprises of each new and the associations of each familiar article, I was perversely and ungratefully blue, simply from disconnecting myself so entirely in thought from prison-life, and then finding it forced back upon me."

To the chaplain he added : —

" Oh ! this cramped page, this lifeless ink-talk ! You know what I would say and what I would do if I were with you. God grant that I soon may be ! Then the box, so full of evidence of your thoughtful kindness ! — who but you would ever have thought of one-half the little articles which make no great figure in an invoice, but are the most valuable of all, because they bring dear ones at the first glance before one's very eyes ? Who but you could have known precisely what I wanted, and anticipated requests already made, but which you had never seen ? I wish we could look over that box together. I want to talk over each article of fifty with you, — and how much have I to say besides ! The skill shown in the selection, the abundance of every desirable thing, and the absence of every superfluous one, so as to make the whole a complete outfit for prison house-keeping, astonished the rest, and surprised even me who knew your ways, and *expected* to be surprised.

"If I could only write,— only *speak!* —but I never could do either."

CHAPTER IX.

LIBBY PRISON, CAMP PAROLE, HOME.

FTER more than three months of siege-work on Morris Island, the 10th Regiment was ordered to St. Augustine, Fla., to recruit for a season. The chaplain rejoined it there. It was a satisfaction to Camp to know that the regiment was thus, in his absence, removed from the probabilities of immediate battle. This point was one on which he was always anxious.

"The one addition to the trials of imprisonment which I am now dreading," he wrote in the opening spring, "is to hear that the regiment has gone into active service without me. All else I have become in a measure inured to,—that will come fresh upon me."

He could not rest in prison. Time was too precious in his estimation.

"A year or a half-year," he said, "is no inconsiderable fraction of any man's life. I would be *doing;* and I am not even preparing. Were my future so settled that I could study with reference to it, my time need not be wholly lost. But I sadly fear that neither German nor phonography [both of which he was studying in prison] will ever be of much practical benefit to me. Still, I have never regretted for one instant the course I have chosen. I do not think I ever shall; but trust to see by and by how all has been for the best."

Rumors as to exchange-negotiations were very tantalizing. The rebel officials declared to the captured officers their desire for a release of the prisoners on both sides; and the precise reasons for delay were never clear to the anxious and interested captives, closely as they watched the correspondence of the commissioners.

"Matters look very dark to us just now," wrote Camp. "Of course we would die here to a man, rather than have Government yield any point involving honor or good faith; but, with no more than our present information, it is impossible to understand why, without any such sacrifice, arrangements can not be made which would set us at liberty."

When the matter was in General Butler's hands, there was strong hope of an immediate settlement.

"We have made up our minds to be exchanged," Camp wrote at that time; "and, if the affair does fall through, you may put strychnine for thirty-one in the next box you send."

But again there was an interruption of the negotiations.

"This suspense is very trying," he then wrote. "We feel like the three egg-gatherers of the Orkneys, whose story used to be in the school-readers, — our rope seems to

be parting while we yet swing half-way down the preci-
pice; and it is a desperate chance whether the last strand
holds long enough to bring us to the top." Many a poor
sufferer dropped from the rope into the dark abyss beneath;
and many more came to crave death as an alternative of
prolonged suspense and suffering in captivity. "If capture is not to be followed by release," said Camp sadly,
"a prisoner loses little by death."

Another escape was contemplated. The plan was made
by the navy officers; but Adjutant Camp was to be one of
those profiting by it. A tunnel was dug from under the
hearth in the navy-room, beneath the yard, toward the cellar of a neighboring house, whence unobserved egress
might with safety have been secured. The tunnel was
dug at the rate of two or three feet a night; the removed
earth being spread under the jail-floor. Steadily the work
progressed, and the hearts of weary prisoners beat with
high hope. But, when only work for a single night remained unfinished, the tunnel was discovered; and the
whole plan was a failure. Then army and navy officers
were together removed to an upper story of the jail, and
their privileges greatly restricted. Yet other plans of escape were proposed, and would doubtless have been
attempted by Camp, had he remained longer a prisoner.

The efforts of those having influence for Camp's release
were at length successful. An order reached Columbia
about the middle of April for the latter's removal to Rich-

14

mond. He was informed of it by the post-adjutant as he came in one morning from the yard at the close of the hour of exercise. The order did not specify that he was to be exchanged; but he had reason to hope that that was its meaning, and his joyful surprise was for a time quite bewildering. He was sent forward at once under guard, by the way of Charlotte, Weldon, and Petersburg, enjoying again the long-forbidden sight of open country, and having ample opportunities of observing rebels in rebeldom, during the frequent stops by the way, and on the crowded cars.

At Petersburg, connection was missed with the Richmond train; and, lest he should lose one trip of the flag-of-truce boat by the delay, he proposed to hire a carriage, and hurry forward over the turnpike the twenty-three remaining miles. The guard was well pleased with this arrangement, as it would expedite his return to Columbia; but, on going to a livery-stable, they found three hundred dollars to be the cost of a hack for the distance. Even accustomed as he was to Southern prices, that charge rather took Camp's breath away, as he said afterward. Several hours of unsuccessful hunting for humbler conveyances satisfied him that, if he should at length succeed in finding any team, its price would be quite beyond his means. So he went with his guard to the Bolingbroke House to wait for the next regular train. His experience, after reaching Richmond, he thus narrated to the chaplain : —

" I was despatched, under guard, to the Libby, marching at the head of a squad of rebs destined to Castle
Thunder. My baggage, which had undergone a merely
nominal examination by Lieutenant Belcher, at Columbia,
received about the same here ; the sergeant observing
inquiringly, that he ' supposed I had nothing contraband
there ? ' Somewhat doubtful as to the character of my
hidden journal, I replied, that I didn't think he'd find any
thing of that kind there, — and he didn't.

"A ladder, substituted some months since for the stairs,
was the means of communication with the upper regions.
Ascending this, I was at once surrounded by inquirers as
to the character of the last haul, and conducted at once to
the room where most of the Connecticut officers were
quartered. You can imagine better than I can tell how
strange the scene appeared to me. You remember the
crowded rooms, the bustle, the confusion, the contrast in
every point, with our old Columbia place of confinement.

"After I had been introduced, and shown the curiosities, — bone-work, sketch for lithograph, &c., — I was considered naturalized, and fit to take care of myself. . . . Our
mess took two meals a day, as in Columbia ; using none
of the prison-rations, except occasionally a little meal, living exclusively upon the contents of boxes from home.
Before I left, their supplies were well-nigh exhausted ;
and we were eking them out with the prison corn-bread,
regardless of the mice, baked whole, in it. After the first

few days, we took turns in cooking. I won't ask odds from any Biddy in the country on a loaf of good wheat bread, — which is, I believe, the test above all others of an accomplished cook, reasoning *a fortiori*.

" Boxes were issued a day or two after my arrival. I attended in the lower room, thinking it just possible that mine might be among them. A blanket was spread on the floor, and the contents of a box pitched into it (the box being then carried away), — sugar, shirts, apple-sauce, boots, coffee, blacking, peaches, and stationery, — all in one indiscriminate pile. Every thing had been thoroughly overhauled, and much stolen. A bag would be torn in preference to untying the string which secured its mouth. Cans of milk or preserved fruit were punched to ascertain the contents. . . . I read a little, played chess a little, sketched a little, cooked a little, paced the lower room a good deal. . . .

" I was warned upon my arrival against standing at the windows. Any one who showed his head to the guard below was liable to be shot. But the exposure was a common thing. Now and then some particularly savage guard would evidently be watching his chance for a shot at a Yankee, — and all would be careful, — tantalizing him now and then with a capital opportunity if he had only been ready for it, but with a prudent regard to the length of time which it would take him to come to an aim.

" There was a story that we were all to be sent to

Georgia; and it was doubtful whether that was not prefer-
able to the starvation which would certainly be the result
of our presence at Richmond during a siege, however
short, and the possibility (much more than what some
thought it) of being blown up, rather than allowed to fall
into Union hands. Altogether we were growing daily
less hopeful; and, about the end of April, had reached
a decided shade of blue. When, on Friday, the 29th,
the old story of 'boat up' came, with better authority,
apparently, than usual, I only thought that, if it was true,
it was in so far encouraging that we might receive some
news. So I went quietly to bed, little thinking that it
was my last night in prison.

"I was roused from a doze the next morning, by hearing
a list of names which was being read, in a distinct voice,
in the center of the room. All the possibilities flashed
upon me at once. I sat up in bed, wide awake. 'What
names are those?' I inquired. 'Names of those who are
going in this boat,' replied Lieutenant Carpenter. So there
were officers going. My breath came a little thick, and
how I listened! I had missed one or two at the beginning,
but no matter; he was still reading names of field-officers.
Then came captains, — a dozen or so; lieutenants; then
an adjutant; and lieutenants again. If there had been
more than one adjutant, wouldn't they have been put
together? 'Lieutenant H. W. Hamp!' A thrill ran
through me. Did he mean me? It must be; but it

wouldn't do for me to allow myself to think so. I *wouldn't* think so until I had asked him.

"As he read the last name and turned away, I jumped to my feet, followed him, and laid my hand upon his shoulder. It was Captain Dick Turner, the inspector. He turned, somewhat surprised apparently, at my appearance, as well he might be : my toilet had not been elaborate, and was deficient in a few minor articles, such as pants and stockings. 'There was one name,' said I, 'which I am not sure I understood, — Hamp, I think you called it.' He opened the list : my eye ran down the page in the tenth part of a second. There it was, — a little too much flourish, — 'Camp, lieutenant and adjutant,' but no room for any doubt. I took a good breath. By and by he found it : it was close to the bottom of the page. 'Camp is my name,' said I : 'is not that what it is meant for?' 'That your name? Yes: Camp, — that's right.' I walked back with a wonderful feeling pervading me ; not so much an intelligent and definite sense of joy as a consciousness of being half-intoxicated, with a necessity of putting myself under restraint lest I should do something absurd. It was the inability of my mind instantly to take in and realize the significance of what had passed.

"I had been told that the names of those who went before had been read an hour or two before they started ; had no doubt that there was plenty of time before me, and leisurely slipping on pants, stockings, and shoes, started for the lower east room to wash before roll-call. Passing the stairs, I noticed a crowd around them, and in a moment more heard some one say, ' They've all gone down now ! ' If I were to be left ! You can imagine that grass didn't grow under my feet before I stood in the office, overcoat on, and valise in hand, — the latter fortunately already packed. I was not the last after all, and should have had time to make my toilet, though without many minutes to spare.

"Those who preceded me, and they were nearly all, were drawn up in line in the lower hall. While we stood there another officer came down. The name of Stewart was on the list, and had been answered to : but his name was Stewart as well ; was not he the man ? How number one looked at him ! But there had been no mistake this time ; and number two, poor fellow, sadly went back up the stairs to his prison. It was enough to make one shudder, like seeing a drowning man clutch at the plank which floats your head above water, miss it, and sink.

"The parole was read to us, not to serve until ' exchanged under the cartel of July, 1862 ; ' and we signed it in duplicate. We passed through a door leading to the outer hall, one by one ; each answering affirmatively the question, ' You declare, upon your honor as an officer and a gentleman, that you have no letter or paper from any person ? ' and there was no examination. Forming by fours in the street, while the guard were drawn up around us, we waited for some time, while those within shouted messages, congratulations, and farewells to us. Every window in the building was crowded with faces pressed close to the iron bars. It was a sad sight: the prison looks far more terrible and prison-like without than within, where, as the 'Examiner' said one day, it resembles the interior of a grocery-store more than any thing else.

"Marching to the landing, we went on board the 'Allison'; and, after some delay, started down the river at half-past eight. Three hundred sick men were with us; and they were an awful sight, in their disease and filth. Stretched upon deck, without blanket or overcoat, some looked as if they would die where they lay. There were piles of mattresses lying close by; but these were not to be used: they were for the rebel sick upon the return trip. I saw them spread before I left the boat at City Point. One poor fellow was deranged, and had to be caught two or three times as he wandered about the boat, and returned to those who were caring for him.

"It was half-past twelve when we reached City Point, and saw for the first time in many months the stars and stripes, as they floated above the 'New York,' which lay there at anchor. I used to think that enthusiasm for the flag was principally a manufactured article, and indulged a philosophical contempt for those who allowed a material object to occupy the place in their minds which should be filled by the abstract principle. But I shall have charity henceforth for all Fourth-of-July orators, knowing myself better than I did; and honest feeling, even if it flies the spread eagle a little too high for my taste, shall have cheers instead of sneers from me. It was some two hours before the transfer of prisoners was accomplished, and I stepped upon our own boat, free. You know how I felt!"

At the very time when Camp was hunting after a conveyance from Petersburg to Richmond, his regiment was embarking from St. Augustine for Virginia. While he was in the Libby, it was at the Gloucester-Point rendezvous of the newly formed Army of the James. When he reached Fortress Monroe by the flag-of-truce boat from City Point, on the evening of May 1, he was met by Chaplain Trumbull, who was waiting his arrival. The joy of that meeting, oh! who can tell?

After the interview, which was but brief, as the boat was on its way to Annapolis, Camp wrote: —

"You have just left me, and I am still in a maze, — whether in the body or out of the body I can hardly tell. So joyful and so astonishing a surprise! For though I had thought of your being in Virginia, as a possibility, I supposed you were still in St. Augustine; and nothing under heaven could have seemed further beyond the range of hope than to actually see you and talk with you to-night. Oh, if we could have a little longer time! . . . Thank God that he has granted us so much! What would I have given, three days ago, for the assurance of it! and the spirit of complaint, which, even now, I can hardly repress, is too ungrateful. I am a thousand times happier than I deserve to be, — almost as happy as I could be. My cup is full: I won't ask to have it overflow.''

Two days later, writing from Annapolis, where he was delayed nearly a week, he said, —

'' I have enjoyed your letter greatly : it is yourself a little way off, it is true, but seen through clear atmosphere, and not the smoked glass of a prison-page toned down to pass rebel inspection. But, oh! how I used to prize the dimmer pictures in the midst of my darkness !

'' I am just beginning to realize that I am free. Until within a few hours, the jesting cry of ' Boat up, three hundred officers on board,' would send the same thrill through me which it did at the Libby. I have still a great respect for enlisted men on duty, and half expect some of them to take me in charge as I pass through the streets. My hand doesn't rise to a salute spontaneously : it requires a distinct volition. Did you jump at once back to your old position ?''

Camp's fear then was that his regiment would be engaged before he could rejoin it. He was yet only paroled, and he longed for a full exchange. '' There is a captain here,'' he writes, '' who has been paroled, and for whom General Butler is going to arrange with Judge Ould a special exchange. - I wish he'd put my name on the same paper. Uncle Sam may take back my leave of absence, and I'll throw in the half-pay, and all he owes me too."

The 10th Regiment left Gloucester Point, May 4th, ascended the James with General Butler's expedition, and landed, on the morning of the 6th, at Bermuda Hundred. On the 7th, it participated in the first attack on the Petersburg and Richmond Railroad. The news of this fight was received by Camp just after he reached his home from which he had been so long and sadly separated. Even in the fullness of his joy at that re-union, he could not repress the desire to be with his regiment at the front; and his affectionate anxiety for his friend manifested itself freely in his letters.

" I know just how you feel about exposure in battle," he wrote. " If I could be there, we would go to the front together; but you have no right to go without me. I can't have you do it. You know I wouldn't ask you to stay back one inch behind the post of duty; but, for my sake, don't go one inch beyond it. Oh! it is hard to think of you in danger which I must not share."

CHAPTER X.

CAMPAIGNING WITH THE ARMY OF THE JAMES.

LATE in the evening of May 11th, Camp heard indirectly that the prisoners paroled prior to April 30th were declared exchanged. At once he telegraphed to a friend in Washington to ascertain the truth for him. Learning early the next morning the report to be correct, he telegraphed to Annapolis for permission to go directly to his regiment, but was informed that he must report again at Camp Parole. But five days of his leave had yet expired. He had been eighteen months away from home, nearly ten of these in prison. Not many, under such circumstances, would have been unwilling to avail themselves of the remaining fifteen days with a loved household, before returning to hard service in the field ; but with Henry Camp the cause of country was the cause of God, and for that cause he was willing to leave father and mother, and brother and sisters, and to lose his life for its sake.

Not stopping even for the completion of the clothing he had ordered made, nor yet for the packing of a valise ; wearing his clumsy prison-shoes of rebel make ; and taking only a haversack for his personal baggage ; trusting to share blankets and whatever else was required with his friend at the front, — he was ready for a start in an hour and a half after the receipt of his telegram, and hurried off, on Wednesday night, for New York and Annapolis ; thence to Fort Monroe and Bermuda Hundred, reaching the latter point on Sabbath evening, May 15.

His regiment had left camp on the 12th, with General Butler's advance to the rear of Drury's Bluff, and, after sharp fighting on the 13th and 14th, was now bivouacked near the Richmond and Petersburg Railroad. The chaplain had left the regiment that afternoon to visit the hospital, and to write from camp to friends of the dead and wounded. The joy of his unexpected meeting with his friend, on reaching the camp, can only be imagined. The re-united friends sat together that night, until 4 A.M., then slept a single hour, and at five were up, making ready to rejoin their regiment.

It was the foggy morning of May 16. The sharp firing of the battle at the extreme right — the position of the 18th Corps — was heard by the friends as they rode out of camp ; but they did not suppose it boded trouble to the 10th Corps at the far left. As they approached the Richmond turnpike, they saw evidences of disaster. Full supply-trains had been turned back ; shirks and stragglers were hurrying to the rear ; rumors of a defeat came down, at first vague, afterward more definite and positive. The friends met an officer of General Heckman's Brigade, an old acquaintance, and from him learned of the morning attack, and the severe losses in the engagement on the right. General Heckman and Captain Belger were prisoners: Colonel Lee was erroneously reported killed, and Lieutenant-Colonel Chambers was mortally wounded: — all these were old North-Carolina fellow-officers. Affairs wore indeed a gloomy aspect. The turnpike was thronged with hastily retiring troops, wounded men, rebel prisoners, ammunition-wagons, and ambulances; and confusion, if not disorder, prevailed. Many of those first met were evidently much alarmed, and gave an exaggerated report of the disaster.

Of the 10th Corps it was not easy to obtain intelligence. Communication with it had been temporarily severed, and the story was in many mouths that it had been cut off and captured, — albeit the friends knew it too well to be disturbed by that report. That it had changed position was confidently asserted, but how to find it was a troublesome question. An officer of rank stated that it had moved down the railroad, and was already some distance in the rear. That assertion was contradicted by another officer, five minutes later. Camp's anxiety to reach his regiment grew greater and more intense continually. In prison, he had more than once expressed the wish that he could rejoin it in the hour of battle; and now it seemed that he might hope to do so. Hither and thither the friends hurried, in endeavors to learn the whereabouts of their corps. Any one who has looked for a missing command in the time of an engagement, and no one else, will understand how next to impossible it then is to secure reliable information of its locality, even from those who would be supposed to know. Again and again the friends were warned of the folly of an attempt to cross to the extreme left, which the 10th Corps had occupied, and told that their capture would be inevitable, if, indeed, they escaped with their lives. The prospect of so speedy a return to the Libby was certainly not enticing to the just-released prisoner; but he had no thought of slackening, on that account, his efforts to reach his regiment.

Moving up the road, Camp met, coming down, Captain Stanton of the 21st Connecticut Volunteers, of Heckman's Brigade, who pulled an oar with him at the Worcester regatta. The captain's bleeding right arm was in an extemporized sling; he having been wounded in the morning's fight. As he had heard that Camp died in a rebel prison, he was as surprised as pleased to find him alive and well. To make sure of the 10th Corps, the friends sought Major-General Butler, and, finding him with some difficulty, ascertained that General Gillmore's Corps was still in position at the left. They then made haste in that direction; and, as they approached it, met wounded men of their regiment coming to the rear. The 10th had been hotly engaged, and lost heavily. It was still at the far front. They still had difficulty in finding its precise location. Sharp musketry-firing was heard just in advance. Other wounded men coming back said it was again engaged. There was intense earnestness in Camp's look as he turned to his friend, and said, in tones of strongest determination, "We must reach the regiment *at once*, in one way or another." Not many seconds later, as the two urged on their horses, the head of the regiment came in view over the crest of a hill the riders were ascending. That Adjutant Camp was recognized a wild shout of joy gave proof. As he drew his horse to the roadside, the regiment filed past; and each company successively greeted him with hearty hurrahs, while he sat, with cap in hand, in all his manly beauty, receiving their gratulations with feelings of grateful pride that atoned for weary months of waiting and suffering in prison. Not alone Colonel Otis gave him greeting, but Colonel (now General) Plaisted, the brigade-commander, hastened forward to bid him welcome; and even General Terry, with all the responsibility of the battle on him in that imminent hour for his division, swung his hat in sympathy with the cheering regiment, and spurred forward his horse to take the returned adjutant by the hand, and express his cordial satisfaction at seeing him once more in his old position. It was but a few minutes before Camp was conveying orders along the line as naturally as though he had never been absent, while the bullets of the enemy whistled past his ears.

"During most of the time after this," he wrote, "we acted as rear-guard, — a very unpleasant duty upon a retreat. To make a stand merely for the purpose of delay, to take positions which we knew we could not hold, to keep the pursuing enemy in check while others made good their escape, — it was harassing and dispiriting work. At one place, forming line with several other regiments, we remained several hours without being attacked, and had almost concluded that we were to march in unmolested, when the order came for us to move forward, and hold the crest of a hill some distance farther up the road. A section of a battery (two pieces) occupied a position just opposite our right flank. We had stood here some time with no sign of an enemy, when suddenly the fierce rush of a shell tore the air close by us. A better shot could hardly have been made in a hundred trials; but, strangely enough, no one seemed to be hurt. The artillerists scattered as if the explosion had blown them away bodily; and it seemed for a minute or two as if the guns were to be abandoned. Their commander rallied his men, however; but even then the hight of his ambition seemed to be to get his guns safely away, and in this he succeeded. I don't believe the same movement was ever executed in less time than it took those fellows to have their section in readiness, and

15

then tear down the road at the full speed of their horses. It was absolutely ridiculous; and our men stood by enjoying and commenting in a style that the battery-commander would hardly have considered complimentary.

" From the same quarter as before, shell followed shell in rapid succession, — some passing far beyond our line, and striking in the track of the flying artillery; some tearing up the ground before us, filling the air with earth and dust; some exploding just above our heads, and sending the ragged iron fragments among us in every direction. Only one man, however, was hit; and his wound was a mere contusion. It is nervous work, this standing target for shells. You can tell a second or two in advance about where the missile is coming, whether high or low, whether upon the right or left, and if it seems to be just about in a line with your own position, and about four feet, say, from the ground, there's a short time during which you are much interested as to the correctness or incorrectness of your estimate."

That night found all of General Butler's troops who remained of the expedition safely within the Bermuda Hundred line of defenses.

The campaign which thus commenced to Camp ended to him only with his death. He hardly knew what it was to rest again while he lived. Battles and skirmishes alternated with tours of exciting and perilous picket-duty, in the face of a vigilant and determined enemy. Being under fire was the soldiers' normal condition in the Army of the James during the summer of 1864.

When the 10th Corps was re-organized at Gloucester Point, the 10th Connecticut was brigaded with the 11th Maine, the 100th New York, and the 24th Massachusetts, under Colonel H. M. Plaisted of the 11th Maine. The brigade was the third of General Terry's division. The 24th Massachusetts and the 10th had been friends in all their campaigning. The 100th New York had been brigaded with both in South Carolina. The 11th Maine, although more recently with them, soon became a general favorite, and that and the 10th were almost as one regiment.

Camp's letters to his home from Bermuda Hundred were full and entertaining as ever. His faithfulness as a correspondent was remarkable. From the day he entered service until he died, his home-letters averaged above three full pages per day. These were written, without prefix or signature, to the family as a whole, and formed a complete record of his entire army and prison life. Of course, much of his writing was by the wayside, or on the battle-field. Seldom did many hours pass without his writing something to the loved ones. The extracts freely made from these familiar letters, written exclusively for family eyes, in this memorial, show the style and substance of his correspondence.

" I'm half afraid," he wrote, soon after his return from

Drury's Bluff, "that my anxiety to join my regiment may have made me seem not to appreciate home; but you know me better than that, don't you? I can hardly recall five so bright days in my life as those five with you. I trust there will be many more like them. It would have been delightful to be longer with you; but none of us would have had it so at the cost of absence from the place of duty."

Tuesday evening, May 17th, Camp addressed his comrades at a prayer-meeting, by the blazing fire-light, in the open air; and again his voice was heard by them in earnest prayer. A few hours later, he was hurrying with them toward the Petersburg pike for a night-attack on the moving trains of General Beauregard. Those who were near him, as the regiment lay in support of the 11th Maine, will not forget how, when an unexpected shower of bullets was poured in among the reclining men, causing a moment's flutter, as if some would seek shelter, the tones of his clear, firm, inspiring voice, saying, " *Steady*, men ! STEADY ! " re-assured all who were within its sound.

"It is a strange life, this," he wrote a few days later, "that we lead here, — widely different from any thing that I have seen before in army service. The constant liability to attack, and frequent skirmishes on the picket-line, close in front of us, make us indifferent to what, in other times, and at other places, would have caused us the intensest excitement. Sharp fighting is going on while I write, just in the edge of the woods beyond the works, — so near that every shot fired comes plainly to the ear; and the cheers of our men ring loudly through the air, — so different from the beastly falsetto roar with which the rebels charge, that we do not doubt that our forces are attacking the rifle-pits which they lost a few hours ago."

Describing a night-attack on the lines, May 21st, when, as on many another occasion, the regiment was hurried from its camp to the works, he said, " The scene, as viewed from the intrenchments which our regiment immediately manned, was a very striking one. Artillery fire by night is a beautiful sight. The red burst of flame from the muzzle of each gun lights up the whole landscape like a flash of summer lightning; the shell describes its long curve through the air, leaving behind a trail of sparks from the burning fuze; and its explosion brings again into momentary sight, sometimes the tree-tops only, above which it bursts, or sometimes, if well aimed, the long, low line of rebel earth-works, near the forest's edge. Then the enemy's reply, — the distant flash, dim in comparison with the startling glare of the shell which explodes, it may be, close at hand, shooting long tongues of fire in all directions from a huge nucleus of intensest brilliance. Add to this the almost incessant thunder of the rapid discharges, the whole in its contrast with the previous darkness and silence of a quiet moonless night, and you have that which, once seeing and hearing, you will not soon forget."

Two nights later, the 10th was on picket when an order came from division headquarters for scouts to be sent out to ascertain if the enemy was still in full force in front. Camp passed along the line conveying these orders from Colonel Otis to his officers. Hardly had he returned to the reserve when sharp firing was heard at the left. Hurrying thither with the colonel, they found it was before the adjoining brigade. Again they returned to their starting-point.

"Before Henry and I had been half an hour at the reserve," wrote Camp, "after our second return from the advance, came the alarm of an attack, just as it always comes, — first the crack of one or two rifles, startling one from his rest, and sounding in the stillness as if it were within twenty feet of him. This comes from the advanced posts, where the men fire the instant they discover an enemy, and then fall back; then the fire of the whole line, — not a solid volley, such as one hears at a drill, but an irregular roll, unlike any thing else when heard close at hand, but sounding at a distance so much like the clattering rumble of heavy wagons over a rough road, that even a practiced ear is sometimes deceived. This time, the sounds were close at hand, and with them came the whistle of bullets.

"We who slept at the reserve were quickly upon our feet, and out of our shelter. One company of our regiment was stationed a short distance up the road; to this the colonel sent me with orders to hold itself in readiness for an immediate move to any part of the line which might be hardest pressed. Henry and I walked toward it through a sharp fire; the message was delivered, and we returned with a most uncomfortable apprehension all the way that we might be hit in the back. The announcement wouldn't read well in the newspapers, however necessary the movement of which it was the result.

" Reaching the reserve, there was nothing more to be done just at present but wait. Colonel Otis must not move forward to the line lest messages sent to him at his post should fail to reach him, and there we remained. It was a far more dangerous position than at the front, being near the central point of a convex line of defenses; so that we had a cross-fire upon us within short range of the rebel works, and we were standing out in full exposure while all others were sheltered behind defenses of one sort or another. I don't know why it is, but this sort of danger affects me comparatively little. Shot and shell, as long as I know that I am not more than others their special mark, I can listen to with a good deal of confidence that none of them mean me; but the knowledge that a sharp-shooter has his eye upon me; is calculating the correctness of his aim, since that last bullet missed its mark; thinking whether he had better take me in the head scientifically, or make a sure thing of it by aiming a little lower down, — this, I must confess, gives me a curious sensation in the pit of the stomach, and makes me cast now and then a wistful glance to the biggest tree-trunk near by. Of course, I don't go there ; but I have a good deal of sympathy with the fellow that does, after all.

" At this time, however, we had no such apprehensions. We had heard, incredulously hitherto, of an explosive bullet, said to be fired by the enemy : now, close by us, nearer than the crack of our own rifles, sounded, every now and then, a sharp little explosion, like that of a pistol. We were inclined, after listening to a few of them, to believe the stories we had heard, though I do not know that any of the fragments have been picked up. As Colonel Otis, Henry, and I stood together, the bullets flew thick and fast ; and we had more than one narrow escape. . . .

" The advance of the rebels was repulsed, Colonel Otis bringing our reserve company into action ; and, by half-past two or three in the morning, all was again quiet."

Until about the first of June, there was little intermission to this skirmishing and artillery fighting. Of one of his earlier visits to a large redoubt at the left of his regimental front, commanded by Major Trumbull of the 1st Connecticut Artillery, he wrote,—

" Major Trumbull invited us this morning to the top of the parapet, to examine the rebel works with greater ease. The interest of the view was increased by his explanations. 'These works in the plain just beneath are our own rifle-pits, those yonder in the woods are theirs. Their sharp-shooters

post themselves in the under-growth much nearer. I don't
know how it will be to-day, but yesterday no officer could
show himself here, without finding himself a mark immediately. You'll see, if we get a shot, it will come from
that thicket on the left. Between where we stand and that
traverse, a few rods distant, eight men have been picked
off since Sunday.' But the discourteous rebels didn't
seem to think us worth their notice ; and we came down
without a salute."

" I think we have been more under fire within the past
ten or twelve days," Camp wrote about the same time with
the above, "than in all our previous army life,— merci-
fully protected, both of us, as always hitherto, and as I
trust it may be in the future, until we reach home together."

It would seem as though such service was sufficiently
active to satisfy Camp's utmost craving for usefulness ;
but when Turner's division of the 10th Corps accompanied
the 18th Corps across the James to re-enforce the army of
the Potomac, and the Bermuda-Hundred front was for a
few days a little quieter, he was again disturbed lest he
should be left where there was not the greatest need of
men ; and, while listening to the thunder of the Cold-Harbor
battles, he wrote in a regretful mood which he never indulged save when denied the privilege of doing more for
the cause he loved.

" Again through the day boomed the heavy guns far to

the northward ; and now, assured that the fight had really reached the gates of Richmond, we listened anxiously, and waited impatiently as we still wait for news. This morning brings the same roar to our ears, but louder and clearer than before,— a hopeful indication we think it. As I stop writing to listen, it seems to have ceased. Oh that we were where it has come from, instead of dozing here, hemmed in by a handful whom Beauregard probably didn't think worth taking with him to meet Grant !

"You can't be having a more humdrum life than we have had for two or three days now. Yet, when I stop to think, we should have called just such days as these a time of the intensest excitement at Newberne, or St. Helena, or in any other place I have ever been. We have been shelled in our intrenchments, we have picketed within pistol-shot of the enemy, we have had word sent that they were massing opposite the right, as if for an attack in force. We have had every thing, except personal participation in a fight, and the narrow escape which was beginning to be a part of the regular programme of each day."

Picket-service was a very different matter at Bermuda Hundred from what it had been at any place before occupied by the 10th. At Newberne and St. Augustine the enemy might make his appearance at any time, at Seabrook Island he was in sight of the outposts, at James and Morris Islands he was within gunshot; but at Bermuda, he was almost within arm's-length, — within speak-

ing distance along the entire front. As a portion of the
line was in the pine-woods, it was not an easy thing to
pass from post to post in the darkness; and a few paces in
the wrong direction after leaving the tree of one vedette
in search of the next would take one into the lines of the
enemy. As much of the posting was done after nightfall,
the duties of the adjutant in conveying orders from the
colonel, and in aiding to establish the line, were responsible and trying. More than one officer or soldier of this
side or the other strayed from his path, and was taken prisoner on that perplexing front; and Camp would have
shrunk far more from the thought of captivity than of
death.

Sociability between opposing pickets was a fresh feature
of outpost life, resulting from the proximity of the two lines.
Describing a walk from left to right along the picket front,
before batteries No. 3 and No. 4, Camp wrote: —

" Crossing the open ground, we entered the woods on
the opposite side of the plain. Here our lines and theirs
converged, so that the posts were as near to one another
as across the front of our house-yard. We stopped and
watched those opposite us for a few minutes; and they
seemed equally interested in us. Very natural they looked
in their gray jackets and pants, just like the fellows who
were keeping guard over me a few days ago. We scruti-
nized their faces to see if we couldn't recognize some of our
old acquaintances among them; but these were North-

Carolina men, — the same, some of them, who had fought us at Roanoke, Newberne, and Kinston: so they said. They invited us to come over and visit them: they had tobacco, which they wanted to barter for what we could give; and very likely we might have accepted the invitation and returned in safety; but we didn't put the question to test. . . .

"The opposing pickets have been on excellent terms for the past few days. On Monday, just before the artillery fire commenced, the rebels at the outposts warned our men, 'Get into cover, boys: our guns are going to open right away!' And yesterday they called out to the men of the Massachusetts 24th, that they had an ugly-tempered fellow on as officer of the day, and would very likely be ordered to fire at any Yankee whom they could see. 'But the *first* time,' said they, 'we'll fire high: after that you must look out.' Good-natured fellows, weren't they? not such as you would care to kill on general principles,— only for special reasons."

The night of June 15th found the 10th on picket at the extreme right, next the James. Soon after midnight, word came to the reserve that the enemy had planted cannon so as to sweep the main road across which ran the picket-line; that he was massing troops as for an attack at the right; and that he had advanced his vedettes as if to make room for an assaulting column. Major Greeley, being in command of the regiment at the time, went immediately to the front, and Camp accompanied him. That there was unusual activity on the part of the enemy there could not be a doubt. The rumble of moving artillery and army-wagons was distinctly heard; and the clatter of swift-riding horses, with the voices of officers giving orders, close at hand, mingled with the rattle of trains over the Petersburg track from far beyond. But whether all these movements indicated an evacuation, or the arrival of re-enforcements for an attack, was an undecided but interesting question to the waiting listeners at the advanced rifle-pits. It was impossible to decide from the sound in which direction the teams were moving.

Adjutant Camp was sent to make report of what was heard to Colonel Voris of the 67th Ohio, division-officer of the day. The latter had received similar reports from all along the line. Orders were given for the entire force to stand to arms until daylight. Just in the gray of the morning came orders for the vedette line to be re-enforced, and every other man of it pushed forward to feel the enemy's front. The thin skirmish-line of the 10th, thus formed, moved out; Major Greeley, Adjutant Camp, and his friend following it closely. It was an exciting advance. The rumble of wheels was still heard, and the voices of the enemy seemed not far in front. There was every reason to expect momentarily a checking fire. They passed the posts where the rebel vedettes stood at sundown. They approached, unopposed, the rifle-pits over which the heads

of the Johnnies had peered at them the day before. The
sounds which were first heard had not yet died away; but
the enemy made no attempt to stay the skirmishers' progress.
They saw before them the line of strong works which had
so long kept General Butler's forces cooped up in the
peninsula; but no signs of life appeared, although the
voices and the rumbling wheels were distinct as at the
start. The abattis was torn aside, the ditch was leaped,
the steep sides of the parapet were clambered; and, with no
little satisfaction, they stood on the crown of the formidable
intrenchments, and, looking right and left, saw that they
were in unquestioned possession.

As yet only fifty or sixty men — extended along a front
of half a mile — had moved out from the 10th; and no
force was in supporting distance. The enemy had not
all deserted the Howlett Redoubt; and the handful of skirmishers nearest to it made haste along the parapet to cut
off the retreat of those still there, and succeeded in
capturing three commissioned officers and nearly thirty
enlisted men.

The few who were participants in that morning advance
and skirmish on the bank of the James will not soon forget
the excitement of its progress, or the satisfaction of its
success. The regiment was ordered up, with other troops
at the left; and soon the evacuated works were fully occupied by a competent force, while General Terry pushed
out to cut once more the Petersburg and Richmond Rail-

road. The 10th, having cleared out the rifle-pits on its new front, and taken a few more prisoners, held a position along the works near the river, where it had made its first captures in the morning.

"Upon the river-bank stood a house, once the residence of a Dr. Howlett, — a pleasant place still, with a magnificent prospect over the river, which winds two hundred feet beneath. From its roof, the spires of Richmond are plainly to be seen, unless, as was the case now, the air is too hazy to permit it. The house has been riddled with shell from our gunboats and monitors, which have made it, and a battery close beside it, their especial target for weeks past. In this battery, forming part of the line of works, was planted the largest and most formidable gun which the rebels had in front of us, — a hundred-pounder Parrott, which we should have been very glad to have been able to silence.

"Near this house we sat down to rest. The ice-house attached to it, still partially filled, furnished us with an unaccustomed luxury. The trees shaded a soft green turf, and we thought ourselves well off in our temporary headquarters. The morning wore away; and, except an occasional shot in front, all was quiet. We strolled about the place, examining the effects of shot and shell. One of the latter, a fifteen-inch plaything from a monitor, lay unexploded half-way down the steep hillside. Our boys amused themselves with rolling it to the bottom.

"Lying down upon the grass, we were waiting the arrival of dinner, when a roar like that of a dozen shrieking locomotives close at hand — a shock which made the earth tremble beneath us; and a tremendous explosion, all nearly simultaneous — startled us, not to use a stronger expression. Looking down the river, a cloud of white smoke, drifting away from the turret of a monitor, showed us what it meant. A hundred-pound rifle-shell had struck the bank just below us, and exploded there. We were supposed by our naval friends to be some of the rebels to whom they had been devoting their attention for a month past. While we still looked, another cloud of smoke rolled out from a second port-hole. We jumped to cover, or threw ourselves flat upon the earth. A second or two, and again the howl and explosion, — the latter not far from overhead; while the huge fragments of a two-hundred and fifty-pound shell from a fifteen-inch smooth-bore flew all around us, — striking the trees close by, burying themselves in the earth, or whizzing past and endangering those who stood in a redoubt some two hundred yards distant, — Colonel Otis and Captain Goodyear among them.

"This would never do. We must contrive to let them know that we were friends. White handkerchiefs were put in requisition, though it was doubtful how clearly they would be visible at a distance of something like a mile; and, while the rest sought cover, the orderly-sergeant of

Company 'H' [now Lieutenant Grinsell] stood upon a tall gate-post, waving his signal, not flinching an inch when the second shell burst above him so near at hand. They saw the sign, fired no more shots, and presently a boat put off, a white flag flying at her bows, and pulled toward us; the officer in charge probably expecting to receive the surrender of a body of rebels. He must have been somewhat disconcerted, I think, when near enough to distinguish our uniform; but took it coolly enough when we met him at the landing, sincerely hoped no one had been hurt, and was pleased to have an opportunity to examine the effects of their fire. We complimented him on the accuracy of his shots, and invited him to dinner. He declined the invitation, but made us quite a call; filled his boat with ice, and then returned, — not to hear the last of it, I suspect, though, for some time. We have been fired at by our own land-forces often enough before ; but this monitor-shelling is a new variety, and throws other artillery-fire as much in the shade as that does musketry. No wonder that the rebels find gunboat-practice, in the rare instances where they are exposed to it, so demoralizing."

The enemy's troops had been withdrawn from the Bermuda-Hundred front to hurriedly re-enforce Petersburg against Grant's attack. Lee was hastening from Richmond to fill the gap. General Butler deciding not to hold the new position, acquired at so little risk, the rebel

16

works were evacuated at sundown on Terry's return from the railroad. The 10th was the last regiment to fall back, being instructed to hold its position "at all hazards," while the other troops withdrew to their lines of the morning. The situation was a critical one; for the enemy was coming down in strong force, charging the no longer defended lines with hideous yells, and being actually over the parapet at the left of the 10th, while severely pressing its front, before word came for the latter to retire. Yet so firmly did the 10th hold its ground, and so steady and accurate was the fire of its skirmishers, that the advance of the enemy was checked, and the regiment finally withdrew not only in good order, but unopposed. The enemy quickly followed up the retiring troops, and attacked vigorously along the line; but were repulsed with ease.

The next two days there was almost incessant skirmishing on the Bermuda-Hundred front. The closing page of a letter from Camp, written on the afternoon of the 18th, illustrates the manner in which his correspondence was persevered in when the only leisure to be found was in the intervals of active movements at the extreme front.

"It's impossible to tell, when one commences a sentence, when and where he will finish it. We are lying here now as a support to the right of our division picket-line, which is in danger of being flanked; the center having been driven in. All had been quiet for some time, until, a moment or two ago, just as I was taking out the portfolio, a bullet or two came whizzing past. 'Ah!' said Henry, 'the time of the singing of birds has come.' 'Humming-birds' our boys call these rifle-bullets. There strikes another now, a little to my left, near where Henry stands talking with a group of men. I doubt whether I'm allowed to write many minutes more. Artillery is pounding away heavily toward the left. Henry returns to sit by me and write. That bullet was meant for him, — a man who stood by him saw whence it came. Their sharpshooters are evidently on the lookout for us. I hope we shall stay where we are long enough for me to finish my letter. They are opening upon us now with spherical case, — pretty good shots too. Our officers and a few of the men sit upon the ground too far in the rear of the rifle-pits to be sheltered at all by them. A shot struck just now within a yard or two of our boys, a couple of rods to the right of where we are sitting : they seem to have our range exactly. I must close this and send it."

The severe shelling which followed that letter-writing he described a few days later : —

" At half-past three Saturday morning, we were ordered out to support the 11th Maine, which held the right of the picket-line. We occupied a rifle-pit a few rods in their rear, and, having taken position, lay down for another nap. The morning, after our waking and breakfast, was chiefly occupied in writing ; a shell from the rebel works every

few minutes giving me subject-matter for an occasional
parenthesis. All these passed harmless by; and we wrote
on, or read the papers just brought up, paying them no
attention, beyond now and then an involuntary start, when
one came lower and nearer than usual. It seemed as if
the rebel gunners now for the first time saw the mark to
be aimed at. Of this we received intimation by the bursting of a shell two or three rods to the left and rear of
where we sat; the fragments cutting twigs and branches
from the trees above us, and the bullets with which it had
been filled (it was a spherical case) striking the ground
in fifty places around.

"Shell after shell now came in rapid succession, and
with the most wonderful accuracy of direction and length
of fuze. Henry and I had thought the first a chance-shot,
and had not moved from our seat under a tree, a little in
the rear of the rifle-pit. But as one after another, at
intervals of a few seconds only, exploded nearly in the
same place, we made up our minds that even the slight
protection of the open rifle-pit was not to be disregarded,
and took position in it by the side of Major Greeley, who
was in command of the regiment. Every man was speedily
ensconced in the same cover. As Henry rose from the
ground to enter it, a ragged piece of iron struck within six
inches of him : he picked it up, hot with the flame of the
powder, and brought it with him.

" Leaning our backs against the side of the trench in which we sat, we thought our danger to be only about one-half that of a position upon the level ground. Owing to the velocity of the exploding shell, few of its fragments fall behind or even under it. Most of them are thrown in front of the point at which it bursts. *Most*, I say; but, after all, it is about as unpleasant to be hit by one of a dozen, as by one of two dozen missiles. So we looked up, and wondered — as each fierce explosion smote our ears to positive pain, filling the air with powder-smoke, and hiding for a moment all that was ' before our eyes — whether this was the one meant for us.

" The air was full of flying iron and lead, pattering in a shower upon the ground, rattling like hail among the trees, cutting off branches and twigs, throwing down the piled-up earth of our shelter, and dashing up little clouds of dust above, before, behind, on all sides at once. Right among us in the rifle-pit they struck: the wonder seemed that any escaped, yet for a time no one was touched. A tree grew above our heads. Among its branches, perhaps thirty feet from the ground, a shell burst, tearing them to pieces, covering us with the falling shreds of wood, bark, and leaves; but the shower was a harmless one. Just before where we sat rose a much larger tree, a pine. Mingled with the explosion of a shell came the sound of a sharper though less stunning crash. 'Look out, boys!' called some one; and down thundered the tree, its trunk shivered, — falling directly toward us, but a yard or two from our position.

"The fire came from several directions. One gun in our front seemed never to fail. Every shell which it sent burst over some part of our line as accurately as if it had been thrown like a hand-grenade. Another, far to our right, flung its shot a few feet above our heads; and on they went, crashing along through the woods, with swift succession of sharp reports mingling with their shrieks as tree-trunks snapped like pipe-stems, their tops whirled in air, the path beneath marked with shivered boughs and limbs rent from their places of growth. Then came the explosion far in the rear, where were posted our reserves.

"This shelling lasted for more than an hour. Narrow escapes were, of course, the rule rather than the exception; still, as yet no one had been so much as grazed. At length there was a lull, — a little time of utter quiet; then came that for which all this had been only preparation. A wild yell sounded through the woods upon our left, and in a moment more there mingled with it the crack of a thousand rifles. Yell upon yell, volley upon volley, nearer and nearer every second. 'Make ready, boys!' called Major Greeley; and at once every man who had not already risen was upon his feet. Just then came one more shell, — almost the last which was fired: it skimmed low, struck the ground a few rods in front of us, bounded just high enough to clear the ridge of earth before the rifle-pit, and strike a man who had just risen in obedience to the order. Poor fellow! he never knew that he was hit. One shoulder, half his neck, and the lower part of his head, were carried sheer away. He dropped without a groan or a quiver. Hardly any one knew it. Henry and I did not, though we were but a few yards from him.

"Each man was leaning over the breastwork, his rifle at his shoulder, his eye fixed on the openings of the wood in front, among whose trees we expected every moment to see the gray coats of an advancing line. I haven't known since I entered the army a moment of more intense excitement. Nor was it over in a moment. Bullets were flying fast above us, but no enemy made his appearance. On our left the fight was raging fiercely; no cessation of the rapid volleys, no intermission of the rebel yells, which, still approaching, seemed to be just upon our flank and close at hand, indicating that our line had been broken but a few hundred yards below us. . . .

"The fight did not reach us. Upon our left, it swayed back and forth, — Colonel Otis commanding upon our side as general-officer of the day. The enemy, in their first rush, gained possession of part of our line of rifle-pits; but were afterward driven back with loss of prisoners, and, at the close, we held our old position. Their sharp-shooters afterward annoyed us somewhat, — several shots being fired at Henry as he stood talking with the men,

several at Major Greeley and myself; but no one was hit.
Henry buried the poor fellow who was killed by the shell
not far from where he fell; and we returned about dark
to camp. At midnight, we were ordered out again, and
remained through the sabbath, — a quiet day. Returning once more to camp at evening, we saw the smoke of a
rebel ram, which had come down the river, now returning
under the fire of our gunboats. A prayer-meeting in
camp closed the day pleasantly."

In modest under-estimate of his power in graphic deline-
ation of these thrilling scenes of army-life, he said, —

"I have described the same thing — or what must seem
so to you — in the same words so often, that I am heartily
tired of the story myself, and mean to quit grinding my
single-tune hand-organ. If I could bring out the distinc-
tive features which individualize similar yet widely different
scenes, and make each one fresh in its exciting interest to
us who have part in it, it would be worth while to attempt
a new sketch for each; but all that is left in my power
now is, in transparent-slate style, to trace over again my
old lines with a pencil that grows duller each time I re-
peat the experiment."

CHAPTER XI.

DEEP BOTTOM. — STRAWBERRY PLAINS. — DEEP RUN.

UNE 20th, the 10th C. V., as a portion of Brigadier-General R. S. Foster's new command, marched down from the Bermuda-Hundred front to Jones's Landing, and thence crossed the James during the evening in the boats on which the pontoon was subsequently laid. It was this movement which gave General Grant possession of Deep Bottom, — his base thenceforward of all operations north of the James. The enemy occupied the position at that time, and on Colonel Otis devolved the delicate and difficult task of establishing, between midnight and morning, a safe picket-line in a portion of country he had never visited before, pressing back the rebel pickets as he posted his own. Adjutant Camp had his full share of duty, aiding in this important work.

Again there were weeks of picketing in close proximity to the enemy, with occasional skirmishes and annoyance from artillery-fire. The pickets were as sociable as before Bermuda Hundred. On one occasion, some South-Carolinians inquired for Adjutant Camp and Chaplain Trumbull, whom they had guarded in the Columbia jail, and sent them kindly greeting. The 10th was on picket when the flag of truce passed out to arrange for the visit to Richmond of Colonel Jacques and Edmund Kirke, and again when the latter returned from their mission. One morning the rebels brought down a light battery to Strawberry Plains and drove the gunboats out of range, killing and wounding quite a number on one of the double-enders; then threw shot and shell across Four-Mile Creek at General Foster's headquarters and the camp of the 10th, exploding shell directly over the tent where the field and staff of the latter sat at breakfast, giving the servants who were bringing in the coffee hair-breadth escapes, and tearing through tents but a few yards distant.

There were days of discomfort in that Southern midsummer, when, as Camp said, —

"The weather we are having is beyond description, — not merely heat, but an enervating influence in the air, that makes it seem impossible to move hand or foot. We should hardly have energy, if we saw the rebels coming over the top of the hill, to get up and form line, without a written order from headquarters."

And there were stormy nights of discomfort on the picket-line. Of one of these he wrote : —

"It threatened rain, and, before lying down to sleep, we made an inner roof of shelter-tents to our booth of boughs. The rain came. We slept quietly; and congratulated ourselves upon our forethought, until the rising

wind warned us that we were not yet safe. Our shelter
was very slightly constructed; it swayed to and fro in
the gusts, and at length, as a fiercer blast swept along,
toppled and fell with a crash, burying us completely.
The materials of which it was built were not heavy enough
to hurt us. We turned over, and went to sleep again.
The wet cloth which covered us, and the branches piled
above, were of no service in keeping off rain, and they
made rather a heavy counterpane; but it was of no use
to think of building a new shelter then, and we lay still.
Our rubber-blanket made an excellent water-proof bottom
for the puddle which was speedily formed around us; and,
before morning, we were as well drenched, and as well
chilled, as need be. It reminded me quite forcibly of my
last December's experience in the South-Carolina woods."

One afternoon, when the 10th was charged with the
duty of pushing out the picket-line on either side of the
Kingsland Road, to make room for the expected 19th Corps,
Camp had a very narrow escape on the vidette-line from a
rebel sharpshooter, close at hand; the bullet striking the
tree at which he stood, just at the hight of his head.

"Strange, how many bullets miss!" he wrote of this,
in coolness; "not only those fired at random, in the
excitement of battle, but those sent with deliberate aim,
and at short range."

His perils and privations seemed only to remind him
that he was doing and enduring something for the cause

he loved, and to give him fresh reason for thankfulness that he was again in the field.

"Ah! those poor fellows in Columbia, and their friends, — am I not grateful, and you for me that I am not there? My prison-life seems to me already like a dream. I don't remember much about it now that the nightmare has left me. How much better to come back here and be shot, if that proves the alternative, than to have stayed where I was!"

He never dwelt on the dark side of his personal lot in hard service. He was never despondent for the national cause. No matter how much he suffered, no matter how much of gloom seemed to others to enshroud the civil or the military situation, he was always contented and hopeful. The pillar by which God led him through the wilderness was of brightness by day and by night.

After a night under arms at the Deep-Bottom intrench-ments, the 10th moved over Four-Mile Creek to Strawberry Plains, near Haxall's Landing, on the morning of July 26, to assist the 11th Maine in retaking a line of rebel rifle-pits on the Malvern-Hill Road, captured some days before by the latter regiment, and yielded again by a portion of the 19th Corps. Then followed a day of sharp skir-mishing; the rebels contesting obstinately every foot of ground, yet gradually falling back. In the forenoon, while the fight was opening, and the 10th had not yet advanced to the extreme front, Camp wrote, —

"The regiment has stacked arms by the roadside where the shaded path winds pleasantly up from the river-bank. Headquarters are under a large tree just in the rear of the line. Henry and I, who always carry writing materials in a little haversack which we keep by us, are writing our letters in the interval of rest. The gunboats are firing over our heads at the rebels in front; and each explosion, so near are we to the muzzles of the guns, makes one feel as if both ears were being boxed with sledge-hammers, and the top of his head flattened with a pile-driver. Field-pieces are being rapidly worked at the top of the bank above us, and the reports are almost incessant. As I write, one of our men is being carried past, wounded in the arm by the premature explosion of a shell. Henry has left his writing to attend to him. He was one of a detachment stationed at a redan in front of our halting-place. It is said the gunboats are using some captured rebel ammunition which doesn't fit the guns. Ten minutes ago, a poor fellow was carried by on a stretcher with his foot torn completely off by a shell which burst short of its mark, and killed instantly one of his companions. How much of this artillery blundering we have seen! Some one ought to be tried and shot for it. Henry returns, saying that our man has only received a slight flesh-wound. He was lying down behind the breastworks, and thought that there certainly he was safe. We are coming to the conclusion that the only place where one is really out of danger is at the extreme front. They are firing now so directly above our heads that I have to stop, and brush from my paper the leaves and twigs cut off by the shot, and falling about us in showers. Hope they have good ammunition on that boat, — no short fuzes, — and that they won't drop any very large branches on us."

The sun and the fire, both artillery and musketry, were very hot that day. Many a brave soldier fell never to rise again, or was carried to the rear maimed for life. It was a trying day. When evening came, the handful of men from General Foster's command held a salient angle in the woods, running into the enemy's position of the morning, where they were fronted and flanked by a largely superior force. The picket-posts were for a portion of the way within a few yards of each other; so that even a heavily drawn breath could be heard across the lines, and conversation in an ordinary tone was distinctly audible. General Grant had telegraphed, just before night, to hold every inch that had been gained, promising help before morning. The pickets of the 10th lay concealed in the low underbrush. If they discovered themselves by the crackling of a twig, they were liable to be silenced by a shot from just in their front; and the preparations for the morning, which they could hear the enemy making, were any thing but encouraging. Artillery was brought down, and so planted that they could almost have looked into the gun-muzzles; while a single discharge of grape from the battery could sweep them away like chaff from the enfiladed picket-line. They could hear the braggart threats of annihilation of the venturesome Yankees when the daylight came, and they realized their danger; yet all who were unwounded remained firm and true. Adjutant Camp crept along that entire line, conveying orders, at imminent risk not only of being shot but of passing within the enemy's lines; the latter being nearer to some posts than the next vedette, and the way found only with greatest difficulty in the gathering darkness.

A pleasant incident to Camp of that evening was the meeting of a college classmate, Wiswell, a captain of the 11th Maine, who had recently returned to his regiment after an absence of some months, and been all that day in the skirmish-line. Glad always to meet a college companion, Camp especially delighted to find one a comrade in arms.

There was not much sleeping that night among officers or men of the 10th, — only an anxious waiting for the morning whose sun must rise in blood. Word was received that the pontoon-bridge was being deadened with straw that a moving column might pass it noiselessly, and that a large force of cavalry was on the south bank of the river. About daylight the 2d Corps crossed over from Jones's Landing, having marched hurriedly from Petersburg. Generals Hancock and Sheridan were present with their commands. Then, in the words of Camp, —

"Soon after sunrise the advance of our forces commenced. From our station at the picket-reserve, we had a capital view of all that was done. A column of men moved forward across the plain on our right; the pickets of the enemy fell back as they approached, and they descended into the valley without serious opposition. Here, sheltered by the rise of ground before them from fire, they formed an open skirmish-line, each man with room to act independently, and moved up the slope. We watched them with intent eagerness. As they rose to the level beyond, a sharp volley greeted them; and instantly the air was white and the hillside dotted with puffs of smoke as each man halted for an instant where he stood, fired, and moved on, loading for another discharge. There is one poor fellow down! and an officer, a surgeon perhaps, bending over him. There are half a dozen more!—not all of them wounded, however: they are lying flat for cover, and we can see them loading and firing industriously. There are two or three mounted officers—one of them with a straw hat—cantering about among the men. That looks to us like recklessness. We are in the habit of seeing officers go into a fight dismounted; but we can't help admiring their pluck.

"Now most of the line has disappeared behind the crest of the hill which slopes down toward the rebel works just beyond; and we can judge only from the rapid rifle-cracks that the fight is being hotly contested. By this time they must be up to the works. But what does this mean? There are men moving the wrong way; there come two or three on the run, and twenty follow them. Is it a panic? No: the men halt as soon as they have gained the partial shelter of the slope, and open fire again. It is plain that the first attack has failed; but they don't mean to give it up yet. They are all on this side of the crest now, in plain sight; and their officers are urging them on for another rush. A good deal of the dash has been taken out of them, however, by that unsuccessful attempt; and they don't like to go beyond the slope.

"The horseman with the straw hat gallops to and fro, waving his sword, pointing to the front, pressing them to come up once more. Some are ready to try it. The color-bearer rushes forward, stands on the highest point of ground where the bullets must be flying like hail, turns, and waves his colors to those behind. We can hardly help cheering the brave fellow, and that noble rider who is in front of all, dashing on, and calling them to follow. We expect every moment to see him go down, and strain our eyes with eager watching. How can men *help* following him? But no: too many hold back; and those who are willing are discouraged, and give way too. Yet the straw-hat man won't give it up so. If it can't be done in one way, per-haps it can in another. He'll try flanking them. There is a little depression in the ground on the right. He plants the colors in a sheltered spot, forms line there, and moves

17

off in this direction, approaching obliquely the rebel works; and his men, ready for any thing except that in which they have just failed, start after him with a rush. They are speedily out of sight.

"Again comes the sound of sharp musketry; but this time there is no falling back: it grows more and more distant, and before long we hear that the works are taken and four Parrott guns with them. Our own men deserve part of the credit, though they won't be likely to get it. That part of the picket-line which was nearest opened an effective fire upon the enemy, and, beside the loss which they inflicted, made the Richmond Road so hot, that horses couldn't be brought down to withdraw the artillery before the works were abandoned.

"We met the officer in the straw hat within the works. Henry talked with him, and learned that he was lieutenant-colonel of the 183d Pennsylvania, commanding a brigade in Barlow's Division of Hancock's Corps, — a very fine-looking fellow, and modest as he was brave. His name was Lynch. His hat had been pierced by a bullet, and his horse shot under him; but he had come out without a scratch. A lieutenant-colonel commanding a brigade! Think how the corps must have been cut up!"

The 10th returned to its camp at Deep Bottom, and resumed picket-duty, with an occasional demonstration against the enemy, or the meeting of an attack on its line. An affair of the latter kind Camp thus described: —

"A week ago Monday (August 1), we were out on picket. The day had passed quietly. Henry, seldom absent at any time, and least of all when the regiment is at the front, had been called away by business on the other side of the river. It was almost time for us to be relieved, — late in the afternoon, — when several shots were suddenly fired upon the line in front. They did not start us; but, when half a dozen more came in rapid succession, Captain Goodyear, who was in command, ordered the reserve to stand to arms. A messenger came; the enemy were advancing. We marched immediately to the point of attack, and re-enforced the picket-line with the reserve deployed as skirmishers. Quite a brisk little fight followed, Indian fashion, — every one, except officers, to his tree, covering himself, keeping a sharp lookout for the similarly protected enemy, and firing whenever he caught a glimpse of a gray jacket.

"Twice the rebels attempted to charge, setting up a feeble yell, which was rather encouraging from its lack of force than disheartening. Finding these Chinese tactics unavailing, our men firmly holding their ground, they finally retired. Then came the turn of our boys; and the complimentary yells, the hoots, and the cock-crowing which followed them as they gave way and left the ground, must have been soothing enough. What their loss was we could not determine: ours was three men wounded,— one mortally, dying the next day; another severely, but not dangerously. The bullet which struck the third was checked in its progress by passing through a stout tin cup and a haversack well filled with hard-tack, — almost bullet-proof, — and inflicted only a slight wound. Henry was on hand before the affair was fairly over, having heard the firing on his way back, and run his horse all the rest of the distance. The boys chuckled over his appearance, believing that, if he had been twenty miles further off, it would have made no difference. Whether I was glad to see him, and he me, I needn't say."

Camp gave the following thrilling sketch of the first military execution which he witnessed, occurring Aug. 8, at Deep Bottom.

"A singular incident took place on our picket-line a short time since. A deserter who came in at the Grover House was recognized by the 24th Massachusetts men, who were on duty there, as one of their old comrades, who had deserted to the enemy two years ago, while the regiment was at Newberne. Tired of the rebel service, and encouraged by former success in shifting sides, he had again run the lines, and thought, on reaching our posts, that his danger was over, little suspecting, until it was too late, that he had walked straight into his old regiment. Had he entered from any other point of the whole rebel territory, had he made the attempt on any other day than the one on which the 24th guarded the line, or, even then, had not a little drummer-boy accidentally present, who was a mem-

ber of the same company to which he had belonged, remembered him, he would have escaped without recognition.
Humanly speaking, his chances were a thousand to one
for safety, after having once passed the rebel vedettes.

"He was, of course, held. Charges were preferred
against him, he was tried, convicted, and sentenced to be
shot in presence of the brigade to which he had been attached while in our service. The orders were received on
Sunday last. Colonel Osborn of the 24th was charged
with their execution. He sent for Henry to talk with the
man, — a hardened desperado, at first reckless, defiant,
professing utter carelessness as to his future, either in this
world or the next. . . . Softened at length, he acknowledged his anxiety and fear, sobbed, broke down utterly,
and desired that prayer should be made for him. The
execution was to take place at four P.M., on Monday. The
condemned man was a Catholic; and a priest had been sent
for on Sunday night, Henry preferring, of course, that the
man's wishes should be consulted in such a matter; but it
was doubtful whether one could be found and brought to
the place in time. He arrived, however, before daylight;
and Henry was spared the exceedingly trying duties which
had seemed likely to devolve upon him.

"At half-past three in the afternoon, the regiments of
the brigade were formed, each upon its own parade-ground,
and then marched to a wide open plain, bounded on one
side by a gentle slope. Here they were formed in three

sides of a hollow square, — the fourth being the vacant
hill-side : there was a newly dug grave, with the fresh
earth heaped beside it.   The proceedings of the court-
martial, and the order for the execution were now read to
each regiment; I, of course, performing the duty for our
own.   Meantime a small column was slowly approaching
the place.   In the center was a wagon containing the prisoner, securely fettered.   The priest rode with him.   A
strong guard marched in front and rear.   At their head,
a band played plaintive funeral music, swelling solemnly
above a heavy undertone of muffled drums.   In the distance, they hardly seemed to move; and the sound of the
dead-march came softly to our ears.   At length they drew
near, approaching with slow measured tread ; the drum-beat
was a deep subdued roll of thunder, the notes of the wind
instruments were a piercing wail as they passed before us
and halted opposite the grave.   Then all was silence.
Every eye was turned toward one spot, every ear atten-
tive.   But for the impatient stamping of officers' horses
and those of the cavalry squadron drawn up on the hillside, there was hardly more sound than if the place was
the same solitary field it had been before armies encamped
and marched upon Virginia soil.

" The prisoner left the wagon ; he seemed to step firmly
and boldly upon the ground ; but we were too distant to
see the expression which his face wore.   The priest was by
his side.   They knelt by the grave, and prayer was offered,

inaudible to any but the condemned. Then a platoon of twelve men, led by an officer, marched out, halted a few paces in front of the spot, and faced toward it. The officer advanced, and read to the prisoner the proceedings of the court and its sentence, — a cruel formality it seemed, a needless lengthening of the terrible suspense. Did the prisoner wait with nervous impatience, as we did, for the worst to come? or did he wish each sentence was a volume, that he might cling a little longer to life?

"The reading was finished, a broad white bandage was bound about his eyes; and, with arms firmly pinioned behind his back, he was made to kneel upon the coffin of unpainted pine which had been placed before the grave. Then for the first time the guard left his side, and all fell back who had stood around him. There was a hush, in comparison with which the former silence had been tumult.

"The officer in command of the firing party waved his sword: each piece was brought to a 'ready.' Again, and they were levelled in aim. The third time, and a quick sharp volley sounded through a cloud of smoke. The blind-fold, pinioned form tottered for a moment; then bent forward, and pitched heavily to the ground. There was a long breath of relief drawn by each who looked on, — it was over, was it? There might yet be a doubt. The officers stepped forward with a surgeon to examine the body, which lay prone and motionless in its suit of rebel gray.

The lungs still feebly expanded, and a low moan seemed to issue from them. Mere mechanical action, the surgeon thought; but a platoon which had been held in reserve was speedily ordered up, a second volley fired, and life at length was pronounced utterly extinct. Then the whole force was wheeled into column, and marched slowly past the corpse, a gory, ghastly sight, lying where it fell, pierced with twenty bullets.

"We returned to camp late in the afternoon. The scene had been one of the most impressive we had ever witnessed; and its effect upon the men, I think, just what it was designed to be. We had never before been present at a military execution; and the death-penalty, so common in the sentences of courts-martial, so seldom hitherto carried into effect, had ceased, in a measure, to possess significance. The case was an aggravated one, and well deserved capital punishment, — not merely desertion, but desertion to the enemy, and long service against his comrades. The man claimed never to have been in action, but was for some months on guard at the Libby. Henry questioned him as to the time: it was between the periods of our visits to Richmond, but including neither. Twenty bullets I said at random: there ought to have been twenty. I have learned since that there were but thirteen, — five of the first volley, eight of the second; twenty-two in all being fired. There were twenty-four men; but, on all such occasions, one in each platoon has a blank cartridge; none but the officer knowing which it is. Any, therefore, who may shrink from the feeling that he has done executioner's duty, and has blood other than that of an enemy upon his hands, is at liberty to believe, if he chooses, that his was not the fatal shot. Does it seem strange to find among soldiers such horror of blood, and such considerate regard for the feelings? Just the place to look for both!"

Sabbath morning, August 14, opened a week of hard fighting for the armies of the Potomac and the James. The latter moved toward Richmond from Deep Bottom to enable the former to establish itself on the Weldon Road. General Terry's division did most of the fighting north of the James; General Foster's brigade losing in the week fully one-third of its entire available force; the other brigades suffering also severely.

Camp thus describes the opening, and some of the later incidents, of the week's operations: —

"Last Saturday, we had orders to be ready for a move. Those who pretended to have any opinion on the subject talked of Washington, the Shenandoah, or Weldon. We packed, and went to bed late and tired. At four o'clock, A. M. (Sunday), came orders to fall in at once (there was great haste), and march to the picket-line. Half-way there, an order to double-quick; within five minutes, the same again. At the front, General Foster was waiting for us; his orders had been to attack at daylight. We must move forward at once, — not precisely like a trip to Washington !

"We formed line, threw out skirmishers, and advanced, connecting with other regiments on the right and left. A very few minutes, and the fight was brisk. The main body of the regiment was halted, and the men lay down ; while officers moved up and down the line ; skirmishers dodged from tree to tree, and bullets pattered fast in all directions. Henry and I had on straw hats, unsuited for a fight, though well adapted for a journey toward the Shenandoah ; and Henry secured caps, first for me, and afterward for himself, — one belonging to one of our wounded men, the other to one just shot dead. A hat was better for the first ; none the worse for the second.

"Going down the line, I stopped to deliver an order to Lieutenant Sharp. We stood for a moment talking ; and I had hardly turned away when a bullet passed through his head just behind the eyes. Officers went down fast. Captain Quinn had charge of the skirmishers. Two of his men, stepping in succession behind a large tree which seemed to offer excellent shelter, fell, — one dead, the other severely wounded. He moved forward to the same place, and was instantly shot dead ; all three within two minutes. It was some time before his body could be recovered. Captain Webb was wounded, and carried back ; and presently we saw two men helping Lieutenant Brown to the rear with a bullet through his leg. A moment after I left Sharp, I came upon one of our men lying on the ground with the blood pouring from a wound in the shoulder. Asking his name of those who stood by, I was told it was Dwyer, of Company F. He looked up as I inquired. 'I'm a dead man, adjutant.' — 'I hope not,' said I; but he knew too well: he did not live to be carried from the field.

"There was a yell from the rebels in front; a louder crash of musketry. Our skirmishers stood fast, and drove back the advancing enemy; but, on our left, men came pouring back in panic. We helped their officers to rally them; the rebels dared not follow them up; the line was re-established, and the fight went on as before. This had lasted more than an hour when the 24th Massachusetts, which had been held in reserve, came marching up in double column: they were to charge through the dense wood upon the rifle-pits beyond. We had orders to follow, and support them. They moved forward splendidly, with well-closed lines and steady step; they passed us a few rods, and the undergrowth hid them from sight. We came after in line of battle. Not very sleepy work, such an advance as that.

"Two or three minutes passed; the same irregular fire in front, and, with a long tremendous cheer, the 24th made their rush. Our boys needed no orders; a shout burst from every throat, and the whole line dashed on. But, instead of the fierce volleys we expected to meet, there, on reaching open ground, was the line of works deserted. The yell and the charge had been too much for the nerves of our friends in gray; and, almost without another shot, they had turned, and made the best of their way to the rear. It was a strong position, and an attacking force might have been made to suffer fearful loss. The 24th took twenty or thirty prisoners, — as contented and happy a looking set of fellows as they marched off as I ever saw. No wonder!"

After a brief rest, the 10th was ordered to a new position; and the day was passed in marching and countermarching, and covering by skirmish-line the movements of other commands. In the evening, during a severe storm, the regiment moved over to Strawberry Plains, — where it had aided in the capture of the Parrott guns a few weeks before, — and there halted until daylight. Monday was intensely hot. The march up the New-Market Road was exhausting; men by the score fell smitten with sunstroke. The only rest secured to the 3d Brigade was during the afternoon under a sharp artillery-fire near Silver Hill. The night again called for picket-duty on an exposed front. Before daylight of Tuesday, the troops were up and in line, ready for a start; and by five o'clock were on the move.

An attack on the enemy's new position was commenced about eight o'clock. Camp's narrative thus continues: —

"A skirmish-line was thrown out to cover the advance;

but the woods were so thick, that it was almost impossible for them to regulate their movements as they should by ours. We marched in line of battle, changing direction by order. They became separated from us, and we from the troops upon our left; so that our flank was swung, entirely exposed, far to the front. Colonel Otis, becoming anxious at this state of affairs, sent me forward to find, if possible, and bring into position, the skirmishers. Twenty paces into the thicket, and the regiment and I were lost to one another. I haven't confidence enough in my own bump of locality to enjoy such exploring expeditions as these, even when nothing serious or important is at stake; and, when I know that lives may hang upon my moving a few yards too far to the right or the left, there is nothing in open battle from which I so much shrink. It was a blind search. I moved rapidly to where the line should have been: there was no sign of it. Then forward, more carefully, through thicket, over fallen trees, across swamps, until I came to a ravine. I halted to listen if I could hear men anywhere moving, parting the bushes, or treading on dry leaves. No sound: the woods were as quiet and apparently as tenantless as if I were in the wilderness beyond the Rocky Mountains.

"The ravine would be a good line of defense; the opposite side a very likely position to meet an enemy. Yet I could not turn back with no other report than that I had found nobody and seen nothing. So I went down the hill, crossed the brook at its foot, and, with cocked pistol in hand, moved cautiously up the opposite slope, keeping a sharp eye upon each tree, each bush, each fallen log, that might cover a rebel picket. Nervous work. Just at the crest was a little pile of fresh earth, — a rifle-pit! It was empty. I satisfied myself of that point, and then went up to examine it. It was large enough to shelter but a single man, hastily dug, and apparently not more than twenty-four hours old; undoubtedly occupied the night before by one of their pickets. I was glad he had fallen back before I came down to the brook opposite his post.

"I didn't feel called upon to go any further, having reached what had been so recently the rebel line; and returned, after a little further wandering, to the regiment, reporting what I had and had not seen. Colonel Otis sent me to General Foster, who inquired if I had been beyond the ravine, and on my explanation, sent word to the division-commander; and a brigade was ordered to fill the gap in the line.

"The skirmishers, who had gone far to the right, at length made their way back to us, and the regiment, advancing, finally crossed the same brook I had been over, and halted in rear of the slope, while the skirmishers ascended. The latter had hardly reached the high ground, when the enemy's line opened upon them from just beyond; and they were immediately engaged in a brisk skirmish.

We lay down; Henry and I sitting together by a fallen tree, while bullets flew fast over our heads. Not all overhead. As Colonel Otis and I were passing down toward the left to examine the position, we came upon an officer lying dead or just dying, — the blood oozing from a ghastly wound. Not a soldier near him : he had either come as I came, alone, or been abandoned by his men. We, of course, could do nothing for him then ; but the colonel afterward had opportunity to speak of him to some of his own regiment, and the body was carried away.

" The officers of our skirmish-line soon sent back word that they were pushing the enemy ; had already driven him from two lines of rifle-pits, and only wanted supports to keep him going. Two more companies were immediately sent. They had hardly had time to reach position, when a cheer rang through the woods far to our right, and came rolling down the line. We knew that Hawley's Brigade was charging. The 24th took it up. Our boys sprang to their feet, and joined in the shout. Colonel Otis gave the word, and the line rushed on, over the brow of the hill, through the undergrowth where the skirmishing had been so sharp, straight on without halt or hesitation, while the rebel skirmishers vanished from before, until the main line of rifle-pits was reached and occupied. But to the left, where our skirmishers extended far beyond the flank of the regiment, the enemy pressed them hard ; and we heard they were beginning to fall back. Henry and

I went in that direction, and, moving a short distance through the low pines, saw before us a few of our men coming in from the front; not in panic, but in steady retreat. We jumped forward, and called to them to halt and stand firm. 'Orders to fall back, sir!' said one. 'Boys!' shouted Henry, 'the 10th *never* falls back!' Ah! there came a staff-officer, terribly flustered, and on a trot toward the rear. 'There were orders,' said he, apologetically, seeming to perceive, as I met him, that I felt something more than mild surprise. 'They came down from the right.'—'I am from the right,' said I: 'there are no such orders there.' He sneaked away; and our men, finding that they need not retreat, promptly advanced once more toward the front.

"The regiment, having halted, formed and dressed its ranks, soon moved forward again to a position near the edge of a second and much larger ravine, on the opposite side of which the rebels were intrenched in strong works curving around our left; so that the ground held by our advance was swept by a cross-fire against which no ordinary cover afforded security. Word came from the skirmish-line that Captain White was wounded seriously, it was feared mortally. Henry saw to his being carried back to the hospital, where the other wounded had already gone, and to which he was himself summoned, a few minutes later, by a message from one of them. . . . In a short time Henry returned : how glad we were to meet in safety !

With thoughtful kindness, he brought for us a huge water-melon. It was speedily cut and divided; General Foster very glad to get his share. What could have been more refreshing under fire? Before it was finished, orders were given for our regiment to swing around, fronting the left, and covering the flank, upon which an attack was momentarily expected. It was comical enough to see officers forming their men, enforcing their orders with brandished slices of melon, and taking a bite between each command.

"The remainder of the day was occupied with continual skirmishing; the main body being so near the advance as to get the benefit of the fire from the enemy. Officers and men sheltered themselves as well as possible. . . . Men fell near us, both in the regimental line and among the skirmishers; but our loss was slight in comparison with that of the morning's advance. There was rain during the afternoon; but we were not in the mood to be greatly concerned about a wetting. At dusk we retired a few rods to the rifle-pits we had captured in the morning, — a much more defensible position than that we had occupied during the day, — and commenced at once throwing up a line of works fronting toward the enemy. Large details from each regiment were set at work chopping and shovel-ing; and by two in the morning a strong breastwork, three or four feet thick at the top, and covered on the inside with well-braced logs, covered the front of the whole brigade.

18

We should have been glad of sleep after such a day as had passed, but we contented ourselves with a morning nap; and slept all the more soundly for knowing that we were ready in case of an attack.

" Our loss during the day had been less in officers, but greater in men, than on Monday. Captain White was one of the finest officers in the regiment. We hear now that his situation is exceedingly critical; [he died in hospital.] Colonel Otis and Lieutenant Savage were each hit, but not severely enough to take them from the field. It was the third bullet or shell contusion, not drawing blood, which the colonel has received in battle, — singular, isn't it? Wounds of this sort are sometimes quite painful and troublesome for weeks or even months.

" Poor Dennis Mahoney was shot through the body early in the day. It was he who sent for Henry to come to the hospital and see him. He was the ideal of a private soldier. Tall and fine-looking; always neat and soldierly in dress and equipments; always cheerful and prompt in duty; brave, to recklessness; never missing a chance to volunteer for an expedition, a scout, or any service of danger; full of fun and dash and spirit, — it would have been difficult to match him in the regiment. . . .

" I was reported killed myself, and talked next day with those who had not only been told by men of our regiment that I had fallen, but who had themselves seen and recognized my body as it lay upon the field, — so they certainly thought. I am glad to believe the story couldn't well reach you."

The hastily erected breast-works were held for forty-eight hours; one or two attempts being made by the enemy, meantime, at different points, to break the line. Thursday noon there were indications of a contemplated withdrawal of the Union troops.

"The movement which we expected," wrote Camp, "commenced late in the afternoon; the troops on the right retiring first, and so, brigade after brigade, down the line. The time for us to march had not yet come. Hawley's Brigade was passing, when a sharp fire opened a little to our right, and speedily became general along the whole picket-line. The enemy had evidently discovered that we were moving, and meant to take advantage of it. Hawley's men were hurried back just in time; for the rebels came on with a rush and a yell. All along our front, the woods rang with their shouts and the rapid reports of musketry; while the pickets, pressed back by numbers, came hurrying in, climbing over the works, and somewhat inclined, part of them, to continue their movement toward the rear.

"Hardly waiting for all of these to come in, two regiments near us now opened fire. The whole line of works was ablaze with rifle-flashes, and the sound was one continuous roar. Our regiment was in reserve, deployed in long open line, ten or fifteen yards behind the others, and deprived, of course, in great measure, of the shelter afforded by the works. There was already some unsteadiness among those who were firing, when our own artillery opened from a position some distance to the rear, intending to fire over our heads, but dropping almost every shell with horrible precision directly among us. Henry was standing a few yards from me, when one of them exploded in his very face, seemingly but a few inches above and before him, knocking him down, blinded and almost stunned, by the flash and the concussion. It was a spherical case. The fragments and the bullets they had enclosed tore the trees and the ground all around, — before, behind, and on every side; but, most wonderfully and providentially, he was unhurt. At the same moment, another exploded among the men in front of our regiment. It was more than they could stand. A dozen started for the rear, a hundred followed, then the whole line broke, turned back, and surged away from the works, through our line, and into the woods.

"Our boys sprang forward to fill, as well as their thin line enabled them to, the vacancy, and with cool determination held the enemy at bay. The 24th Massachusetts stood firm on our right, — New-England Yankees, every man; all this was like a flash. As the break commenced, our officers rushed among the fugitives, shouted encouragement, entreated, threatened, seized them, and flung them back to the front, — all did our best to turn the tide. I haven't worked so since the Worcester regatta. We were in some degree successful. A dozen looked on hesitatingly while our major flogged an officer, a six-foot skulker, back to the works with the flat of his sword, and concluded to stay there themselves. Indeed, I ought to say that many of the regiment stood fast from the first. . . .

"Having persuaded the enemy not to interfere with us, the movement was resumed. Our regiment formed the rear-guard, as so often before; and, retiring but a short distance, established a new picket-line, behind which the rest of the army kept on its way toward the river. No advance was attempted by the rebels until morning, when they occupied, without resistance, the works which we had abandoned. It was about three A.M. when we lay down.

"A rainy night was followed by a rainy day. Our pickets had some sharp exchanges of shots with the rebel skirmishers. Six bullets struck the tree behind which Sergeant Peck, of Company A, sheltered himself; and one or two of our men on advanced posts narrowly escaped capture. At dark on Friday, our pickets were all gathered in; and we marched over roads of horrible mud, through the rain, until we reached, about midnight, the rest of the brigade, again behind strong works, at no great distance from the river. Our tired men stretched themselves upon the soaked ground. We had a little fire built, and our shelter-tents stretched. Henry and I, however, had been, without our rubber-coats, to gather in pickets at dark, and were too thoroughly drenched to be dried in one night. So we lay down, and, once asleep, it made no difference. Saturday was another quiet, rainy day. We marched at dark; reached Strawberry Plains; again established a picket-line to cover general movements.

"Establishing a picket-line at midnight, stretching a mile or more from right to left, especially if the weather is dark and stormy, is no joke; but we are pretty well accustomed to it now. A short sleep and we were up again at daybreak. All was safe. We were the only troops who had not crossed the river. Falling back in skirmishing-line, lest the enemy should attack at the last moment, we assembled on the river-bank; marched down to the water's edge, across the pontoon, which workmen were already taking to pieces, and stood once more upon the neck of land along which lay the safe road to camp. It was the first time for a week when we had felt secure from immediate attack, — a pleasant relief from the continued strain of watchful anxiety. An hour more, and the early sabbath morning found us in our pleasant old camp, weary with a week of toil and of battle, rejoicing in the day of quiet and of rest."

The 10th had taken out from camp fifteen line-officers and about three hundred and forty men. Its casualties, during the week of absence, were seven officers and sixty-five men killed and wounded, and three men taken prisoners.

Of the twenty-four hours succeeding the return of his regiment, Camp wrote, —

"Sunday, Aug. 21, we had a quiet day of rest; though there was too much to do, in the way of re-establishing ourselves, to allow us to lie down and sleep, as we would gladly have done. We looked forward to the night, determined to go to bed as soon after dark as possible, and sleep a good ten hours before rising again. Henry held a prayer-meeting, unusually interesting and well-attended, at dusk, in our large commissary tent; and we returned to our own quarters. Wouldn't we have a good rest now? Orders had arrived to be ready for an immediate march! The explosion of a mine under us would have been nothing to it. Not that there was any burst of indignation, or any considerable degree of grumbling. I have known five times as much over trifles not worth speaking of; but it seemed to finish up whatever of cheerful energy was left by the weariness of the week among officers or men. There were the orders; there was nothing more to be said. We made our preparations in a dogged, mechanical kind of a way. Henry and I took a bath, — more refreshing than sleep, — and lay down for a nap before word came for the march. It arrived just before midnight. Where we were bound, no one knew; but it was rumored that we were to charge the works in front of our old position at Bermuda Hundred, — works which once before, when the enemy had voluntarily abandoned them, we could not hold against his return; works behind which, with approaches swept by cross-fire of artillery and infantry, impassable abattis, and deep ditch, a brigade might hold at bay an army-corps. . . .

"We marched silently and gloomily. More than one man fell from the ranks and was left by the roadside; not because he shrank from sharing the risk of his comrades, but because, from mere exhaustion, he was unable to go further. So we moved slowly along our way, until about half the distance was accomplished; then came orders, unexpected as the first, to about-face, and march back to camp. A much more cheerful and free-spoken set of men promptly complied with them; and we reached our quarters again about half-past four, A.M.

"It was true that Birney had issued orders for an attack upon those works, — why countermanded we do not learn, — and there was reason to believe that our brigade would have had the advance in the storming party. Our men, had they been led to the assault, would have fought well, but almost hopelessly; and a small part of us only would ever have left the field."

In this expression of opinion, Camp shadowed forth the result of the assault in which, two months later, he lost his life.

CHAPTER XII.

IN THE PETERSBURG TRENCHES.

NOT long after the return of the column from New-Market road to Deep Bottom, General Foster left the latter point to assume command of a division elsewhere; and the 3d Brigade was again in charge of Colonel Plaisted of the 11th Maine. Aug. 26, this brigade was relieved by the colored troops of General Paine, and left Deep Bottom for the Petersburg front, where the 10th Corps was ordered to relieve the 18th Corps.

"We had a tiresome march," wrote Camp of that move. "It is about as fatiguing to ride at a walk for ten or fifteen miles as to march the same distance on foot. It was cloudy overhead, muddy underneath, and, in the pine-woods, pitchy dark.

"We reached the Appomattox about 11.15, P.M., and, after difficulty and delay in finding the road which led down to the pontoon, learned upon reaching it that we should have to wait for the passage of a wagon-train. Meantime, the rain came down in torrents; but we wrapped our rubber-coats about us, lay down on the muddy ground, and slept soundly. About one o'clock the road was clear, and we started again. It is a long distance from one bank to the other, the bridge crossing several low islands before high ground is reached on the farther side. We went but a mile or two beyond; the darkness, solidified by blinding flashes of lightning, making it impossible to distinguish the road. Our bivouac was cheerless enough; though a tent-fly, thrown over a couple of rails which leaned against a tree, gave us such shelter as few or none besides had.

" Saturday morning was bright and clear, and we marched early. The country was very pleasant: high, rolling ground, sloping down toward the winding Appomattox; fortifications everywhere; pleasant residences not a few, — abandoned, of course, — beautifully shaded by huge old trees, and commanding fine views of the river valley. Petersburg was plainly in sight, during a part of the march, directly in front of us; and, not more than two or three miles distant, its streets and houses distinctly to be seen. Henry and I wondered, if, with a good glass, we couldn't have picked out the Bolingbroke House, where we had each stopped in passing through the place.

" About ten A.M. we reached the position assigned us, — the deserted camp of a negro-regiment. I have hardly seen so filthy or repulsive a spot since I have been in the army; every thing in the most shocking condition imaginable. The main works were perhaps a quarter of a mile in front of us, and on higher ground, so that we could see nothing beyond. Parallel to them, where we were, a brook ran through a shallow valley. It was this stream that rose so suddenly, a few weeks since, as to drown fourteen men of the 18th Corps, whose place we had now taken. That side of the slope nearest the front was full of burrows of all shapes and sizes; some nicely faced with logs, some mere rat-holes. One of the best of these we made headquarters; and the men dug and built for themselves strong shelters on the level ground in front of us.

"Before the precise spot for our camp had been indicated, we halted upon the plain near by, and stacked arms for dinner. 'You can't stay there,' said an officer to us, 'every one who stops there is killed.' The regiment dined in peace, however, and was marched off by the senior captain; the field and staff waiting to finish a little more at leisure. By and by the enemy's artillery opened. No shells came very near, and we paid no special attention to them. One, bursting some rods distant, called forth a remark; but we had ceased to speak or think of it, when, with a fierce whiz, down came a fragment, — it must have been thrown high in air, — and buried itself in the earth about six feet from Henry, and precisely where Colonel Otis had been sitting a few minutes before. We began to think the place might deserve its reputation; but the firing ceased as suddenly as it had commenced, with no more close shots. . . .

" At dusk, artillery re-opened on both sides. Mortar-shelling at night is a beautiful sight. The burning fuze of each projectile marks its course for the whole distance of its flight. It rises like a rocket, moving apparently only half as fast, sails slowly through the sky, sometimes a mile above the earth, at the highest point of its enormous curve, and descending, one would think at a distance, as gently as a snow-flake; but it strikes the earth with a concussion which shakes the ground for many yards on every side, and explodes with a report like that of the mortar from which it came. One can see in the darkness precisely where it is coming,— it seems as if a good ball-player wouldn't find it a difficult catch, — and there is no need, if a bomb-proof is within a few rods, of any one's being hit by the shell before explosion; but the fragments fly in all directions, and fly far, striking sometimes, as in the case I mentioned, long after it seems as if all danger must be over. None of our men were hurt on Saturday evening, though there were some narrow escapes. The 7th New Hampshire, a little distance to our left, lost one killed and several wounded. The man who was killed was sitting near the breastwork, watching the shells. One came directly toward him; those who stood near scattered, and called to him to hurry away; but he gazed at it as if fascinated, — moved not an inch. A moment more, and the shell tore him to fragments."

The weeks passed by the 10th before Petersburg were

weeks of seldom intermitted peril. On the picket-line, in the trenches, and in camp, there was constant danger of death. Rifle bullets were whizzing past or striking near one, wherever he went; and rarely a day passed without a few hours of artillery-firing from the enemy. Even when there was a tacit truce on the immediate front, sharp-shooters at right or left kept up their diagonal fire ; and, during most of the time, active hostilities prevailed along the entire line.

The position of the 10th was in front of General Meade's headquarters ; its picket duty ranging from the opening of the exploded mine under Cemetery Hill to the right of the Second-Corps line, near the Jerusalem Plank Road.

" Near the right of our line," wrote Camp, of his first tour of picket duty at Petersburg, " was a hollow, running from front to rear ; and through this, more or less, bullets were flying during a large part of the day, and all the evening and night. One of our companies was stationed beyond this, and its position connected with the rest by a long and exceedingly crooked covered way. Sometimes for an hour or two there would be no firing, and one would be tempted to take the short cut above ground ; but a bullet was very apt to whistle by when the experiment was tried ; and the only prudent course was to take the long way round, lest the other should prove emphatically a short way home.

" It was evident that rebel sharpshooters were watching

this place, and that they knew its every crook and turn. The passer must move quickly, or his momentary appearance where a side path branched off and left an opening, or where an angle brought him for an instant into sight, was the signal for a bullet too well aimed to be called a chance shot. Henry and I convinced ourselves of this before we had been long at our new station, and others had the same experience."

Some of the incidents of the artillery-fire he thus described : —

" They are shelling us again here in camp this afternoon ; making pretty good practice, too, within the last few minutes. No one hit yet. A shell struck just now in the road, behind a fellow who was carrying a pail of coffee. It was amusing to see the coolness with which he slowly turned round and took a good look at the spot, then trudged along his way, without having spilled a drop of coffee, or been apparently any more discomposed than if a snow-ball had struck near him."

And, of another date : —

" In the afternoon, we were more heavily shelled than at any time before, since that day at Bermuda Hundred ; being compelled to leave our tents and take shelter in our bombproof. The rebel gunners seemed to have our range as accurately as if the ground had been measured for target practice. Henry, who was visiting the men in their tents, had his regular narrow escape, — a shell bursting close to him, and the fragments striking everywhere, except where he stood. The men begin to think he is bomb-proof himself. A beautiful ricochet shot struck in the field behind us : it could be seen, bounding along in half a dozen successive leaps of 20 or 30 yards each, as distinctly as if it had been a cricket-ball. Our mess-tent was hit, but not a man in camp struck from first to last, wonderfully enough. The Morris-Island experience of our men is useful to them now ; they know just when and how to cover.''

But men of the 10th often were hit. A sharp cry at dead of night more than once gave indication that some one had been wounded while asleep in his tent ; and casualties came to be so frequent, that officers and men moved about with an ever-present consciousness that they might fall the next minute. Frequently, one on stepping from his tent would ask his friend to forward an open letter, to attend to an unfinished business item, or to remember some former request, in case he did not come in again ; and every nerve was kept on tension by this sense of personal peril, during the waking hours, — hardly quieted even in sleep, when the patter of bullets gave shape to troubled dreams.

Pickets were relieved only after nightfall, and there were times when no man at the advanced posts, or even at the main works, could show himself by daylight save at the imminent risk of his life, so vigilant and accurate were the rebel sharpshooters.

"Just before evening," wrote Camp of one such day, "Lieutenant Hickerson was struck in the face by a bullet. He had seen the flash of the rebel rifle, and stooped long enough, he thought, for the bullet to pass; but it was an enormously long range, and he lifted his head again just in time to be hit. The ball struck the upper part of the check-bone, close to the eye. Almost spent, it made only a flesh-wound, painful, but not dangerous. An inch higher, it would have entered the eye, and blinded or killed him. The videttes coming in when relieved at dusk brought with them one of their number who had been mortally wounded at ten o'clock in the morning. He was still living, though his brains were oozing out of a bullet-hole through the head.

"So sharp had been the fire, so positive the certainty of being hit, on those advanced posts, with the slightest exposure, that it had been impossible to move him. None but his companion in the same rifle-pit, and those on the next post, to whom he called out the information, knew until night that he had been hit. It was Henry Lyman, of Company K, one of our tried and reliable men. His companion — Bunnell, one of the same sort, scout and sharpshooter — would have done for him any thing that man could do; but it was of no use to make an attempt. Think of him spending the day in that rifle-pit, with his dying friend, helpless, unable to lift his head without bringing certain death upon himself!"

There were hours of sociability between the Petersburg pickets, in the intermissions of firing at one point or another. In a cornfield between the lines in front of the 3d Brigade, they sometimes met for a friendly chat, or to barter, or for a game at cards. One afternoon, while the 10th was on picket, after an hour of lively shelling and some musketry-firing, there was a rest from active hostilities. Then a rebel soldier showed himself on the parapet of his works, and, shaking a newspaper as a sign of truce, sprang over into the cornfield. At once a hundred men from either side were over their lines and side by side, exchanging papers and coffee and tobacco, and renewing old acquaintances, or forming new ones. Old schoolmates and fellow-townsmen were, in several instances, found over against each other. When, after a half-hour of this friendly intercourse, fire was opened from one of the batteries, over the heads of the cornfield party, officers and men hurried back to their lines again, and hostilities were active as before.

"For my own part," wrote Camp of these times of truce, "I have an uncomfortable sensation when I'm in a situation where my safety depends on the good faith and fairness of rebels. Our Morris-Island experience was one not readily to be forgotten; and I sha'n't be likely to lead them again into any unnecessary temptation."

Here is an extract from another letter, written when no truce existed : —

"I have just been out to watch the sharpshooting.

19

There is no longer any truce opposite our position, and one can not safely raise his head above the parapet. I watched for some time the shots which our boys made at a rebel who had a capital position from which to fire, and made good use of it. His head only was to be seen, and that seldom. Half a dozen of our men would take aim at the aperture where he appeared; and one, with a field-glass, would give notice when to fire. Then the dust would fly all about the place, and he wouldn't come in sight again for some minutes. When I left the trenches to return here to our bomb-proof, he seemed to have left his post; whether hit, or only having come to the conclusion that it was too dangerous a place, we couldn't tell. It was too long range for accurate shooting with ordinary rifles, — some five hundred yards between the main works, which, at this point, are widely divergent.

"The rebels have a few sharpshooters with Whitworth rifles, who are dangerous fellows to be seen by. One of our men this morning had his hair lifted by a bullet, fired, like many others, through one of the apertures of the parapet: another's face was grazed. As Colonel Plaisted and I were standing close to the parapet, a bullet struck it just in front of us, and so near the top as to throw the dirt over us. As I was coming up the hill toward our bomb-proof, another — chance, I think, for I could hardly have been in sight — passed before my face so close, that I involuntarily threw back my head, feeling the wind of it, or fancying I did, as it went by. They are constantly whizzing by our splinter-proof. Our orderly, who occupies a smaller one near by, said that he saw three strike ours within a few minutes. I presume many are buried in it. Down in the ravine, there is a tree in whose trunk over two hundred bullet-marks have been counted; and there are probably twice as many, if it could be carefully examined. Within the last half-hour a rebel battery has opened upon one of ours a little to our rear, which answers vigorously. We are directly under the line of fire, and are in hopes that neither side — (Well, they did, just that minute; fired low, our own side; struck the earth between themselves and us, ricochetting overhead, but a little to the left. Awkward experiment! — don't want 'em to try it again. The first rebel shot passed very near us, — too low for the battery at which it was aimed : they are doing better now. Still, if the rebel gunner should depress the muzzle of his piece a quarter of an inch, it would probably finish us. It is a sixty-four pounder, and one of its balls would knock our splinter-proof into a cocked hat, and bury us under the ruins. I hear now that the same man who had the bullet through his hair a little while ago has been hit in the arm; nothing very serious, though it will lay him up for a few days. Henry has been down to the 24th camp to bury a man killed yesterday. I was anxious about him, going and returning; for bullets fly thick along the whole way; and just in rear of our bomb-proof here, is one of the worst places within a mile. Something of a parenthesis I have made of it, haven't I ?)"

Of the Sunday night after the news came of Sherman's capture of Atlanta, Camp wrote : —

" We lay down early, and slept quietly until midnight. Then suddenly broke forth such a cannonade as we had heard only once before in all our experience, — the evening of the attack on Wagner. We rose, and looked around : our whole line was lit up by the flash of the guns, and the roar was incessant. The rebels answered, though with a fire of by no means equal intensity; and the sight was a magnificent one, — the blazing shells cutting the sky in every direction, bursting sometimes at the very summit of their curve, and flashing the red glare of their explosion on all beneath. Impressive pyrotechny ! What it all meant we were at a loss to understand. There were no signs of an attack by either party; and when, after half an hour or so, the exhibition closed without any apparent results, we went back to our blankets more mystified than ever. Next day we learned that it was a salute for the fall of Atlanta. Thirty-six midnight guns from each battery ; and, not to waste ammunition, the guns were shotted, and Petersburg and its fortifications given the benefit of them. The whole thing must have been gratifying to our friends opposite. During the whole time, the bands were playing national airs, — the music, of course, adding materially to the effect."

Of the shotted salute with which the rebels greeted the passage of trains over General Grant's railroad from City Point to Meade's extreme left, Camp wrote : —

"In the afternoon, we stood for awhile watching the rebel artillery practice on our railroad-train. Nearly opposite our camp is a place where the new military road toward Warren's position passes in plain sight of the rebel works, and within range of rifled-guns, though nearly a mile to our rear. They fire frequently at the cars, and have made some capital shots, though never yet hitting them. We can hear the bolt hum through the air overhead, and have plenty of time to step out of the tent and look toward the train before it strikes. Of late, our guns have opened on the rebel battery every time a train approached; but they can't prevent the one shot which comes almost as regularly as the train passes. The range is probably a mile and a half; and the shooting has been accurate at a moving object, — a pretty difficult job."

In one of Camp's letters from the Petersburg front is found almost the only expression of wearisomeness in his work which escaped him from the hour he entered service until his death. It gives evidence of the terrible pressure of the prolonged and bloody campaign of 1864, even on the bravest and truest.

"The activity of this life has intense pleasure," he wrote; "but it has weariness too. The strain of excitement and of anxiety, the wear and tear of such work as ours, begin to tell upon me. Not that I am breaking down under it, or ready to abandon the task which *must* be accomplished, or even that I would return to such play-day, pleasant soldiering as our occupation of Newberne. But I am beginning to long for the end on personal as well as patriotic grounds. I used to feel differently, you know. Home would seem very attractive to me now, rest very pleasant, could I feel that my place was any-where else than here, my work any other than this. Perhaps I should be restless and uneasy away from ex-citement. I certainly should while the war lasts; but, when peace comes, I think I shall be ready (if I am alive then) for at least a few months of quiet. There was none in prison-life, — less even than now; and the time since I last knew what it meant begins to seem long."

———

It was soon after the 10th went to Petersburg that Camp received from Governor Buckingham his well-deserved commission as major of the regiment. The number of men on the rolls of the 10th being below the standard required for three field-officers, there was some delay in Camp's muster-in; but General Butler, being made acquainted with the facts, issued a special order directing his muster, as demanded by the necessities of the service; and on the 25th of September, being duly qualified, he assumed the duties of his new position.

Saturday afternoon, Sept. 24, brought orders to the 10th Corps to be ready, that night, to be relieved by the 2d Corps, — a portion of which had been some time in reserve in the rear of the line at the left of the 10th. Preparations were hastily made; and, at midnight, the troops of the corps were withdrawn to the level ground in the rear of General Birney's headquarters. There was a halt, and a delay of several days; the time being occupied in drilling, and in parades, — a service almost unknown since the campaign opened in May. It was with a restful feeling that the tired troops found themselves out of reach of the enemy's guns, and permitted to move about without expecting momentarily the hiss of a bullet or the whiz of a shell. The rest was needed, both in view of what had gone before, and what was so soon to come.

CHAPTER XIII.

LIFE AND DEATH BEFORE RICHMOND.

SOON after noon of Wednesday, Sept. 28, the 10th Corps was again in motion. From its camping-ground before Petersburg it moved hurriedly, yet with the tedious slowness of any long column, toward the Appomattox, over the pontoon at Broadway Landing, across the Bermuda-Hundred Peninsula, and to the north bank of the James, from the Jones's-Neck pontoon to Deep Bottom.

The 10th Regiment had commenced its march soon after three P.M. It was half-past two A.M. when it halted at Deep Bottom ; and those of its heavily laden men who had not fallen out exhausted by the way dropped, foot-sore and weary, on the wet grass of the familiar ground, where, before, they had camped and picketed and stood fire and fought, and buried their dead, and from which, a month previous, they had gone out with no thought of a return.

As they lay down, word came to them that they must move again in light marching order, at four A.M.; and to move was to fight, where the enemy held his lines as closely as about Deep Bottom. With such an announcement, but little of rest was secured in the single hour allowed them for sleep ; and it required true moral courage to lift men up when the line was formed in the darkness of the early morning, and to carry them forward in the hurried march to the very front where so many of their comrades had fallen on that remembered sabbath of battle in August.

But the morning move was less bloody to the 3d Brigade than was anticipated. The 18th Corps, having crossed the river at Varnia Landing, made a successful advance against the strong works at Chaffin's Bluff, while the colored troops of the 10th Corps pushed out beyond the Grover House, driving the enemy, and causing him to fall back from before the front of Colonel Plaisted's Brigade, which advanced on the extreme right along the bank of Four-Mile Creek, until the entire fortifications on and about New-Market Hights were carried. For several hours, the victorious lines pressed steadily on, driving all before them. Only Fort Gilmer checked the advance in any direction. General Terry's Division, including the 10th Regiment, moved, during the afternoon, up the Central or Darbytown Road toward Richmond ; the head of his column reaching a point within three miles of the city, of which the roofs and spires were in full view. Had it been deemed advisable, he might, doubtless, have pressed directly into Richmond ; but the condition of affairs on other parts of the line rendered this inexpedient. He retired at nightfall to the new line established by the 10th and 18th Corps, where intrenching was already going on rapidly.

The next few days were days of activity and of privation. The enemy made several attempts to retake his lost works at Chaffin's Bluff, and to drive back General Terry's lines near the New-Market Road. The troops stood to arms much of the time, and were frequently under fire. The officers of the 10th Regiment had left all their baggage, even their blankets, at Deep Bottom, on Thursday morning; and the field and staff had come forward without their horses. Thursday night was cloudy; but no rain fell. On Friday it commenced to rain. Without shelter of any kind, and no bed save the soft clay of the traveled road, but comfortless sleep was secured during the drenching storm of the following night; and Saturday morning, when it came, gave only the opportunity to rise up, and take the rain perpendicularly instead of horizontally.

Of a bold move by the 10th, on the afternoon of that day, up the New-Market Road to Laurel Hill, unsupported on either flank, Camp wrote as follows : —

" On Saturday afternoon our regiment was ordered out alone to make a diversion in favor of General Terry, who, with two brigades, was demonstrating upon the rebel lines further to our right. It was still raining, as it had been all day, and the mud was beyond description. All of us footed it. Passing by the picket-line, we halted where the road ran through thick woods, and threw forward skirmishers. They speedily came upon the enemy's vedettes. We heard the cry of 'Halt, halt!' followed by a dozen shots; and presently a prisoner came back, one of our men hurrying him down the road at a double-quick. Two others had succeeded, although fired upon, in making their escape. The only anxiety our chap seemed to feel was to be taken out of the way of any further fighting. He was afraid, perhaps, of being recaptured.

"Colonel Otis now went forward to the skirmish-line. Henry went up to a house near which the captured vedette had been posted. I, of course, had to remain with the regiment. In the house were some poor, sadly frightened women, whom he, as far as possible, re-assured, and to whom he returned a few minutes later with hard-bread (for they said it was very difficult to obtain food); and afterward the colonel sent them some coffee, a luxury to which they had been long unaccustomed. The division-officer of the day [Major Randlett of the 3d New Hampshire] speaking of a good position near this house, I moved the regiment forward, and occupied it; and, Colonel Otis soon returning, the skirmish-line was strengthened and still further advanced.

"Presently our men reported themselves flanked upon the left, and a cross-fire poured upon them. Sergeant Williams was shot through the small of the back, the bullet grazing the spine and inflicting a mortal wound. A private of the same name was shot through both thighs. These men were brought back upon stretchers, attended by Dr. Hart on the spot, and sent away to the field-hospital. A wounded rebel, left by his comrades in their retreat, was also brought in, moaning and groaning most piteously, even when treated with all possible kindness, and assured that he would be well cared for. Our men had not uttered a sound in their pain : it is rare that a wounded man does. This one claimed to be a Union man, forced against his will into the ranks, attempting to join us when he was shot; said that papers in his pocket-book would prove it. So Henry opened it for him, and there, tucked away in an inner pocket, was a little wood-cut of the American flag, and a cautiously worded statement that —— was *reliable*, and might be trusted by any friend of the subscriber, signed by one whom inquiry showed to be a known friend of Government. Henry went down to General Butler's in the evening to see about it; and, the poor fellow's statement proving true, he is well cared for. Hosts of such men are fighting us on just such compulsion as brought this man to it.

"Company K was sent out to drive back the enemy on our flank : they did it, and we sustained no more loss. Reaching a good position for the purpose, and having moved forward quite as far as was prudent, considering that we were entirely without support, and that a force of the enemy could be seen pushing toward the right, where they could flank us more safely than on the left, we halted, and waited for dark ; keeping up a continual skirmish-fire with the enemy, who occupied the crest of a little slope just in front. At dusk, I went up to the line, withdrew it, and, returning to the reserve, we marched into camp.

" We had in this affair but *one* line-officer [Lieutenant Benjamin Wright] with the regiment ; the rest being absent, sick, or excused. But our men can't be prevented from fighting well when they are once sent forward, with orders or without. They know what's wanted, and have such an inveterate habit of removing any thing that stands in the way, that it would be hard to break 'em of it. Colonel Plaisted is enthusiastic about the regiment, and never fails to speak well of us in his reports."

On Monday, Oct. 3, upward of one hundred of the old men of the 10th, whose term of service had expired, left the regiment for their homes, — several of their officers accompanying them. This seriously reduced the battalion, and increased the pressure of duty upon the few remaining officers. Camp was on Wednesday division-officer of the day, having an oversight of the picket-line on either side of the New-Market Road, and receiving a flag of truce borne by Major Wood and other rebel officers, with letters for Lieutenant-Colonel Mulford.

On Thursday, Colonel Otis being corps-officer of the day, Camp was in command of the regiment, which was that day paid for four months' service by Major Holmes. In the evening, a wayside prayer-meeting was held by a blazing camp-fire. Although the day had been a busy one, and special duties devolved on him, Major Camp was present at that gathering for worship; and the pleasant tones of his inspiring voice were heard in prayer, as so often before, but as never again, in the presence of the regiment.

Deserters from the enemy had announced an attack as contemplated for Friday morning (Oct. 7), and arrangements were made to receive it. Yet so many announcements of the kind had proved incorrect, that few anticipated trouble, even while they faithfully obeyed the orders received; and when, after a night of vigilance, the morning came with no disturbance, there was many a joke cracked over the last needless scare. But about eight, A.M., sharp firing was heard over at the extreme right, soon followed by orders to be ready to move in heavy marching order. The firing increased; artillery and musketry were heard, — all in the direction of General Kautz's cavalry-position. Flying horsemen were seen coming in from the right, through the swamps and thickets, in wild disorder. The command came to move rapidly down the road toward the rear.

All seemed to indicate a retreat. The camps and breastworks were being deserted, and the road was already thronged with retiring columns of cavalry, infantry,

and artillery; while ambulances and baggage-wagons dis-
puted progress with the mass of moving men; and along
either side of the way hurried cooks with their knapsacks
on their backs, and huge coffee-kettles swung on poles
between them; invalids limping as rapidly as their feeble
limbs would bear them; officers' servants "toting" heavy
loads of personal baggage; surgeons driving their patients
before them, or starting up those who were already dropping with exhaustion; sutlers' clerks and runners with
their extra supply of "truck," brought up in view of the
recent pay-day; and shirks and cowards pushing ahead of
their regiments, on one plea or another, as they fall behind
on an advance.

Officers and men exchanged disturbed, distrustful looks,
as only on a retreat, when trouble is anticipated, and there
is chagrin at apparent failure. But no retreat was really
contemplated. The right flank of Major-General Birney's
fortified position, held by General Kautz, had been turned,
with a considerable loss to the latter of men and guns;
and the enemy, in strong force, was now pressing down to
follow up the advantage he had gained. General Birney
had withdrawn troops from the left to enable him to form a
new line of defense at right angles to his works, and thus
resist the progress of the enemy. General Terry's division
had been selected for this duty; and Plaisted's Brigade
was merely being sent down the road to the right of the
new line. Reaching the Cox-Farm Road, this brigade

deployed, and moved forward *en échelon*, connecting on the left with Hawley's Brigade. Camp's description of the battle continues from this point.

"Heavy firing was going on in the direction of the place we had left, — principally artillery; while the almost continuous roar of musketry nearer, and upon our left as we stood, seemed to show that the rebels were feeling for the end of our line, — each successive attack coming nearer and nearer. When the brigade next us became engaged, including the 7th Connecticut, with its seven-shooting rifles, the crash was beyond any thing I had ever heard. We shook our heads as we listened : ammunition could hold out but very few minutes at that rate ; and we knew that, as always, nine shots out of ten must be wasted. Yet, as it afterward proved, that tenth shot did fearful execution.

"We hadn't long to wait and comment. A rattling volley in our own front showed that the skirmishers were engaged ; and, in a moment more, they came hurrying back through the dense pine-woods before us, — the rebels close upon them. (These were not our own men, who had been left far to the right when the main body of the regiment last moved.) There was a brief delay while they were gaining a place of safety. One poor fellow staggered toward where I stood, the blood pouring down his face from a wound just received. He was behind the rest ; perhaps he could not move as fast as they. We would have waited longer, but could not. While the bullets of the rebel skirmishers flew among us, their main body was forming line just behind for the attack, — their feet plainly to be seen beneath the low-growing foliage, which concealed their bodies as they dressed their ranks. It was no time to stop for one man's life, whether friend or foe : our line opened fire, and he dropped. Probably it was only to avoid as much as possible this new danger. I do not think he was hit ; but I did not see him again : and, looking for him after the fight was over, he was gone.

" The rebels opened in return, and the bullets flew fast. Colonel Otis stood near the right of the line ; I at the left. We had hardly a hundred men in the ranks ; and the regiment looked like a single company, with a captain and lieutenant to manage it. The men needed little in the way of orders or instruction, — they knew just what to do, and did it. At the first fire, the regiment on our right turned and ran. Our men saw it ; knew that their flank was now exposed ; nothing there to hinder the immediate advance of the enemy. Nothing is so apt to strike men with panic. Our men paid no other attention to it than to give a rousing cheer just to show the enemy that they had no thought of giving ground, then turn steadily to their work. Each man stood fast. Where a comrade fell they gave him room to lie, — no more. There was no random firing in air, but rapid loading, cool aim, and shots that told. It was good to see such fighting.

20

Those whom we met were no raw recruits. They fought well. For awhile, though unable to advance, they stood their ground. Broken once, they rallied again at the appeal of their officers, and once more tried to move forward through the fire that mowed them down. It was of no use : again thrown into confusion, they fell back, leaving their dead and wounded upon the field. Among the former was a captain, said to have been in command of the regiment ; while opposite other parts of our division-line lay officers of different ranks among the bodies of their men. Surgeons said that they attended as many rebel as Union soldiers ; and when it is considered how many must have been carried away, or hobbled off themselves, the total rebel loss must have been very heavy. It is said that among them were two generals, — one killed and one wounded.

" There is no doubt that they had at least two divisions, — Field's and Hoke's, — probably more. Prisoners reported Lee in person superintending the movement. A woman at a house close by speaks of meeting him there, and describes his appearance. Possibly it was so. Two rebels who gave themselves up voluntarily to one of our men just after the fight told us that the woods were full of others who were anxious to come in, but who feared to attempt it, lest they should fall into the hands of the negro troops, who, they believed, would give them no quarter.

" Although our loss was not large, the affair was, while it lasted, a very brisk one. Our fighting hitherto has been almost exclusively skirmishing. It was the first time since I have rejoined the regiment that simultaneous fire has been opened by the companies of the battalion-line. We have seldom had an opportunity to stand and receive an enemy; and even now, we had to leave our intrenched position, and meet them without any advantages of defense. But we are well content with even terms, and would ask nothing better than to have them always. Now, if we could only have a full regiment of men like this handful left to us! — there's nothing which we shouldn't feel as if we could do. The three New-England regiments of our brigade are as good men as ever fought.

" Deserters reported that Lee was coming down on us again this morning, this time with three army corps; but he didn't make his appearance. The rumor now is that he only postponed operations twenty-four hours, and will certainly attack at daylight to-morrow. Don't believe, now that we are ready for him, that he'll give us a chance to fight him behind works. Still, he may find a weak spot somewhere between here and Deep Bottom. As the mail doesn't go until to-morrow afternoon, perhaps I shall tell you about it in a P.S., or somebody else may."

Camp never finished another home-letter. In this, he failed to tell of himself, as he appeared to others in that hour of sharp conflict. Calmly and quietly he moved along the battle-line while the fight raged fiercest, saying firm and encouraging words to the brave men before him, pointing with his sword in the direction whence the enemy's fire was sharpest, and enjoining a low and well-aimed return-fire as coolly as he would have superintended harmless target-practice. Hidden once or twice, in the dense smoke, from the friend who watched him with intent and anxious gaze, it seemed for a few burdened seconds as if he also had fallen; but while the breath of the watcher was stayed, and the heart suspended its throbs, again his flashing sword was seen through the rifted smoke-cloud, and his form stood erect and noble as before. And, when the firing ceased, his face showed no flush of excitement, his voice betrayed no unusual emotion: his only impulse was to thank God for victory, and to bless the brave boys whose unflinching steadiness had won it.

The next few days after the battle of the seventh were occupied by the troops of Terry's Division in finishing breastworks along the front they had then so nobly defended. On the evening of Sabbath, the ninth, Camp attended a preaching service at the regimental bivouac. On Tuesday, the eleventh, he deposited with the commissioners appointed to receive the votes of Connecticut soldiers in the field, his second vote for Abraham Lincoln as President, — a vote which was never counted at home, because of his death prior to the day of election.

Soon after noon of Thursday, Oct. 12, orders were received for the regiment to move at once in light marching order. At half past four it left camp, and, with the remainder of its brigade, passed out, through a sally-port of the works, near the New-Market Road. The whole of the 1st Division, temporarily commanded by General Ames, — General Terry being in command of the corps, — was in motion. On the broad fields of the Cox Farm there was a halt, the three brigades resting in successive lines of battle. Rain commenced falling. The afternoon was dreary. General Ames and staff, and the brigade-commanders, sat or stood on the piazza of the plantation-house. Regimental and company officers gathered in little knots, and chatted in the dismal storm. The men lolled on the wet grass, talking and laughing as merrily as though they had no wish for better quarters.

Major Camp and his friend joined Colonel Rockwell of the 6th Connecticut Volunteers; and the three indulged in conjectures as to the nature and probable results of the new and sudden move. Then, looking about them, they spoke of how many now in careless ease were unlikely to see the termination of this advance. The trials and anxieties of the prolonged campaign were referred to, not sadly but seriously; and cheerful words were also uttered, and a hearty, mutual laugh was enjoyed. An hour passed by. Then there was a new start. The column once more in motion wound its slow way along the hillside, around to the left; and, to the surprise of all, back to the works again, and in through another sally-port than that by which it had passed out. The troops returned to their several camps. A flag of truce coming in from the enemy had suspended the move for the time being, and a night of rest was to be substituted for one of fatigue and exposure. The friends sat writing and talking until past midnight. Then, for the last time, they read their evening chapter, prayed together, and lay down side by side, as so often before.

At three, A.M., they were up again; and at four, the regiment was once more in motion. In the darkness of the early morning, the column passed out beyond the works, by the Cox Farm, through the woods, across the ravine, on to the Johnson Place; thence, after a brief halt, to close up the lines, over the Darbytown Road, to the extensive plains between that and the Charles-City Road. There was another halt to form for an attack.

The morning was delightful. It was the opening of a bright October day. The air was clear and bracing. The first rays of the rising sun were reflected from the frosted surface of the wide-reaching grassy fields, and from the many hued forest-trees beyond, as the skirmishers of three brigades deployed, and moved in their wavy line, extending far to right and left, up toward the belt of woods where the enemy's mounted vedettes were distinctly seen. General, staff, and regimental officers rode hither and thither. Corps, division, and brigade flags were in sight. Long lines of infantry with flashing arms and waving standards were coming up by the flank or advancing in battle-front. Cavalry, with rattling sabers and fluttering camp-colors, clattered along the road, and the brilliant guidons of the artillery — yet far at the rear — signaled the approach of the rumbling batteries. The scene was exhilarating and inspiriting ; and no one more thoroughly appreciated and heartily enjoyed it than young Major Camp as he rode back and forth, conveying orders and bearing messages.

The first fire of the skirmishers opened. The enemy's advanced line was easily pressed back to his strongly intrenched position beyond the woods. There his skirmishers were re-enforced, and the progress of the attacking party was stayed. For several hours, the fighting was brisk between the opposing skirmish-lines ; the main force halting in line of battle in close reserve. Four companies of the 10th skirmished under Lieutenant Linsley ; the other six were in reserve, in charge of the three field-officers. The forenoon dragged along slowly. Artillery-fire was sharp for a time, and the rattle of musketry was incessant. Men were killed and wounded close at hand as the little group of officers of the 10th sat chatting together; and word came frequently that one or another good soldier had fallen on the skirmish-line. An occasional narrow escape to some of the party from a flying bullet or shell fragment would cause a passing remark, or, perhaps, raise a laugh. No one expected to be hit himself, for he had escaped so many times before. Dinner was brought up and eaten under fire. Then Camp stretched himself on the ground, and was lulled to sleep by the sound of the battle.

Soon after noon, he was started up to lead a party of men down the road on a mission from the corps-commander. While he was away, Colonel Otis received orders to report at once with the remainder of his regiment to Colonel Pond, commanding the 1st Brigade, at the extreme right of the division. No sooner was the new position reached, than the formation of troops was seen to indicate an assault on the works in front; and a chill ran over many an old soldier's frame. The enemy was known to be strongly intrenched; and an advance could be made at this point only by a dense thicket of scrub-oaks, and laurels, and tangled vines, through which a way could not be forced save slowly and step by step. A dashing, resistless charge was impossible; and the small force ordered forward was not likely to prove any match for the now heavily re-enforced lines of the foe. There was a disturbed look on the face of every officer, and from many outspoken protests were heard.

When the chaplain saw the condition of affairs, his hope and prayer was that his friend would not return in season to share the perils of the assault, since he could probably in no way affect its result. But, while the column waited, Major Camp appeared, wiping from his face the perspiration caused by his exertions to rejoin his regiment without delay. As he came up, the chaplain's face fell with disappointment. Reading the look, Camp said quickly and tenderly, "Why, what is the matter, Henry? has any thing happened?"—"No; but I'm sorry you've returned in time for this assault."—"Oh! don't say so, my dear fellow; I thank God I'm back."—"But you can do no good, and I'm afraid for you."—"Well, you wouldn't have the regiment go in with me behind, would you? No, no! *In any event, I thank God I am here!*" Then he moved about among his comrades, with a bright and cheerful face, like a gleam of sunshine through gathering clouds. Never a word of doubt or distrust did he express as to the pending move, although his opinion was probably the same with the others as to its inevitable issue. Many near him were as regardless of personal danger as he, and would go as fearlessly into the thickest of the fray; but few, if any, showed such sublimity of moral courage, in meeting, without a murmur, his responsibilities at such an hour. "I don't like this blue talking," he said, aside to his friend. "The men see it, and it affects them. If we must go, we must; and the true way is to make the best of it."

The shattered remnant of the 10th had the right of the assaulting column, which was formed in two lines of battle. Colonel Otis led the right and front. Lieutenant-Colonel Greeley led the right of the second line,—the left of which was assigned to Major Camp. "May I not as well take

the left of the *front* line, Colonel?" Camp asked in his
quiet way. "Certainly, if you prefer it," was the reply;
and he took his place accordingly,— not that the advanced
position was more honorable, nor yet *because* it was more
exposed, but from the belief that it gave him a better opportunity to lead and encourage the men. As he drew
his pistol from its case, and thrust it loosely through his
belt for instant use in the deadly struggle, and unsheathed
his sword, he said to his friend, "I don't quite like this
half-hearted way of fighting. If we were ordered to go
into that work at all hazards, I should know just what
to do; but we are told to go on as far as those at our
left advance, and to fall back when they retire. Such
orders are perplexing." And they were; for the men
of the 10th had never yet failed to do the work assigned
them, — never yet fallen back under the pressure of the
enemy.

The two friends talked of the possibilities of the hour,
speaking freely of the delightful past and as to the probable future. "If we don't meet again here, we will hope
to meet in heaven," said the chaplain. "Yes," replied
Camp; "and yet I have been so absorbed in this life, that
I can hardly realize that there is another beyond." After
a few more words on this theme, the friends clasped hands,
and Camp said warmly, "Good-bye, Henry! good-bye!"
The words sent a chill to the other's heart; and, as he
moved to the right of the line, they rang in his ears as

a sound of deep and fearful meaning. Good-bye! that farewell had never before been uttered in all the partings of a score and a half of battle-fields. It was first appropriate now.

The signal was given for a start: the men raised the charging cry with a tone that rather indicated a willingness to obey than a hope of success; and the doomed column struggled forward, through the impeding undergrowth of the dense wood, through the crashing sweep of grape and canister, and the fatal hiss and hum of flying bullets. Those latest words had so impressed the chaplain with the idea that this hour was his comrade's last on earth, that he felt he must see him yet again, and have another and more cheering assurance of his faith than that natural expression of inability in the present to fully realize the eternal future. He turned once more to the left, and pressed on to overtake the major, whom he saw in the advance, pushing his way along toward the furthermost front of death. Every step was an effort. The struggle to reach his friend was almost as the hopeless chase in a nightmare dream. Oh for some superhuman arm to remove the intervening thicket ere the one or the other fell prostrate! At length they were side by side in the deadly race. As the chaplain laid his hand on the other's arm, Camp turned with a loving look of glad surprise. "You said, Henry, that you could not realize you had a home in heaven. You do not doubt your Saviour, do you?" asked the chaplain as they

pressed on together.   Camp's face lighted up inspiringly,
all aglow with excitement, expressive in its story of tenderest affection, of true courage, and of firmest faith.   It was
never more fair or bright or beautiful than in that hour
and place of death, as the peerless Christian soldier said,
with warmth and earnestness, "No, no! dear fellow! I
do not doubt.   I do trust Jesus, fully, wholly."   With
another good-bye, the two friends parted.

The chaplain turned to his work among the many dying
and wounded.   The major struggled on, through the thicket, out to the open space before the enemy's works; and
there, when all at his left had fallen back, when only the
brave men of the steadfast 10th at his right were yet pressing
forward, he stood for a moment to re-form the broken line
which could not be maintained in the tangled wood.   The
rebel parapet was but a few rods in his front.   From the
double battle-line behind it, the rifles poured forth their
ceaseless fire of death.   His tall and manly form was too
distinct a target to escape special notice from the foe.
Waving his sword, he called aloud cheerily, "Come on,
boys, come on!" then turned to the color-sergeant just
emerging from the thicket, that he might rally the men on
the regimental standard.   As he did so, a bullet passed
through his lungs; and, as he fell on his side, he was
pierced yet again and again by the thick-coming shot.   His
death was as by the lightning's stroke.   His eyes scarce
turned from their glance at the tattered, dear old flag, ere

they were closed to earth, and opened again beyond the stars and their field of blue.

The few remaining veterans of the 10th were alone before the enemy's well-defended stronghold. They had performed the part assigned them. Had the order been to go on at all hazards, they would never have turned about, even though no man of their number had crowned the bristling parapet in their front. But the brigade-commander who directed their movements had already fallen back with the remainder of his troops. Seeing this, Colonel Otis and Lieutenant-Colonel Greeley retired in good order their little band of now less than fifty men, and reached again their starting-point; having lost more than one-half the battalion, dead or wounded, in the fruitless charge. Major Camp's body was left where he fell. It was in vain that his stricken friend sought to reach and recover it. The enemy closely followed up the retiring column with a skirmish-line, and held the bloody field, with its dead and wounded. This closed the aggressive movements of the day. General Ames's division shortly after recrossed the Darbytown Road, and withdrew to the line of works it had left in the morning.

Before Camp's body was really cold, the enemy — as was afterward learned from the wounded who were near him — took from his person his sword and pistol, his watch and regatta-ring, his money and papers, and even stripped him of all his outer garments. The next morning, Colonel Rockwell of the 6th Connecticut, accompanied by Chaplain Trumbull and Lieutenant Shreve, bore out a flag of truce with a communication from Major-General Terry to the Commander of the Confederate forces on the Darbytown Road, requesting the return of Major Camp's remains. The party were halted at the foot of the hill on the road beyond the Johnson Place, at a point midway between the opposing picket-lines, and there made to wait until a reply could be received from the request they brought. Captain Simms, of South Carolina, an officer of the general's staff, soon responded to the communication, and stated that the desired remains were being exhumed without delay; having been already several hours buried. When they were finally borne down the road, Captain Simms expressed his sincere regret that the clothing and valuables had been taken from the body; and, when the chaplain expressed a strong desire for the personal diary of his friend, courteously promised to seek and recover that if possible. Subsequently, having obtained it by no little search, he kindly sent it through the lines, informally, to the great satisfaction of the home-friends of the fallen soldier.

CHAPTER XIV.

MEMORIAL TRIBUTES.

THE chaplain accompanied the remains of his friend to Hartford, — reaching there on the evening of Wednesday, Oct. 19. The funeral-services were attended the next Friday afternoon. Of these a sketch is copied from the columns of the "*Daily Post.*"

"A prayer was offered at the residence of his father on Woodland Street, whence the remains were taken to the North Church. The Rev. Mr. Spaulding, pastor of the church, opened the exercises with prayer, and then read the most beautiful consolatory passages which the Bible contains in its sacred pages. The choir sang the hymn commencing, —

> "'Why should our tears in sorrow fall
> When God recalls his own?'

"Rev. Henry Clay Trumbull, the chaplain of the 10th Connecticut Regiment, an intimate friend of this young officer, delivered a splendid but most just eulogy upon the character of Major Camp. Even from his youth, he said, he

319

had gained the respect and esteem of every one who knew him. He grew up with this same purity of life and manners. During the whole period of the chaplain's intimate acquaintance with him, in the bivouac and battle, in hospital and in prison, he had never known him to say or do any thing inconsistent with what he believed to be his duty; always a Christian, without obtruding his piety, patient, enduring, courageous in the discharge of his duty, not hesitating to expose himself to danger if he could accomplish the most by so doing. Just previous to his going into his last battle, he expressed his perfect trust in his Saviour, and then took his position in the front line, and went forward calmly and gallantly to death. The words which he addressed to his friend, the chaplain, telling him of his reliance upon his God, were the last words he uttered, except those of encouragement which he shouted to his men in the midst of the fierce conflict. Mr. Trumbull concluded with a most eloquent tribute to the extraordinary beauty of the moral and religious traits of this excellent soldier and splendid man.

"A few words of consolation and prayer from Rev. Dr. Hawes, and the services closed with the magnificent funeral anthem, ' Blessed are the dead who die in the Lord.'

" The body was borne by the intimate friends and college classmates of the dead, from the church, through an open line formed by members of the City Guard in citizens' dress; and, under the bright October sky, one of the noblest, truest men that ever lived a pure, manly, holy life, or ever died a generous sacrifice to a cause which such deaths sanctify, was laid away, together with all that was dear to ' friends and sacred home,' except the blessed memory of the grandeur of his goodness."

The wide-spread sorrow which the death of Major Camp occasioned, in the army and home circles of his admiring comrades or attached friends, found expression in many a warm and eloquent tribute to his acknowledged ability and worth.

Said Colonel Otis, in reporting the action in which he fell, —

" The memory of Major Henry W. Camp is deserving of more than a passing notice. The service has never suffered a heavier loss in an officer of his grade. Brave and cool in every emergency, of spotless character and refined intellectual culture, he was one of the brightest ornaments of the volunteer service, — a soldier 'without fear and without reproach.'"

Brigadier-General Hawley wrote of him to a friend : —

" He is deeply mourned by all who knew him, — a gentleman, a soldier, and a Christian. He was, indeed, a young man of rare excellence and promise."

The " Hartford Daily *Post*" said, in its announcement of his death, —

" Thus has perished one of the noblest young men whom this city has ever mourned. He possessed some rare characteristics : prominent among them was a Christian manliness

21

that impressed itself palpably upon every one with whom he came in contact. He had a robust, vigorous moral strength, and a keen conscientiousness, ever vigilant against even the shadow of wrong. His entrance into the army was the result of a deliberate conviction of the right and justice of the cause to which he consecrated himself. He did not wish to pass through this epoch of grand events without participating in them; and, governed by the same motives throughout, he patiently, sincerely, and bravely performed his every duty. And the iron discipline of the war wrought in him a still bolder manhood and a more marked Christian character. His filial reverence, his social kindliness, his firmly outlined integrity, were traits for which he was loved, and by which he will long be remembered. A victim to the accursed ambition of the slave-power, a noble sacrifice to the country which he loved, subjected, when powerless, to the insults of the barbarous enemy, he died — undoubtedly, as he lived — a true Christian gentleman, joining the goodly company of our young and brave and beautiful who have gone down to death with the war-cry of the Union on their lips."

And thus the editor of the *"Evening Press"* described him : —

" He was an unusually fine and accurate scholar, with a free, open mind and large capacity. From his solid acquirements, his industry, his versatility and energy, his happy facility as a writer and impromptu speaker, — his friends were justified in expecting great things from his maturity.

More than almost any one we knew, his character was

one of mingled strength and sweetness. He was thoroughly manly and noble, with the clearest conscience, and the highest sense of duty ; and, in disposition and manners, most lovely and winning. To natural graces of no ordinary sort, refinement and amiability, he added the piety of a devout Christian. A strong, cultivated intellect, a large, warm heart, a gracious, attractive manner, — what he might have been to the world we shall never know. We know he was brave and beautiful in death ; and we believe that, giving his life for the noblest cause in history, he already knows that the sacrifice was not in vain."

The following sketches show how Henry Camp was viewed as a law-student and as a soldier by his legal instructor and by his brigade-commander.

"HARTFORD, Dec. 14, 1864.
"REV. H. C. TRUMBULL.

"MY DEAR SIR,—You desire me to give you some account of our lamented friend, Major Camp, as a student of law with me. He studied with me from the spring of 1861 till the following winter, when he left for the war. During this time, he frequently came to my house in the evening to recite, as it was more convenient to me to hear him there. There is little that I can say of him in this relation beyond the fact, that he exhibited a remarkable facility in the acquisition of the science. Of the many students whom I have had in my office, I never had one who seemed to comprehend legal principles so readily. I certainly found difficulties myself in my early study of the law which he did not encounter. He seemed to understand at once, not merely the refined distinctions of the law, but the relations of one principle to another ; and, so far as he went, to take in the science in all its proportions. He thus manifested, not merely a highly discriminating mind, but a generalizing and philosophical one. I was so much struck with this, in the more leisurely recitations of the evening, when I often extended the instruction beyond the mere lesson into the adjacent and related fields of the science, that I repeatedly spoke to my family about it after he had left. I am sure that, if he had lived, he would have made a very superior lawyer. His mind was calm, clear, and self-poised, and his judgment sound. He had, I think, in a high degree, the judicial faculty ; and would have ultimately made an able judge.

" His faculties, naturally superior, had evidently been improved by thorough education. He seemed to me to have felt, while in college and earlier, the value of education ; and to have improved his opportunities well. He thus came to the study of his profession with a mind remarkably disciplined, as well as with a rare literary culture. His reading had also been systematic and well-chosen, so that his mind was well furnished, both with thoughts on the most important subjects, and with information.

" When the war broke out, his whole soul became enlisted in the cause of the country ; and he could not bear to fail in his full duty and his full measure of sacrifice in her behalf. Still he had no taste for military life. He had been brought up to look upon war as one of the great curses of the world ; and military ambition and displays had always had with him an unpleasant association with the wickedness of war. He had no misgivings, however, as to the righteousness of the war which had been forced upon us; and prepared himself at once for what might be found to be his duty, by joining the City Guard — a finely organized home-company — for the purpose of learning military drill. There was probably nothing that made him hesitate so much, as to joining the army, as the distress that he knew it would give to his mother, who idolized him, and who had long held, as well as instilled into him, a horror of all war, as essentially unchristian. As the call of duty grew more and more emphatic and unequivocal to him, the voice of home, coming to him no less tenderly, and falling on no less loving ears, yet lost some of its potency; but it was not till he had obtained the full yet agonized assent of his mother, that he left his home for the field.

" This completes the particular duty which you had assigned to me, of giving a sketch of him as a law-student. I can not help, however, expressing to you my admiration of him in other respects than his rare intellectual powers. He was, physically and morally, as nearly perfect as any young man I ever saw. Indeed, as a splendid specimen of a physical, intellectual, and Christian man, I do not know whom I could place by the side of him. While earnest and devoted as a Christian, and of a sensitive purity that would have adorned a maiden, he had yet nothing of religious assumption or obtrusive meekness in his manner. He was one of those muscular Christians who could swing an almost irresistible arm, and a defiant one, if necessary, as well as utter the gentlest words of love. The very caviller at religion could not but respect and admire him.

"I have never seen one more full of life and strength, and ready to do battle with hearty vigor for truth and right; never one with whom it seemed more incongruous to associate the idea of early and sudden death. Few deaths ever extinguished more of *life* than went out when he died. It is almost impossible for me to satisfy myself that there is not some illusion about it; and that he is not, after all, still living. The exuberance of his vital energy seems to me to have been an overmatch for any ordinary power of death.

"I last saw him as he was hurrying to the cars, the last time he left home, to join his regiment at the front. He had been many months in prison at the South, and had just been paroled and had reached his home. A few days after his return he heard, unofficially, that he had been exchanged, and could return to active service. He had a furlough for twenty days, but a small part of which had passed. Without waiting to write, he left his home to hurry on, that he might not lose a day in getting to his regiment. I happened to be riding with my family through the street on which his father lived; and, as we approached the house, Henry came out on his way to the cars. On seeing us, he came up to the carriage to bid us good-by. We exchanged a few words, and shook hands with him, and said 'God bless you!' and he hurried on. I never saw him again. As he left us, we all spoke of the remarkable beauty and grandeur that seemed to rest upon him. His face was flushed and glowing, and his eye dilated; his form almost majestic in its size and elegant proportions; and the whole man bore the impress of the nobleness of purity and patriotism and self-sacrifice. It was a grand view for the last one I was to have of him. It seems to me now to be less like an earthly and mere human vision, than like that glorified presence which he already bears, and which I hope, some day, to see in the heavenly world.

" Very truly yours,

" JOHN HOOKER."

" HEADQUARTERS 3D BRIGADE 1ST DIVISION 24TH ARMY CORPS, Before Richmond, Va., March 20, 1865.

" FRIEND TRUMBULL, —

" You desire me to speak of your friend as I saw him and knew him. I can not say that I knew him; but I can speak of him as I saw him.

"It was at Drury's Bluff, May 16, that I first saw Major Camp, under very interesting and somewhat exciting circumstances. The Army of the James was retiring before the victorious enemy. There was a momentary lull in the conflict; and the gallant 10th, having repulsed the onset of the enemy on its front, was in the act of taking up a new position, when I saw two horsemen abreast, coming through the slashing, straight to the front, — yourself and Major (then Adjutant) Camp. I had heard of Adjutant Camp as ' the chaplain's friend,' and that he was expected. At a glance, I saw that the long-imprisoned adjutant had returned. How will this young man accept this state of things?

thought I. How will he be received? The dead of his
regiment were lying in the road, — the wounded being
carried past him to the rear. He took no note of the dead
or of the wounded; none of the gallant boys of his regiment.
His eyes were on the field, — right, left, and front, taking in
the scene; for the battle was not over. His face was pale,
his lips compressed, and his every feature seemed like iron.
One of the soldiers of the 10th exclaimed, ' There is the
adjutant!—Adjutant Camp!' Then the brave boys gave
at once a shout of recognition, throwing up their caps, and
cheering. Instantly his features relaxed; his face filled with
hot blood; and the iron man the moment before appeared
as modest as a girl; and when he took off his hat, sat erect
in his saddle, while the 10th moved past as it were in review,
' the young man' dwarfed everybody present.

"I was impressed by Major Camp's bearing on that occasion. I felt that he was a power, an embodiment of will,
force, genius; and that opportunity alone was wanting in him
for the display of great qualities. He gave such assurance
of a true soldier, my first impulse was to wish for an occasion
for him, — one equal to the man. They were knightly
qualities that showed forth themselves in him.

" Subsequent acquaintance with Major Camp never
effaced, never diminished, the first impressions of him. He
ever seemed to me the fittest man for the choicest occasion,
— hence I was chary of exposing him, felt he was not one
to be killed in a skirmish. The day he fell, this feeling was
strong in me. ' I have no officer,' said Colonel Otis, ' to send
with the skirmishers, unless I send Major Camp.' I felt
averse to sending him against a thicket where any skulking

rebel might take away his life. Later in the day, I wanted a field-officer to take charge of the skirmish-line of the brigade-detachments of the several regiments, which were doing a good deal of fighting, but disliked to expose the major, and delayed sending for him on that account. But, when the order came to send the 10th to report to Colonel Pond, I immediately sent for the major, but he was away. I had placed the 10th in reserve that day, its ranks were so thinned, wishing to spare its gallant officers and men; and that very circumstance devoted it to the bloody service which I wished to spare it. It was the will of Heaven.

" After the affair of Drury's Bluff, I never saw Major Camp excited, — never saw him except in repose. In all our subsequent engagements with the enemy, he was the same quiet, composed soldier he was in camp.

" Oct. 7, he moved along the battle-line of the 10th, among the file-closers, the only commissioned officer Colonel Otis had, with perfect coolness; and, when the fight was hottest, as one almost without occupation. He seemed a little moved; and I never shall forget the light of victory in his eye, as the boys of the 10th gave their shouts for victory. He thought nothing would express his sentiments so well, just at that time, as ' Hail Columbia,' from the band.

" At Petersburg he was detailed by General Terry as Acting Assistant Adjutant-General of the brigade. The regiment had three field-officers, and he could be spared. He received the order as the brigade was in line, ready to move across the James, on the eve of the battle of New Market Hights. He came to me with a most troubled expression of countenance. ' Colonel,' said he, ' can not this be changed? I have been absent from my regiment so much : I have just been promoted, and we are now going into action. It will not do for me to be away from my regiment.'

"He could not rest until he saw the general, and received permission to accompany his regiment.

"Major Camp's modesty, his purity and simplicity of character, seemed not to belong to one of his years, but rather to the innocence of childhood. Entirely unconscious of the powers he possessed, he would hardly seek responsibility; yet he was not the man to turn from the path of duty to avoid it. The only question in his mind would be, 'What is duty?' But, with a great responsibility thrown upon him, he would have been an inspired man, and equal to any emergency. For my part, I believe him to have been as good a man — as good in head and heart — as was George Washington in his youth, or David when he kept his father's sheep or slew Goliah.

"However contrary to our desires the manner of his death, we must believe that it was best, and that some great good will come of it. May it not be realized in the pious labors of your hands in giving to the young men of our country, in his Life, the example of such a character?

"I have the honor to be, chaplain,

"With the highest regards,

"Your most obedient servant,

"H. M. PLAISTED,

"Col. 11th Me. and Brevet Brig.-Gen. Comd'g Brigade.

"REV. H. C. TRUMBULL,

"Chaplain 10th Conn. Vols."

Thus closes the record of a brief and beautiful life. "All of us who were about him," said a college friend, "perceived that Henry Camp was a Christian who followed Christ. All things that were true, honest, just, pure, lovely, of good report, shone in his walks and conversation among us. Not more pleasing was his manly beauty to the eye than was his piety to the hearts of such as communed with him." "True always," adds a classmate, "and faithful unto death, the sudden stroke that quenched all our bright hopes for his future opened to him a new life of nobler aims and higher services. Such a death closes such a life with all fitness. The suddenness of heroic death rivals the blessedness of translation. No waste of energies, no sad decay, but a Christian soul rising to heaven while the heart is still intense with the fire of purified passion, and the body girt for battle."